"Pretend... I'm going to have to pretend?"

She stood speechless, unable to move or breathe, or think of anything but the sweet ache building in her, wanting, hoping....

"You think it will be an act?" Tal pressed her, his voice soft, dangerous.

Mary-Anne managed a shaky whisper. "Don't lie to me, Tal. Lie to the world if you need to, but not to me."

"All right—you want the truth?" He took a step closer to her, his sudden grin half-savage, highlighting his scars. "I've forced myself to think about kissing you, touching you and pretending to want you, oh, about two hundred and forty times since I saw you yesterday. Just in case I needed the scenario for a mission, of course." He smiled at her, his eyes dark, unfathomable—his body too close. "I must have been training for this mission for a long time, honey, because I've been *pretending* to want you ever since I was fifteen."

Dear Reader,

What better way to start off a new year than with six terrific new Silhouette Intimate Moments novels? We've got miniseries galore, starting with Karen Templeton's *Staking His Claim*, part of THE MEN OF MAYES COUNTY. These three brothers are destined to find love, and in this story, hero Cal Logan is also destined to be a father—but first he has to convince heroine Dawn Gardner that in his arms is where she wants to stay.

For a taste of royal romance, check out Valerie Parv's *Operation: Monarch*, part of THE CARRAMER TRUST, crossing over from Silhouette Romance. Policemen more your style? Then check out Maggie Price's *Hidden Agenda*, the latest in her LINE OF DUTY miniseries, set in the Oklahoma City Police Department. Prefer military stories? Don't even try to resist *Irresistible Forces,* Candace Irvin's newest SISTERS IN ARMS novel. We've got a couple of great stand-alone books for you, too. Lauren Nichols returns with a single mom and her protective hero, in *Run to Me*. Finally, Australian sensation Melissa James asks *Can You Forget?* Trust me, this undercover marriage of convenience will stick in your memory long after you've turned the final page.

Enjoy them all—and come back next month for more of the best and most exciting romance reading around, only in Silhouette Intimate Moments.

Yours,

Leslie J. Wainger
Executive Editor

Please address questions and book requests to:
Silhouette Reader Service
U.S.: 3010 Walden Ave., P.O. Box 1325, Buffalo, NY 14269
Canadian: P.O. Box 609, Fort Erie, Ont. L2A 5X3

Can You Forget?

MELISSA JAMES

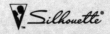

INTIMATE MOMENTS™

Published by Silhouette Books

America's Publisher of Contemporary Romance

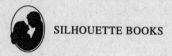

SILHOUETTE BOOKS

ISBN 0-373-27342-8

CAN YOU FORGET?

Copyright © 2004 by Lisa Chaplin

Visit Silhouette at www.eHarlequin.com

Printed in U.S.A.

Books by Melissa James

Silhouette Intimate Moments

Her Galahad #1182
Who Do You Trust? #1206
Can You Forget? #1272

MELISSA JAMES

is a mother of three living in a beach suburb in New South Wales, Australia. A former nurse, waitress, store assistant, perfume and chocolate (yum!) demonstrator among other things, she believes in taking on new jobs for the fun experience. She'll try almost anything at least once to see what it feels like—a fact that scares her family on regular occasions. She fell into writing by accident when her husband brought home an article stating how much a famous romance author earned, and she thought, "I can do that!" Years later, she found her niche at Silhouette Intimate Moments. Currently writing a pilot/spy series set in the South Pacific, she can be found most mornings walking and swimming at her local beach with her husband, or every afternoon running around to her kids' sporting hobbies, while dreaming of flying, scuba diving, belaying down a cave or over a cliff—anywhere her characters are at the time!

To all those who love Beauty and the Beast stories,
and to those who prefer healing and peace to war,
yet know the realities of this life demand that some of us
give our lives to protect others—I hope you enjoy this
one. And to Maryanne, my dearest friend
and natural healer, this is for you.

Special thanks must go to some of my dearest friends
in the world, for making this story what it is: my
critique partners, Maryanne Cappelluti and
Diane Perkins, for putting aside a month of their lives
to help me through my first deadline with style, grace and
love, and a little cyber champagne at "the end." Thanks
also to my dear friends Olga Mitsialos and
Anne-Louise Dubrawski for reading, encouraging and
making suggestions. Very special thanks to Tracey West,
reader, fan and suggestion person extraordinaire. And big,
big thanks to Susan Litman, my editor, and to Gail Chasan
and Leslie Wainger, for taking a chance with this book
when it had so very much wrong with it at the start!

Prologue

Tumah-ra Island, Arafura Sea

"There's fresh blood in this." Flashing a torch around the top of the cliff face, Tallan O'Rierdan, Nighthawk code name Irish, pointed out the stain to his team partner: a skidding footprint with a small dark pool near the heel.

Braveheart, the enormous bear of a man beside him, grinned, his teeth startlingly white against the camouflage-darkened face. "So you nailed him. That was one hell of a shot in the dark, Irish."

Tal shrugged, squelching the instinctive surge of guilt. "Nowhere vital, by the looks of it." Yet his gut roiled. Shooting people went against all he believed in. Even hitting scum like Burstall, a renegade Fed who'd committed murder and almost killed a fellow Nighthawk, cut deep in a place he didn't want to analyze right now. But his objectives were clear: treat anyone injured by the rebel militia's free-for-all attack, find Burstall and bring him in—or down. "He's still on the move—toward Ka-Nin-Put."

Braveheart nodded. "Let's go."

The black camouflage paint on his face drove him nuts, but his training forced him to not scratch. He had to be invisible, unrecognizable in the jungle fatigues Nighthawks wore on recon in Search and Rescue assignments: just another soldier in a faceless army.

But the people in his secret army were SAR experts, non-official hunter-gatherer spies in a network only the top brass of any government knew existed, in a world few dared enter. The shadowy world of the Nighthawks.

"I'll go this way. You take that path and get to the village from behind. That way we cover our bases and block off escape."

Braveheart looked doubtful, but Irish's word was law on the field. "Meet in the middle?"

Tal nodded in detached interest, thinking how he'd treat the injured left to rot by the rebels. "ETA fifteen minutes."

The whining of bullets came closer as he ran, half crouching, toward the village, slinging his assault rifle behind him. Mortar bombs dropped not far off, thunder-filled quakes beneath his feet. The night sky blazed with the hail of silver and bloody fire, harbingers of death outshining the stars.

Sudden eerie silence all around Ka-Nin-Put told him the rebels had bolted. The brave, strong rebel army walked the walk and talked the talk with harmless villagers and young girls, but bolted when a few men with guns came near.

Just as well. If I found any of the little bastards now... He kept the rifle firmly behind him. Temptation clawed at him as it was, the gnawing need to avenge what couldn't *be* avenged.

Keep it together, O'Rierdan. You're Search And Rescue, not search and kill.

From house to ravaged house, he found them all burned, with fallen and hanging doors and shattered windows bearing mute testimony to the rebels' attack—almost no evidence remained of the lives that once filled this quiet jungle village.

Please, let the Navy have got them out first. He didn't know if he could handle seeing any more people left for dead in a gaping, rubble-covered hole, or to find half-starved shivering kids hanging on to a cliff shelf until they fell into the sea. He had the skills to save them—and he would—but the nightmares the rescues engendered left him sleepless for months.

A pall of gray smoke hung beneath the night air, obscuring the stars. The stench of blood, fire and death lay everywhere. Casualties of war, they called this. Collateral damage. "What a load of crap," he muttered. There was no *acceptable* number of dead when you walked in the shoes of the people who'd lost *acceptable* family members or you found the bodies of the *casualties of war* hanging from trees or hacked to pieces. He couldn't let it happen if he could do anything to change it.

A long, quiet groan alerted him. He wasn't alone here.

"Kumusta po kayo? Doktor po ako," he called in Tagalog, hoping he got the words right and wasn't asking for something stupid like an umbrella or a cat skin. *Hello, are you okay? I am a doctor.* *"Gusto ko kayong tulungan."* I want to help you.

"Ai," came a weak call to the left.

The man was old, frail, very thin. His sallow dark skin hung in loose folds all over him. His almond-shaped eyes held no pain. "I cannot move," the old man said in his native language.

A puncture wound in the upper stomach, deep and lethal. The powder around the wound told him they'd shot this defenseless old man at close range: enough to have a near-identical wound coming out his spine, leaving him crippled. His vital organs would empty themselves out as he bled internally to death.

Tal didn't dare move him. "I will help you," he said in Tagalog, and gave the only help he could: a whopping shot of morphine. Then he sat beside the poor old guy and held his hand as he talked about his family and his lifetime in Ka-Nin-Put.

Ten minutes later Tal closed the man's eyes, got to his feet and punched the tree the body rested against. It shouldn't be like this! It was so bloody *wrong* to—

Sudden rustling let him know he had company in the steaming, acrid darkness. Probably Braveheart. But it could also be a villager hiding until the danger passed…maybe a child, injured, or dying… *"Kumusta po kayo? Doktor po ako,"* he called again, unpacking the rest of his kit in case of serious injury. Yeah, he'd blow his cover if it was Burstall or even a Nighthawk, but this was why he'd left the Navy to join the elite spy-rescue group. It wasn't the worst risk he took on assignment. If the rebels found him, they'd take him as hostage to tend their injured—then barter him for a very high price. If he lived.

But the only answer was silence: no one called back, not in any language. "Hello? Who's there?"

In the quiet punctuated by the whine of bullets, his scalp prickled. No time to pack up his kit. Even if it was a Nighthawk out there, he'd blown his cover as a burned-out ex-Navy guy turned beach bum pilot, with mountain climbing and rappelling experience. Only Anson knew he was a doctor. He was so fanatical about Nighthawk security no operative knew anything about each other's life or background.

Except Songbird. An imp inside him gave the reminder. *She knows more about you than Anson ever will.*

Damn it, would he never stop thinking about her?

"G'day." A man dressed in black limped out from the tangled undergrowth around the village. With the night goggles, Tal saw the blood flowing down the man's left leg, and his savage grin. "Nice greasepaint on the face. Are you the bastard who shot me?"

"Yeah, and I can do it again." Tal scrambled up to come face-to-face with him. He whipped his night rifle from behind, praying Burstall wouldn't take up the challenge. In automatic mode, he checked Burstall's injury. Crikey, was that a cracked patella? Knees were so tricky to repair—

"Don't move." His eyes glittering in the darkness, Burstall held a grenade right in front of Tal's face. "Don't move, all you painted-up boys playing spies in the bush, or this one's dead meat. You shoot me, the pin's gone.''

Despite the dank, sultry heat, Tal broke out in cold sweat. One year of psych training was enough to tell him this guy had a serious mental problem. He had to convince Burstall they were alone, then talk him down. "There's no one there.''

Burstall sneered. "If you think I can't hear your mates belly-crawling through the undergrowth, you're even dumber than you look in your flak jacket and war paint, Rambo. So tell them to stay where they are,'' Burstall said softly, holding the grenade right in front of Tal's sweat-soaked face.

A lightning second to weigh his options, then he yelled, "Do as he says." If Anson or Linebacker tried to play the hero, or Braveheart did something smart with one of his pyrotechnic gadgets—talk Burstall down, now.

Tal spoke with quiet persuasion: the soothing tone he'd always used for his unstable or distressed patients. "You're surrounded. Give up, while you can. You may have some legal leverage now, but if you kill someone—''

"Yeah, I have leverage after trying to kill one of yours. I was a Fed, Rambo,'' he sneered. "All you emergency service and government goons stick together. You're one of them, this Mission Impossible group McCluskey's involved with. You kept me from getting to McCluskey, and taking Lissa.'' Burstall's eyes narrowed in the dark. "I don't like losing.'' He took another step back, pulled the pin on the grenade, threw it and a smoke bomb to the ground right beside him. "'Bye, Rambo.'' He laughed as he dove out of sight.

Tal bolted, but the grenade was already exploding beneath his feet. He flew through the air, feeling the flesh on his thigh sear, his bone crack and burst through the skin. His cheek tore apart when he hit the low branch of a tree face-first.

There's no other doctor to patch me up, no chopper close enough to here to take me to Darwin in time. I'm gonna die.

And strangely, only one regret stabbed him about his pitiful circus of a life: he should never have given in to Anson's dictate about leaving Mary-Anne alone, even for the sake of her safety. He should have kept asking about her. He should have found her, gone to her...made things right. Now it was too late.

I'm sorry, Mary-Anne. I'm sorry for everything.

When he landed on the ground, he was already out.

Chapter 1

She took the massive bunch of dark red roses with a gracious smile, to the beat of thunderous cheers. Turning to her backup singers and the dancers, she handed each a rose and took her bows with them, knowing they'd resent the hell out of her for the audience's enthusiastic response to her generosity.

Oh, Verity West is so magnanimous...

They'd all kill to have her life.

And all she wanted was to kick off the heels making her feet ache, go home, make a hot chocolate, curl up with her faithful dog Charlie Brown and sleep. Invite the family to stay. No hellish workouts or starving herself. No long hours in rehearsals and with stylists and couturiers. No adulation, groveling or saccharine-sweet impertinence from agents or producers, reporters, wannabe socialites or begging visits, letters, emails or tapes from singer-songwriters in her mould.

And best of all, no men showering her with compliments

and gifts, all hoping to be the one to brag that they'd broken the Iceberg's famous cold shell and gotten her in the sack.

Final night of the Sydney tour. Here we go. Party time...

Backstage, she donned a simple white sheath. The famous twisted curls glowed with flame, so the media said—better than the schoolkids' taunts of "better dead than red"—pulled up in a clip, tumbling down to her waist. A gold rope pulled in the dress at her waist and showed off her breasts...and no one knew how much unflagging discipline it took to keep her glorious figure.

Fat girl, fat girl!

She plastered a smile on her face and headed for the limousine, smiling and waving, signing autographs. Wishing Gil was here to laugh at the absurdity of her life, to help her survive the predators—to hold her when she cried. For cool-as-ice, touch-me-not Verity West was a marshmallow inside. A shy girl living in the public eye. A stranger inside her own life.

The heart of the girl who hid from the world was still beating within the slender, lovely shell. Still sickly sweet, trusting and vulnerable Mary-Anne Poole somewhere deep inside, seven years after becoming Verity West.

She spent the evening encouraging hopeful singers, talking to kids who'd won contests to meet her and fending off men's smug I-know-you-want-me advances with her trademark cool smile and quiet wit, counting the minutes until she could leave.

Then a waiter passed her. Inconspicuous; there one moment, gone the next. Pressing a note into her hand.

Change your key, songbird. In the shadows of the alley, a ghost from your past awaits.

Escaping through the kitchen and service elevator of the exclusive hotel, she ran past the blinding glare of flashing bulbs in her face and slipped inside the leather-lined luxury of the darkened car. "Thank you," she sighed. "What's the deal?"

Nick Anson, her secret boss, smiled at her. "Sorry, darlin', but you're getting a throat infection. You need a fortnight off."

She sighed with the intense relief she always knew when she had to drop work for a mission. "My agent and manager will have collective heart attacks. Could be fun. Where am I going?"

"This is the most vital mission I've ever given you, Songbird." Nick threw it at her, hard and blunt. "You'll spend the first few days in Mekalong Island in the Torres Strait—and you know why, since you stole his file when my back was turned."

Her heart stalled, then kicked again. All she could think of was, *What can I say to that—sorry, yes, it was me?* But she didn't think she *could* speak right now. God help her, even in shock her body was primed already, pounding with excitement. She had to fight to get one croaked word out. "And?"

"And we need Irish back pronto. He's refusing to answer my calls or messages. It's up to you. Make him want to do it."

She jerked up in the seat. "Me? But...his wife—"

"He's been divorced for three years." He slanted her an odd, probing look. "Wasn't that in the file I let you steal?"

She kept her mouth clamped shut. He knew damn well it wasn't on file. Nick Anson was too much a rabid perfectionist to leave it off file—unless he'd had a damn good reason to do so.

No point in drawing this out. "So you know about our past." She drummed her fingers on her leg, the only visible sign of the internal explosion of her heart. "The tabloid stories, right?"

"It's how I came to recruit you in the first place. I saw the possibilities in case a mission like this ever came up—and so I sought you out." Silence filled the car as she absorbed, then accepted, her ruthless boss's reasons for first contacting her to join the Nighthawks. Then he went on in his smooth-as-molasses Southern drawl.

"The future of the Nighthawks depends on this mission. No one else can possibly handle it, so the American office sent the request to me." He hesitated. "Irish broke into the office several times to access your file, after you two ran into each other at headquarters that day. I believe you two have a mutual chemistry that, together in one place, would create an explosion big enough to rock the planet."

God help her, Nick was right, and she didn't know if Earth was ready for the explosion. Nick Anson had to be the gruffest, most irascible and unwilling Cupid ever to plague man and woman. She'd thought she'd never want to see Tal again, nor he her, yet it seemed neither of them could forget...

"Will you do it?" Nick asked quietly. "Will you work with him? This mission won't be an easy one, on any level."

Was she shaking with excitement, or fear of what seeing Tal again would do to her? "You don't know what you're asking."

"You're not Mary-Anne now. You're Verity West, and aside from your phenomenal talent, you're a brilliant, brave and beautiful woman whose skills have saved more than one operative in the past. I'm proud to have you on my team. I know you can do this."

"A penny looks pretty when you shine it up, but it's still a penny." She bit her lip, feeling rimmed by shadows of the past. Going to Tal would mean inflicting deeper cuts on old scars...and exposing her long-hidden heart—being Mary-Anne again. But Nick couldn't know that: only Tal would ever know. She took a harsh breath, squared her shoulders and lifted her chin. "All right."

He nodded, having expected no less. "This is going to be harder than you know." He pulled a bundle of photos from a folder and passed them to her. "I kept more than his divorce out of that file I let you steal. I've kept a secret from you about Irish for the past fourteen months.''

Mekalong Island, Torres Strait

No time left! No time! The typhoon's gonna knock them off the cliff shelf into the sea. There's only one chance now! If I don't get the kids into the bird in time—

Tal woke with a start and a hard, guttural curse.

Would he ever be able to put the memories behind him?

Rolling jerkily off the lounge, he laid a towel over the sweaty plastic before he resumed his position, hat over his eyes to block out the violent sunlight. Not bad, the deal Anson made with him. For the hardship of hiding out under an assumed name—finally being the beach bum pilot his cover had always been—he got a massive payout and all operations paid for, past, present or future. Only two left to go to finish the muscle layering on his leg, and one to inject more collagen and massive doses of vitamins beneath the slow-fading scars on his face.

After the last op, he'd be almost as good as new…ready to face Mum and Dad with his new look. He couldn't go home yet. The folks had all been through enough with Kathy's sickness and death. Sending a few postcards from nonexistent Navy ships in different ''postings'' was better than telling them the truth.

The squeaking sound of feet shuffling over the hot, creamy-white sand gave him thirty seconds' warning. Someone was here. Time again for the stares, the sidelong looks and whispers. ''The poor thing, he must have been so handsome once…''

To add another twist to the rack, the stranger had a CD player on—there was no radio station on this remote island—and of course, it was *that* song.

'''I never thought we'd break up, at least not for good. When it came to goodbye, I never thought we would. But I was wrong about you, you found someone new, and you were wrong about me, I found someone too…'''

''Farewell Innocence.'' *Her* song…perhaps *their* song. Would he ever know? The jackhammer hit his guts with the first wistful refrain. Words and voice, so strong and incredibly pure, woven together like the strands of harp and violin and transposed into human sound. Sheer perfection. There was no way in hell he'd ever forget that voice—or the girl who'd owned it.

Had they made a new version of the song, without background music? Seemed even more haunting without harmony. She sounded so scared, so lost. As she had ten years before when—

He couldn't escape her, no matter where he went. Even without the constant dreams of her, with constant radio airplay of her nine worldwide hits from three albums, avoiding the memories was the impossible dream. Her first smash hit— "Farewell Innocence"—had taken up permanent residence inside him from the first time he'd heard it...wondering every time if she'd written about their life and his betrayal of her ten years ago.

Mary-Anne, oh, honey, it wasn't like that!

The singing stopped the same time the foot-squeaking ended. "Hello, Tal. Nice shorts—more casual than the Flying Doctor, Navy or Nighthawk getup. You do get around, don't you?"

Great, now he'd upgraded from dream to hallucination. Her songs did that: he'd spend the next few hours creating scenarios where they'd meet again. So many years wasted in insane hope, hearing her voice, turning around so damn fast he got dizzy only to meet emptiness, the darkness of ghosts taunting him.

She'd never come to him. They were both different people now. *He* sure as hell was different—as was she. A reversal of lives. The cruelest joke ever played on a man.

But it didn't stop his body from lighting like a blowtorch, filling with instant heat, his heart bounding up into his throat with useless, stupid hope against hope. From praying that this time it would be real—it would be her, his Mary-Anne, standing in front of him, with that sweet, high-lipped smile of hers.

Can it, O'Rierdan. She's never coming back to you.

"Well, I see you're as rude as ever. Don't you say hello to old friends anymore?"

Well, that was new to his reunion scenarios.... In his dreams she'd been furious, smacking him as he deserved, or running into his arms and kissing him senseless. But the gentle amusement in this voice confused the hell out of him. He really was losing it...

"Aunt Sheila would be ashamed of your manners—and Uncle Dal would clip your ear, boyo."

He frowned, blinked slowly beneath his hat. He'd all but forgotten that silly joke of hers. "Mary-Anne?" he croaked.

"Either that or your worst nightmare, O'Rierdan."

The silver-gold shimmer of laughter rocked his soul. Now that his prayers had finally come true—she was here—what did he do, yell at her for taking so long, or pin her beneath him and love her until he'd slaked half a lifetime of aching fantasy?

Uh-huh. One look at the scars on his face and leg and she'd be begging him. Yeah, that was gonna happen.

"G'day, Mary-Anne." He didn't have to lift his hat to see her: she was a tattoo burned on his brain, seared on his soul with a branding iron. She'd lived and breathed, gasped and moved beneath or above him in his dreams every night in hot, vivid color, since he was sixteen. He lifted his knees to hide his hard, primed body, ready for her to say the word. Man, he *hurt* already, and she'd only been here a minute. "So Anson's bringing out the big guns to make me answer his summons? He must be desperate to convince *you* to come to me." He heard the guttural rasp in his voice, the hot, essential male-to-female thrust-and-parry he'd only ever known on this gut-deep level with her.

Another soft ripple of laughter, full of heart and soul and fire. "That's what I said, but even though we've never worked together, we both know Nick. Never say die."

"Yeah." He grinned beneath his hat. Man, he loved her laugh—almost as much as he'd loved the gentle touch of her silky-soft fingers on his skin, as innocent and sensual as the kisses they'd shared as boy and girl. The unbidden fantasy was so intense he almost felt the tender glide of her hands…the kisses so saturated in love they filled all the empty places inside.

Can it, O'Rierdan. It wasn't going to happen—and he didn't want her here, re-igniting hungers that he'd never explore. *Who are you kidding? They're in permanent ignition, ready to explode.* "Tell him you tried. Want a drink before you go?"

He could hear the grin in her voice. "I'm booked in at the local B and B for three days, so cut the rude stunts. I outgrew being hurt at them by the time I was about twelve."

Despite the roaring inside him, the exploding Molotov cocktail of fury at his life and her expected rejection, he chuckled. Ah, it felt so good to talk to her outside the bondage of sleep. Never, in all their long history, had she let any of his gauntlets lie unchallenged, defusing his quick rages with a smile. It was refreshing after a year of overdone kindness born of pity and the sidelong glances of people unable to handle imperfection. And having her finally here, with him in the flesh, made him feel like more of a man than he had in years.

And what good is that going to do me? He'd spend the whole time she was here in knife-edged, gut-gnawing hunger. Variety might be the spice of life, but right now this particular life had all the pepper it could handle.

So find out why she is here and get rid of her. Fast. "So spill. What does he want from me? Whatever it is, the answer's no, but what the hell, I can listen for a few. Entertainment's kinda self-made in these parts."

He heard the shrug in her voice. "Sure. But I'd like that drink. In private. I'm booking your services for the afternoon."

His laugh sounded rusty from disuse…and its feel-good release unleashed hungers he'd worked long and hard to lock away in darkness. Yet the response in kind came, dragged from him against his will. "Baby, watch your terminology. There could be a journo behind any shrub, if they know you're here. I can see the headlines now. *Verity West Writes A New*

Song. 'I go for banged-up bush pilots and pay them for their services.''

She laughed again, its pure sound vibrating with the serenity his soul had hungered to know the past ten years—yet he heard the stress beneath. So it wasn't any easier for her to face him than it was for him to know she was here... "Well, at least I know you, and you're my age."

"I'm more attractive, too," he remarked blithely, hiding his pounding heart. Mad, crazy—totally certifiable—but the hope wouldn't go away. She didn't say no or retreat behind embarrassed silence at the thought of being with him...

He heard the sorrow in her voice as she replied, "Nick only told me about your accident two days ago. If I'd known—"

Sudden cold rage made him grit his teeth. "Yeah, right. We both know you wouldn't have come. Anson must've painted you into a corner to get you to come here. But it's a good revenge, seeing Tallan O'Rierdan, walking freak show, huh?"

"Oh, grow up, Tal," she snapped.

His hat suddenly flew over the sand, leaving his unprotected face exposed to her gaze. Refusing to back down, he stared up at her, blinking against the harshness of the hot sun and its silver reflections off the water and bright sand all around. "Well?" He knew what she'd see: the destruction of the face women once compared to a blond-haired, brown-eyed, living angel.

Yeah, right. An angel with pink puckered scars down the left side of his face, perfect on the right. Sorta like those half-man, half-woman carnival freaks people used to pay to gawk at in horrified fascination.

Come on, Mary-Anne, do it. Gulp. Cry. Turn away. Just do it and get the hell away from me!

But he couldn't drag his gaze from her. Oh man, she was more beautiful in real life than in her promo and society shots, or even his most erotic dreams. Her vivid, wildly curling hair fell free, tumbling over her shoulder blades and full, sweet breasts. Her face glowed pale and soft-freckled in the tropical sun, dominated by a sweet, high-lipped pink mouth, sleepy cat's eyes and a delicately wide jaw, lending feminine character and strength to a pretty face: the vividness and fire she'd once had in abundance beneath her shyness. She wore a loose tie-up flowered cloth as a skirt and a sapphire-blue bikini—striking against her silky skin, glowing hair and eyes. A floppy straw hat half fell over her face, flat sandals on her feet. A smudge of zinc cream covered her pert nose to stop further freckling.

Lovely. Entrancing. *His* girl as he'd always wanted her, fat or thin, shy recluse or world-famous ice queen, because she'd never been an iceberg for him. Just natural, unadorned, innocent Mary-Anne, who took in all strays and came out of her habitual hiding with both guns blazing to take a passionate stand for the rights of any underdogs she took into her heart.

His girl, as God made her.

And true to form, her direct gaze stayed right where it was, traveling from his eyes to his messed-up cheek and back again. "Did you think Nick would send me to you without showing me the pictures first? He might be hard, but he's not a sadist." Her face softened then. "He wouldn't hurt you after what you've already been through, Tal. And neither would I."

It took all he had to not grit his teeth. "Thanks, but you can leave the pity at the front door," he drawled.

"Pity? For what?" Her slumberous eyes blazed with the flaming *aliveness* that had always made her a goddess in his eyes, no matter what her weight happened to be at the time. "You chose your path, like all of us did when we joined the Nighthawks—I'm sorry you've paid the price for your dreams, but you did what you love best. Yes, I hurt for what happened to you, but I don't pity you—and why would I hate you for marrying Ginny? There were no promises between us, just a lot of dreams on my part." She sighed. "And even if Nick hadn't shown me the pictures, I never had hang-ups about physical perfection. I was a nurse—and with my childhood, I can't afford to judge people by their looks. I'm not Ginny. You should always have known that."

The mention of his ex-wife released a store of anger buried

deep beneath lazy mockery for months. "Oh, I don't know. You both did a runner when life didn't work out the way you wanted."

She tilted her head, utter perplexity now mingled with the dark flash in her eyes. "What reason would I have to hang around home, except my parents? I had college to finish, a job in the city, friends, someone to love me." Her hands fluttered up. "We used to be best friends, Tal. I thought you'd be happy for me." She spoke the words with genuine confusion, but they hit him like a careless blow right to the gut, and his heart—what was left of it. That was the crux of it: he'd never spoken the words. All the promises he'd wanted to give her remained locked inside a boy's heart, filled with dreams of their future. His father's son, all right. He'd never had the gift of the gab like Kathy, who'd been the only O'Rierdan to escape the family's introverted, take-it-on-the-chin genetics.

The name jabbed at him, an uppercut he took in silence with the other blows life punched out. His cute, funny little sister was gone and he'd lost Mary-Anne, the only girl who'd just—

No use thinking, or feeling. He heaved to his feet. "You're right. I was happy for you. Okay, I'm yours for the afternoon, for the minimal fee of one hundred dollars per hour including tax." He picked up his Akubra, jamming it over his head—keeping one side of his face in shadow.

"You know, you could earn that much an hour working as a doctor—or back in Search And Rescue with the Night-hawks—and you'd get a lot more job satisfaction," she said softly.

He wheeled around on her, his throat burning like the sudden prickling heat behind his eyelids. Damn it, didn't she *know* he had to fight the longing every day? "Don't go there." His voice was harsh and as tortured as a crow in a bird-catcher's trap. "I'm not coming back. Anson can go to hell."

"Why, you want him to join you?" She stood him down, defiant, lovely in radiant emotion, and, like a flicked switch, a compass turned north, he was where he needed to be, with her—and it turned him on even more. "So it seems your life-long hatred of self-pity suddenly looks good from the other side of the fence?"

He almost flinched, remembering his careless, thoughtless, get-over-it remarks about her size—then he understood. The unaccustomed gibes were deliberate, designed to make him think, feel—and fight back. "Call it self-pity if you like. I call it accepting life as it is." He took a few steps. No hiding the limp. No exaggerating. "SAR operatives run, free-fall out of choppers, climb down cliffs and belay into caves. They climb trees to hide from the enemy and drop out of them to attack. I'm what you might call 'out of shape.' I don't do that any-more."

He finally obtained his first objective: she turned away.

In the awkwardness of sudden silence, laughter filtered from the other end of the beach from kids splashing, families play-ing together in the tropical warmth of the late-summer day. The scent of frangipani and fallen coconuts filled the air. It was picture-perfect, a secluded tropical paradise, and she was finally here—yet he felt so damn *alone*. Aching, needing to reach out, to have the sweetness of contact with her for the first time in more years than he could count.

She tugged at an errant curl dancing in the warm breeze. "So you're just giving up? Leaving the life behind that once meant everything to you?"

The darkness unleashed…the trembling started deep inside, the damn-fool useless *longing* to go back. All he'd ever wanted was to be a doctor, to help those in desperate need.

The flash of agony ripped through his leg, the faceless en-emy, the constant reminder that his life was over.

He had to get out of here before he fell down.

He tipped up her face, denying the searing heat that raced through him with the simple touch. He couldn't afford to think about it. "Don't go there," was all he said—but even he heard the anguish, the need, and he didn't have a clue which need it was right now, to have his life back or to have her.

Didn't matter: his dreams were gone and he couldn't have them back. He dropped his hand, ready to run.

Limp, his mind corrected in sardonic self-mockery.

The tender touch on his face halted him with the force of a Mack truck. She'd always had that way with her; her power all the stronger because she had no idea what she did to him. "Tal," she whispered, holding him captive with warmth and caring. "Don't go. Please."

He turned his face back to hers and aching hunger ripped through him: the need to fall inside her arms, lips and body— and just maybe, lost inside her, he'd find himself once again.

"We'll talk tomorrow." Desperate, his voice sounded thready now, weakening under the relentless jagged hell in his thigh.

He couldn't face her like this. When he could walk again— when he'd got his head together, drowned the roaring need under the force of a few cold showers—he'd feel more in control.

"All right." Then both hands touched him, cupping his face. Her silky-soft fingers trailed over his scars, unconsciously erotic on the exquisitely sensitive skin. "You didn't lose it all. Dreams change shape. You can still help. You can be so much more than you are now." And the soft brush of her mouth on his shocked him to the core. "We'll talk tomorrow."

He swallowed down the ball of hot gravel in his throat. What a man—he wanted her like hell, but could barely stay on his feet. He couldn't stand for her to see— "Just go, okay?"

As if she knew, she dropped her hands. "Okay. But we have to talk. Consider your services hired for tomorrow—all day."

With a massive effort, he grinned. "I'll look forward to that, Miss West."

Already walking away, she flicked a strange, intense look over her shoulder. "I hope you still feel the same when you know what services the world requires from you—Dr. O'Rierdan.''

When she'd gone, he grabbed the walking stick he kept hidden behind the deck chair near the wooden shack he called his home-office. Gritting his teeth, he hobbled slowly into his cabin. As soon as he was inside he fell to the bed, pulling his legs up, fighting the fisted knuckle-punches gutting him from the inside, from thigh to groin. When he could finally pull it together, he rolled to the bedside table and grabbed the full syringe he kept there and injected his leg, right beside the scars.

He forced himself to lie flat on the bed, waiting for relief. He only took enough to take the edge off, never often enough to get addicted. But when it came, he had two choices: this or puke and pass out where he landed. If he was flying when the pain hit, he settled for a local anesthetic until he got back here.

At least he had a choice today: he could feel sorry for himself or think about why Mary-Anne was here…why she'd gotten mad with him, why she'd touched him—kissed him.

Could it be that maybe, just maybe, beneath the cool, controlled, icy Verity West persona that she presented to the world, *his* Mary-Anne—lovely Mary-Anne, so sweet and caring, so fiery and passionate as she'd only been with him—still existed? And if she did, maybe…God help him for even hoping—

Don't think. Don't go through this. She'll be gone soon, back to her latest album or concert or high-society party, and your life will go back to crap.

Yet as he drifted into restless sleep he knew that, no matter why she'd come to him or what happened after, life was going to be a hell of a lot more interesting this week than it had been over the past fourteen months.

Chapter 2

But she slipped farther down…poor baby was hanging on to his knees, screaming, her eyes begging for help while the boy on his shoulders began to topple, flung against him in the gale-force wind. Held up by lines suspended from the chopper, they kept slamming into the cliff face. A man, three kids and a split-second choice: which kid did he save? Or did they all die?

Drenched in sweat, he jolted up in bed.

Five-thirty. Would he ever break the habit of jerking awake the second the sun peeped above the horizon?

At least it broke the nightmare.

If he'd never joined the Nighthawks, there'd be no blood-soaked visions stalking him whenever he closed his eyes. He'd be a hardworking Flying Doctor, helping people in isolated areas—

Stupid. I left the Flying Doctors and joined the Navy to make Ginny leave me—and I left the Navy for the Nighthawks because it was my dream to work in war zones, helping those in greatest need. I jumped at the offer, knowing all the risks.

Tal limped to the bathroom, gritting his teeth hard when he

had to balance himself to use the john. At least he was walking again this morning—hell, he was lucky he could still walk at all. The docs in Darwin saved his leg from amputation when putrid infection set in, and the most up-to-date plastic surgeon put his face back together—but all the medical magic in the world couldn't make his femur knit as it had before, or stop the pain. So this was life, Jim, but not as he'd known it.

You could be so much more than you are...

He stood face-up beneath the stinging spray of a cold shower, half wishing it would drown him. Why wasn't it cold enough to freeze the mess in his head and douse the raging fire of turbulence inside? Just yesterday his life was quiet, serene—

And boring as hell. You know you want to do whatever this mission is. Any reason to be with Mary-Anne again is worth it.

No, damn it, he couldn't afford to want her here. She'd gone light-years out of his reach...and there was no way he could be *friends* with her. The white-hot chemistry that confused and embarrassed the hell out of him when he was a kid was still in full force. He'd never be able to look at her without wanting to drag her somewhere and make fast, furious love with her.

Dripping wet, he looked at himself in the mirror. The daily grueling upper body work had done its job: he was in top condition. The days in the sun left his olive skin glowing with health. Even his other leg looked good thanks to the one-legged skip-rope jumps he wasn't supposed to be doing. As good as he was going to get—nowhere near good enough for a star like her.

So get over it.

Yeah. After half a lifetime of obsession with her, *that* was gonna happen.

Fifteen minutes later he left the shack and headed for the massive garage-style hangar that housed his little Cessna. A solitary sunrise dip and swirl with Harriet, the one faithful love of his life, would do him good.

He jammed his Akubra on his head as he limped down the

soft, sandy dirt track bordered with wild hibiscus and azaleas. If any of the few tourists here got up this early, they'd be off on the high bush tracks or running on the sand to worship nature at its finest: an unspoiled sunrise over a calm, pristine reef ocean. They wouldn't even notice him.

The irony of it. All he'd wanted once was to be overlooked, unimportant, faceless—but he'd wanted it by his own choice.

Not like this. Never like this.

Passing the nearby B and B on a palm-shadowed, winding path near the beach, he heard soft, peaceful Eastern music. He turned to find its source—and lost his breath.

She stood gracefully on one leg on a towel on the creamy sand beneath a swaying palm tree. The other leg extended back, her arm forward in a balletlike stretch movement. Her hair glowed in the gentle morning light, roped down her back in a simple plait. Barefoot, wearing shorts and a lemon tank top, breasts free of restraint—*Don't go there*—her face scrubbed fresh and shower-clean, she resembled the simple, natural girl she'd once been.

And he was gone. The old ache, the helpless longing he always knew when he'd see her waiting for him at the billabong between Eden, his family's farm, and Poole's Rest, filled him again.

Mary-Anne had been his since she was six and she'd first seen his face. He'd been hers from the same day, climbing a tree for her against his will, a sulky eight-year-old putting a nest of dead swallow's eggs back up in the branch to stop her tears for the task she was too chubby and ungainly to perform herself.

Not wanting her then—but wanting to be like her. A timid girl hiding in the shadows of life, she still had the courage to love, to give, never anything but herself. She'd needed him to help with her makeshift hospital of limping wildlife rejects, and he'd needed someone to need *him*. Just…a friend.

When his feelings changed, he didn't know.

Maybe when Kathy died of leukemia when he was fifteen? Mary-Anne had left him speechless with gratitude when she'd sneaked through the window into his room the night of the funeral and held him all night in empathetic silence, letting him cry.

The erotic dreams of her started that night, a crazy wildland fire out of control—but, confused and ashamed, he hadn't called it sexual love for his best friend.

Perhaps he'd known on his eighteenth birthday. His parents, close friends of her parents, had invited her to his private party with just the families, knowing she wouldn't come to face the town kids' taunts in a pink fit. Yet, knowing how much it would mean to him if she showed up, she'd stood outside the door and fumblingly handed him his favorite coconut-cream cake. Ginny, rich, pretty, spoiled and his try-hard-wannabe-girlfriend, had seen the pride on his face for his best friend. Spiteful and jealous, she'd said the name Mary-Anne suited her, since she was straight from "Gilligan's Island." All the kids laughed, but Ginny couldn't work out why Tal didn't. She didn't know he'd always had a secret crush on the more famous Mary Ann, for being so sweet and kind to dopey Gilligan.

Three months later he'd turned down a major football contract in Sydney—and of all the kids in town, only she understood. "Oh, Tal, I'm so glad I'm not losing you," she'd whispered…and, seeing her unashamed love for him in her eyes, he'd kissed her for the first time. It was gentle, sweet, awkward and terrifying—a fragile moment of beauty he would never forget. A son of four generations of blunt-talking, hardworking farmers who didn't know how to communicate, he'd prayed that his touch, his kiss, told her all he could never bring himself to say.

But he'd known he loved her the night his loving, distressed parents and Ginny's rich, smarmy father, holding the mortgage on Eden and having ambitions for the boy he'd hand-picked to be his son-in-law, had backed him into a corner with two words. "Ginny's pregnant." They hadn't had to say more: they'd known he'd stand by her, even if Ginny had had to find him in a drunken stupor after a college party to seduce him. Well, she'd claimed he'd been enthusiastic, but since his mate Carl had had to carry him back to his dorm, and the remains of his puke had lain on the floor beside the bed, it hadn't seemed likely.

Years later, Ginny had taunted him with the truth—but he'd never questioned at the time that the baby was his. She'd suckered him, grabbed the chance to get a ring from the boy Daddy had planned for her to marry. The boy she'd known could barely stand her.

As the families planned his wedding, only one thought filled his mind. *How the hell do I explain this to Mary-Anne?*

He'd given a quiet, unemotional promise to marry Ginny and left them to the champagne Max had brought—refusing to lie or to act happy about it—and he'd run to the tiny billabong, desperately needing comfort. Home from nursing college for the summer, Mary-Anne had come to him—but with tears streaming down her face for what they both knew would be their last time together.

"Ginny's pregnant," she'd cried, her pure, clear voice sweet even in her severe distress. "The whole town knows—and they're all laughing at me. How could you? Why didn't you make love to *me?* Why her? I thought...I thought—" She'd broken off then, her face ravaged and white, her eyes dark and burning.

He'd ached to comfort her...and to get comfort himself. Caught like an animal in a trap from one damn time he couldn't remember. But he'd been in it then, for better or worse. Much worse. "I don't love her. I—I don't even like her," he'd stuttered, desperately needing someone to talk to...aching to hold her, one last time...

"But you slept with her. You gave *her* your baby." She'd flung off his touch, his pleading hands. "Go on then, marry her—have your baby—have a nice life with your skinny, pretty wife—but she'll never love you the way I love you!"

The words he'd always longed for her to say as woman to man, said a day, a week, a year too late, while Ginny listened in from the shadows. Ginny, who'd thought she could cheat and lie to get him, and he'd love her anyway.

Ginny had made him pay for the love he'd only given to Mary-Anne. She and Max had made him pay every hell-filled day of the five years he'd been forced to stay with her, long after their mythical baby returned to the world of fairy tales and any real baby she might have had could have been any guy's in town.

And Mary-Anne had disappeared into a fairy-tale ending. She'd hooked up to the stars, and dropped his Mary-Anne carelessly in some other galaxy where he'd never find her again.

As if dragged by magnets, he limped over to her now. "Well, I never thought I'd live to see this sight. Mary-Anne Poole is exercising of her own free will."

"I didn't lose those sixty pounds by crying in my coffee." She turned her face to smile at him, sweet and unselfconscious. "And it's rather hard to keep up a schedule of two hours of dancing and singing almost every night without some basic fitness skills."

"I thought you famous pop-star types slept 'til midday."

She smiled at that, too. "You're still a farmer's son, why shouldn't I be a farmer's daughter?" In a movement shimmering with tranquil beauty, she lifted her arms to a sky alight with the colors of sunrise. A gentle scent of rose and lavender floated to him, filling him with a sense of peace and rest.

"What are you doing?" he asked gruffly, gulping down a ball in his throat at the sight of her effortless grace, the fluid movements of her body. *Oh, man, I'm losing it already…*

"Tai chi. I finished my yoga a few minutes ago." She sighed. "I feel like a sloth. I usually do an aerobic dance workout, run five kilometers and do an hour of weights, but I 'officially' have a throat infection, so I'm taking a week or two of R and R."

He shook his head, laughing. "Mary-Anne Poole running five Ks every day and working weights. Is this the same girl who hid behind the equipment shed during phys ed?"

"No, it's Verity West and Songbird." Her tone measured, even. "I work out every day. I have to stay fit to keep my jobs."

"And the jobs are so important to you?"

She gave him a look hard to interpret. "Verity West is my cover, like being a beach bum pilot was yours until you quit. I have to work hard at getting it right, but the life I lead for my cover is no less important to me than yours is to you."

"Right. You lost the weight *first.* You were famous four years *before* you joined the Nighthawks, and you reveled in it!"

She didn't blink at his knowledge of her life. "So you asked about me," she said softly. "You found out about me after that day we passed each other in the hall at headquarters."

He flushed. Had Anson told her about his attempted theft of her files, the suspensions he'd endured for refusing to drop what Anson called his obsession with her? Had she asked about him, or was the gnawing need for them to be together again only in his mind and heart? "Can you answer the question?"

"Fame was important once." She swung her body around in another motion of unselfconscious confidence. So unlike the girl who hunched over to hide her breasts, walking with a shuffle, as if apologizing to the earth for being such an unwanted part of it. "I thought I'd feel better about myself, being accepted. But being chased and photographed by the press, or enduring endless speculations about my sex life—no, I don't revel in it." She shrugged. "I just wanted to be like everyone else."

"Why?" To him, she'd always been a miracle, a true human in a world of wannabes. A girl who just loved him for what he was, in a town where everyone adored him in an awed manner as Cowinda's sports star and valedictorian. In their anxious eyes, he was only as good as his next performance or exam result, his university entrance mark and the beautiful girl on his arm.

"Being normal has its merits, Tal." She lunged down, her

arms reaching out, fingers reaching to emptiness—but it didn't seem to bother her, the emptiness. But she'd never had the emptiness inside, like him.

"Why are you here?" He had to end this farce, the pretense that they were still friends, soul mates—anything but the lovers he couldn't stop aching for. "What does Anson want?"

"Are you sure you're ready to hear it?"

He shrugged. "I know Anson. Always expect the unexpected."

She scouted the area to be sure they were alone. Then she looked him in the eyes with her usual directness. "Here's the deal. We have a whirlwind public courtship, then do a fake marriage ceremony in either Sydney or Cowinda within three days. Then we begin a European honeymoon where, under the cover of a happy couple, we investigate the activities of a black market arms dealer and an apparent houseguest wanted for murder."

The world swung around him like her body in that Tai chi movement. Oh, man. Was this a twelve-year dream coming true or yet another king hit from life? Trying to reorient himself, he lifted his brows and sucked in a breath. "O-kay," he said for the sake of saying something, vaguely proud of the fact that he hadn't fallen over. Yet. "Why us?"

She gave him a resigned grin. "The tabloid stories Ginny sold. What else?"

He felt the flush creep up his neck. After he'd left her three years ago, Ginny had made a fortune by selling stories to TV, radio and the print media that her husband had taken the Iceberg's virginity by a billabong. When the story grew cold, she'd added her belief that Mary-Anne was cold to all other men because she was still, and had always been, wildly, madly, deeply in love with Tal O'Rierdan—even when she was married to Gilbert West.

"But the stories are lies," he argued.

"And no one knows that but you, me and Ginny," she said quietly. "You and I won't argue, and Ginny's not likely to recant the story. Nick thinks we can use it to our advantage."

He shook his head. "But it's breaking all his you-can't-know-your-fellow-operative rules—and it's bloody dangerous for both of us. We know too much about each other—homes and families, our backgrounds, strengths and weaknesses. This is crazy. The mission had better be something right outside the box."

"Um, you could say that." She looked around the beach again, checked the path. When she spoke, it was low and urgent. "One of the Nighthawks is working with the arms dealer and his houseguest—an international criminal who's out to destroy us. Operatives are dying or disappearing on the most basic missions. Some found alive were loaded with a chemical cocktail that left them with no memory of who they've been with or what they'd been doing. Top-secret information's reaching the wrong people—stuff that could only come from a Nighthawk. It can't be us, since you've been in hospital and here, and I was on the *Blue Straits* tour. Through a few loyalty tests, Nick's narrowed the field down to three probabilities—Solomon, Angel and Jack."

"I don't know any of them," he remarked, frowning.

"That's why it has to be us. Neither of us has worked with them. They're among the few who *don't* know I'm a Nighthawk. If we go undercover to find the rogue, they won't know who we are."

Feeling as though she'd loaded *him* with some chemical cocktail that had robbed him of the ability to think, he rubbed his scar. "Why do we have to appear married? What's the full deal?"

"Think about it. Verity West is the most famous iceberg since the one that sunk *Titanic*. 'The woman so faithful to Gil West's memory she lets no man touch her,'" she parroted, mimicking her press. "Taking a lover would bring on rumors and speculation that could blow my cover. But marrying my 'first lover' should be a reasonable marriage in the eyes of the world."

"And?" he pressed, trying to focus on the mission rather than the old obsession with them finally becoming lovers—

and the instinctive knowledge telling him they'd be lovers hotter and more eternal than the fires of hell, as infinitely beautiful and unforgettable as the gates of heaven.

"And anyone can check our supposed history. Ginny's version of our hot little teenage affair is documented in a hundred places." She shrugged, but the soft rose touching her cheek and throat told Tal that, if she didn't want him now, she sure as hell had back then. Did she hate herself for loving him once or—*yeah, right, O'Rierdan*—was she hiding the fact that she wanted him still? "So we're legitimate. Our marriage won't be questioned, nor the fact that we're hiding out for a honeymoon."

"Bloody hell," he muttered, just to fill the silence. For the sake of saying *something* because he could never say it, could never ask her... *Will it be real, Mary-Anne? Will we be lovers, as we both wanted so badly to be, once?* "I guess they're right."

She held herself tense for a moment before she relaxed. He could feel her palpable relief, but he didn't know why. What had she been so afraid he'd ask her, or say? "The certificate looks so real it will pass any scrutiny. The registry will keep it on file for a month. The press won't find the celebrant— Nick's flying in some Nighthawk friend or relative. Not that we'll ever know who she belongs to, or where she lives." The ironic twist to her smile told him she found Anson's never-know-your-fellow-operatives rule as frustrating as he always had.

"And after?" He watched her closely. "What happens after the mission? Taking a lover might destroy your cover—but so will the act of getting married again. Even if we make the breakup look realistic, it shoots your reputation to pieces. Imagine the tabloids. Verity West's Marriage Fails After Only A Week."

"I know." She sighed. "This is the most vital mission we'll ever do. If it has to be my last, it's worth doing. It's more important than my feelings or yours, or even the rules on secrecy between operatives. If the Nighthawks are destroyed—"

He tapped his foot. "I know the drill. I did the introduction course, too. Nighthawks come first or regional stability is in peril. Lives could be lost."

Her eyes burned into his. "Why are you talking like you don't care? You always cared too much before, taking stupid risks to save people! Flipper and Braveheart told me about the time you belayed down a two-hundred-foot cliff during a freak storm to save six kids on that island off East Timor. None of the others would touch it, not even Braveheart. You nearly died, yourself, you broke your shoulder and severed your Achilles tendon, and got a severe concussion, but you saved them!"

He flushed again, stuffing balled fists into his pockets. "The guys are exaggerating again." And he hadn't saved them *all*.

"Why, Tal?" she insisted, her face vivid, alive with her lifelong passion to help others. "Why don't you care now?"

He turned away, fighting the old longing again. "You tend to get less emotional when you've become a statistic, too."

"I don't believe it!" she cried. "You know how many people died the night the grenade hit you—but do you know how many innocent Tumah-ra people lost their homes and families? They're not *statistics* any more than you are. I was there before the war, gathering information—I knew their names, I'd been to their homes, ate and drank with them, cuddled their kids…and now they're gone! I—" She choked and wheeled away, dashing at her face—and she gave a wobbly little hiccup of distress, one that melted his heart, that made him care, made him want to be something better. For her. And, if he was honest, for them: the faceless sufferers that his girl took into her heart and soul and made real to him.

He couldn't stand there as she ached and cried for the fate of people she didn't know. The statistics she made so *real* by her vividly stark words. "Mary-Anne?" He touched her shoulder.

"Linebacker died last week," she muttered, scrubbing at her face. "Shot through the head at close range."

He staggered back until he found something to lean on: a

rough-hewn post on the beach path. "My *God*. Linebacker was twenty-two, twenty-three at the most. He was a real nice kid—"

"He was such a sweet boy. He wanted to save the world." Tal watched her tears well up and overflow without shame: a purity of grief he'd always associated with her. "I don't want anyone else to die, Tal—not if I can do anything to stop it. I *know* what these people are feeling—and I'd do anything to stop it. Anything." Without warning she turned into his body, burrowing against him, gulping so hard he could almost feel it hurting her throat. "I've lost someone I loved so much I wanted to die…"

The unforgettable Gilbert West. She'd met the pathologist at her last teaching hospital before graduation. Gil had adored her from first sight, married her within six months and created the legendary singer-songwriter Verity West from the cripplingly shy Mary-Anne Poole, by the simple act of believing in her. He'd entered her in a contest where she'd sung the haunting "Farewell Innocence." Within weeks a major recording label picked her up, and when her first album, *Nobody's Lolita*, went triple platinum, Gil gave up his career to manage his wife, to be beside her through good times and bad. And he was, until the day he died.

No wonder she'd written the poignant hit, "Making Memories," when they'd got the shocking diagnosis of Gil's impending death from multiple, inoperable brain tumors. Gilbert West had made all her dreams come true.

And this was totally the wrong time to be reacting, burning with the feel of her breasts pushing against his chest, the soft mound of her femininity pushing against him as she cried. *Can it, O'Rierdan. She wants comfort from an old friend, that's all.*

But his rock-hard mate inside his jeans didn't have a conscience, just one hell of a long-denied need for her—and an intense instinct that he'd finally find his way home in her soft warmth, so close beneath those flimsy layers of clothes.

A couple of tourists emerged from their huts. Turning the

scarred side of his face away, he watched from under the protection of his hat. Did they recognize the famous trademark hair and statuesque beauty of Verity West? Was that the Iceberg, burrowed into the body of some island hick?

He could see the headline: The Iceberg Melts On The Cripple.

The reality of their situation cooled his libido in an instant. He'd be *damned* if she'd have to face another sleazy tabloid headline because of him. "Let's get out of here."

She nodded as he snatched up the bag beside her towel, grabbed the tape deck and towel with it. "We don't want tourists grabbing free Verity West souvenirs," he said dryly.

He took her along the path to his plane's steel hangar and, once inside, slammed the roller door behind them. "So you'd do anything to help those people—even marry me?"

Had she flushed again, or was the color rising in her cheeks because of the heat of the day? "If that's what it takes, yes." The huskiness in her voice lingered. With the gentle flush in the valley of her cleavage, it made a lethal chemical catalyst for his libido, sending it right back into hyperdrive.

"We'd have to make the marriage look like a real one in case any paparazzi break in," he said bluntly, struggling to keep focused on the mission. "We can't use two beds."

"I know." It might have been a trick of the light, but the rose in her face and throat seemed to deepen as she looked anywhere but at him. "It doesn't have to be awkward, does it? We…we've slept together before."

He chuckled. "Slept being the operative word, Mary-Anne. We were kids. We haven't *slept* together since that night we camped by the billabong when I was sixteen—and I never touched you."

"I know that," she said—too quiet—and he wondered what was going on beneath the surface. Gentle, smiling, cool and calm one minute—erupting with mini explosions of passionate emotion the next. It was like playing Blind Man's Bluff or Murder in the Dark. "We didn't touch then, we won't now."

He wheeled around to look at the half-dark hangar wall,

watching shadows of waving palms chasing each other through the window's early morning light. "You might be able to control your passion for me, sweetness, but you'd better ask before you assume the same for me. I'm a man now, even if I don't look like much of one—and I've still got a man's needs."

"I heard about your needs." He jerked his head around to look at her. A flash of ancient pain, the sense of a wound too deep and raw to touch, crossed the banked fire in her eyes. Yet she met his gaze without flinching or apology. "Ginny made sure I knew all about those needs of yours. She gave me every detail."

A helpless curse ripped from his throat, strangled fury that had nowhere to release. "Mary-Anne—"

"There's no need." Another careless shrug: a flimsy defense against this too intense conversation in a hangar that was way too hot, humid with diesel fuel, morning mist and late summer sun. She was all rosy now, flushed and damp, as if they'd spent the past hour— Oh, man, was he trying to *kill* himself? Why keep fantasizing about what he'd never have?

"What matters is stopping Darren Burstall and his rogue from taking down the Nighthawks one by one."

He went totally still. Something cold and slimy touched him, slithering into his soul like hideous poison. "Burstall?"

She licked her upper lip, taking the sweat beading it, he noted absently. "Yes."

"You're telling me he's not dead?" he muttered through stiff lips. "Anson left Burstall alive—and he didn't tell me?"

"They chased him, but they had to save you, then he shot some villagers. They couldn't leave innocent people there to die. Then Burstall hooked up with the rebels in Tumah-ra," she sighed. "It seems he's made interesting connections, rendering him useful to people Interpol would like to take down—people with billions in offshore accounts and vested interests in the oil off Tumah-ra's shore. Too many reasons to keep those dumb rebel kids on the island rigged with weapons and stop the UN taking control."

He barely heard her. Burstall was *alive*. Anson didn't get him! Burstall was alive—the insane bastard lived and breathed, killing and maiming innocent people to feed his mania—and Tal's rage, cold and flippant for so long, boiled over.

"Anson's a noble, interfering, self-righteous *jerk!*" His fists slammed into the hot steel wall so hard it buckled outward and his knuckles scraped raw and bleeding. "Why the *hell* didn't Anson tell me all this? Didn't he *know* I'd want to go after him myself—and not just for me, but for what he did to Skydancer, Countrygirl and all the poor villagers he shot in Tumah-ra?"

"I don't know. You'll have to ask him." With folded arms, she watched him destroy the hangar wall, her high-lipped rose mouth rimmed with a touch of fastidious distaste.

"So the Iceberg's wondering what sort of husband she's got after the sainted Gilbert?" he sneered, baiting her. "Well, look on the bright side, sweetness—it's all a game of pretend. You can dump me at the end of the mission, guilt-free."

She didn't bother to answer his taunts. Instead her lips curved in a slow smile. "I've got something more constructive for you to do than breaking walls, Tal," she breathed, "and I think you'll agree that it's a lot more fun."

She moved a step closer, her eyes dark and slumberous, her body radiant, as if in the afterglow of hours of scorching-hot lovemaking. "It's something I want—something I wanted so badly for years—but I never found the courage to go after."

Rage took wings as he watched her move toward him, her eyes alight, her mouth curved in promise. His heart slammed against his ribs. His head spun with the hope his body wouldn't let him ignore. What was she saying—that for all those years, she wanted him…that even now, looking like he did, she'd—

Uh-huh. He got real turned on looking at himself in the mirror every day. Why wouldn't she?

But the cynicism wouldn't take hold. His man's need, hot and hard and urgent, kept hammering at him, *Do it, do it, do it. Ask her. Touch her. Take her. So many years wanting her,*

*needing her, and she's so close…so damn beautiful it hurts.
Do it!*

It almost killed him to speak, but he managed to say,
"Well?" in a strangled croak.

She moved to him, step by slow, sultry step. She lifted her
mouth to his ear and whispered, in the gentlest, most seductive
of tones, "Revenge…"

Chapter 3

"I'm on. I'll take Burstall down—for Linebacker's sake, if nothing else."

Mary-Anne—for though the rest of the world saw her as icy Verity West, she never had, could never think of herself as anything but plain old farm girl Mary-Anne—sighed in quiet relief at his words. She'd been pretty sure he was hooked even before she spoke Darren Burstall's name—but it was hard, so *hard,* proposing this mission to Tal.

She couldn't show him how she ached for him, that she had all the empathy in the world for his suffering. Growing up different, plain and overweight but with extraordinary talent, gave her some insight into how he must feel about his injuries. Golden-haired, olive-skinned Tal, handsome, athletic and brilliant, Cowinda's pride and joy, must be chafing so hard against the physical restrictions he couldn't change.

But the harsh, dark-souled man in front of her, so unlike the sweet, caring, tongue-tied boy he'd been, could still fire her rebellious body's response to him like fast-melting honey...

With the exception of her poignant four years with Gil, she'd only ever wanted one man to be her lover—and if anything, his scars made her want Tal more. If he was less of an angel now, he was all male—all strong, dark, tense *man*. The brooding depth gave him a raw, pulsing sexuality that left her screaming for fulfillment. Tal was her sweetest taboo, the forbidden fruit: her best friend, confidant and rescuer too many times to count, pain and rejection and dark, hot temptation rolled into one man. Fantasy and reality in blue jeans and black T-shirt, his muscles bunching in riveting, superb maleness as he buckled the hangar walls with a punch.

How could she tame her heart or stop the midnight call of her body? Within a year of Gil's death, the dreams she'd had of Tal all through her teen years started again—and all the guilt in the world couldn't kill off the wanting. And five years later, Gil was a faint, sweet memory…and she called another name when she woke up at night in a sweat of fevered, aching need, after white-hot erotic dreams of the man she could never have.

"Okay, let's get out of this sauna and make arrangements. I have the license. Nick faxed it to me last night," she said crisply to hide her pounding heart and sweating palms.

"He always counts on getting his way," was all he said. Then he gave her a curious look. "Nick? That's…unusual. He's always Ghost or Boss to the rest of us—or sir."

She shrugged. "We have an unusual relationship, because of my fame. I call him Ghost or sir on missions, of course."

But he merely shrugged. "Who's our backup?"

"Ghost is taking this one. It's been ranked top secret, and apart from Braveheart and Wildman, all the other operatives are coming in from Virginia, hand-picked by the brass and absolutely trustworthy," she answered, lost between relief and a kind of sick despair. Once upon a time, Tal had always known when she went into hiding and he'd always come to her, made her talk out her fears or pain. He'd made her love him more every time, just by caring so much. But it seemed he'd lost his radar with her. They were drifting further apart every moment, and she couldn't do a damn thing to stop it, unless she wanted more operatives to die.

He frowned. "I'd have thought Skydancer would want to be in on this. This whole thing started because of a private show between Burstall and Skydancer, right?"

"Skydancer does want in on this—so does Countrygirl—but she's pregnant and they have kids. Ghost won't bring them in because Burstall's primary target's still Skydancer. Skydancer's also worked with Jack and Angel in the past. And Burstall has an obsession with Countrygirl. We traced a call he made to her through four computers and two different satellites."

"Nice complication," he remarked, frowning in concern. "If Burstall ends up taking one of us, he's likely to demand hostage exchange to get Countrygirl."

"You're right." She looked in his eyes, willing hers not to show the aching hammer of desire hitting her. She could die and not care, when she looked into his eyes... "This whole assignment will be dangerous, without the complication of being conducted in the public eye. My fame is the only ticket we have to get into where Burstall's hiding—but it's a flimsy cover at best. We'll be lucky if they don't suspect us from the get-go."

Tal frowned. "Where is he? Where are we going?"

She grinned at him. "That's one advantage to this—we've hit the jackpot. He's in Amalza. One of the smallest Mediterranean islands outside the Mallorca group off the coast of Spain—"

"Where famous honeymooners hide out, and tax cheats, illegal arms dealers and financial wizards from the wrong side of Wall Street abound," he filled in with his own special blend of unique grinning irony. He leaned against the hot wall, folding his arms across his tight, muscled chest as he smiled still, making her gulp. "So are we going to an 'Embassy' do?"

Grateful for the distraction, she laughed. The "Embassy" was infamous among those in the know. The Embassy was an enormous white *castillo* of indecent luxury owned by Robert

Falcone, an illegal arms dealer who absconded with billions of dollars when his British financial empire collapsed. Anyone who was someone on the international black market partied there—and any spy worth their salt longed to infiltrate it. Every Interpol operative or connected agent dreamed of being the one to take the slippery-smooth Falcone down. A party there was a potential gold mine for the arrest of the century.

"That's the point of us going, Irish," she shot back with a lifted brow and a quirky grin. "Why do you think Nick wants me in on this? Burstall's in Amalza. We've heard rumors he's in hiding out at the Embassy. Falcone has made it obvious he'd love to get up close and personal with me. Falcone's *castillo* has tighter security than the White House, but if I go to Amalza—even on my honeymoon—you think he won't send me an invite?"

"Oh, he will," Tal retorted dryly. "The question is, will I get an invitation to come with my lovely wife?" He limped to the roller doors and with a bunching heave he let fresh air in, tropical-warm and sweet-scented. "It's too hot in here."

Oh, yeah, baby, it was hot all right...she was so *hot* she could barely think. Those well-worn jeans molded his butt like a loving glove... "Doesn't matter," she made herself say through a lump in her throat that felt like sticky tar in summer. She'd had a love affair with that butt for more years than she wanted to remember. "I can't afford to go without backup."

He turned back to her and frowned. "Mary-Anne, this is your venue. What use will I be in this beyond window-dressing? I am—was—Search And Rescue. A field operative and medical officer. I might be a doctor, but I'm a bush kid. Tact and subtlety, or sophisticated man-about-town, I don't think I'll handle well."

"Maybe it's time to stretch your skills." She hoped her lifted brow, her cynical smile, would stop the unwanted question forming, unbidden, on her rebel lips. "I learned to play the game quick enough. I'm sure you'll pick it up."

He gave her a strange, intent look. "Are you willing to risk your life on me being able to do that?"

"As much as you are, I guess." Could she handle a fake marriage with Tal, when it could all end in a week and she'd never see him again, except on trips home to see the family—

The thought slammed into her like a truck hitting a kangaroo on a dark Outback road. She felt the blood drain from her face. "Tal," she whispered, "our parents—"

He jerked around to her, taking her words and running with them. "Not just them. Your brother. My grandparents. Bloody hell, the whole town of Cowinda."

"My mum and dad and Greg always wanted us to get married," she whispered, her mind racing along with the horror of the scenario unfolding in her mind.

"My family, too. Dad dreamed of Poole's Rest and Eden being one property, after Greg chose vet science instead of farming. And you know how much they love you." He looked at her, his face dark as a sudden Outback storm. "We can't do this to them."

"Ghost wants our families as part of the thing, to make it authentic. They're to come to the wedding, but they can't know the truth about us being Nighthawks, or our marriage being for the mission…" Her mind went blank. "It would put them at risk."

"The media will hound 'em as soon as the mock-up starts. Our mothers would give the lot of 'em the scoop on us, along with a bang-up dinner to celebrate." His muscles bunched again as he leaned both hands on the metal wall. "They won't just be heartbroken when we break up—they'll be publicly humiliated."

Tal always called a spade a spade. A hand lifted to her mouth. "When we break up after the mission…if it leaks out later that our wedding was a fake, I don't think they'd get over it…"

Still leaning on the wall, he turned his face to her, his eyes burning. "It's crunch time, Mary-Anne—regional stability or the people we love. We either let someone else handle the assignment or we break our parents' hearts and shatter the illusions of everyone in Cowinda."

More ramifications Nick couldn't possibly have taken into account, because he wasn't born and raised in a tiny, close-knit Outback town of less than eight hundred people. "We're the shining kids of Cowinda. We put the place on the map."

"I was just a doctor. You're the one who put Cowinda on any maps that matter, sweetness," he interjected dryly.

She waved that off. "Our marriage would be a fairy tale come true for everyone in town—well, except your ex-wife, her daddy and a few of their followers," she added, just as dry. "There's no way everybody wouldn't know, or find out. The wedding being leaked to the papers is a vital part of the assignment. The paparazzi would bolt to Cowinda to get the scoop. Everyone's going to have a point of view, want their moment of fame. And when we break up, it'll make them all look like fools."

Still slow and thoughtful, he said, "I don't know about you, but I can't do this to Mum and Dad. Not since Kathy died. I'm all they've got left—and they want me to remarry and have kids." His mouth twisted in a cynical slash as he finished.

Mary-Anne almost gaped at him. "You haven't told them about the accident, have you?"

He shook his head. "Anson wanted it kept secret until my contract runs out. I wanted to wait until after the final operation, anyway. After Kathy's death...I couldn't scare them like that, or wreck their dreams of me finding another wife."

She clenched her jaw shut. The man was stone blind, deaf and stupid...he had to be. A woman stood right in front of him, almost dying with the pain of wanting him, and he couldn't even see it...

Don't make a fool of yourself over him again. Once is enough.

"Tal, people have died." Though a tad croaky, her voice was calm, a thin cloak hiding her anguished desire. "The Virginia office is right—only you and I have any chance at all of pulling this mission off. My fame will give us bona fides. Falcone's interest in me guarantees us an invitation into the

Embassy. Ginny's lies about us will help make our marriage look above suspicion. Any other newcomers to the island would be too heavily scrutinized.'' She couldn't stop the words tumbling from her mouth like falling dominoes. "It's not only the Nighthawks that will be destroyed with this, Tal. Falcone's latest arms cache is big enough to start a war or three. The rumor mill inside Interpol has it that he's not just sending guns to Tumah-ra, but bombs. He's got caches ready to send to rebel militia and fractious religious groups in volatile countries in Africa and Eastern Europe.''

Tal bit out a gritty epithet. "Then what the hell do we do? I won't sacrifice our families, but I can't risk innocent lives for them, either.''

She bit her lip and held on to the too warm wall, feeling the discomfort vaguely as she took on possibilities and discarded them. "I don't know.''

"There's only one thing to do.'' The note in his voice made her heart hammer. He tipped up her chin, and looked deep into her eyes. "We sacrifice our feelings, and get married for real.''

Chapter 4

"W-what?" The world shifted around her. She staggered and almost fell. Tal lifted a hand to steady her, but she moved a step back, hating the delicious, pulse-pounding sweetness that filled her whole body when he touched her. "W-what did you say?"

He shrugged, obviously seeing no need to repeat himself.

Marrying Tal. Was this a dream come true or a nightmare about to descend on her? From meeting him again to fake marriage to reality, in the space of three days—

"Are you all right with that?" he asked, his tone grim. "If it's too much for you to go through—"

Disoriented, she blinked up at him. "T-too much…?"

"Marrying me, sweetness." He touched his scarred cheek and then made another tiny sneering motion with his mouth. "I know it's a big sacrifice for you—I realize that I'm a huge step down in standards for a star like you, Miss West—but I thought you cared about saving lives, and our families."

"I do!" God in heaven, he *was* blind. How could he not *see* how much she wanted him? "If we get married, *sweetness,*

I'll try to make the sacrifice if you do,'' she snapped. "You make yourself pretend you want me, and I'll pretend you're still the love of my life.'' She used the same cynical, flippant curtness he used on her. *Damn* him! Why couldn't he be happier about this situation? It wasn't as though he had to put up with—

A caressing touch on her shoulder startled her. "*Pretend* I want you? You think I'm going to have to pretend?''

She stood speechless, unable to move or breathe, or think of anything but the sweet ache building in her, wanting, hoping...

"You think it will be an act?'' he pressed her, his voice soft, dangerous.

She managed a shaky whisper. "Don't lie to me, Tal. Lie to the world if you need to, but not to me.''

"All right—you want truth?'' He took a step closer to her, his sudden grin half-savage, highlighting his scars. "I might not look so good these days, sweetness, but I'm still a man. Everything that needs to functions just fine, and the thought of kissing and touching you—for the mission, of course—isn't a big hardship.'' He moved on her, his face like a savage angel's, tender and taunting. "I've forced myself to think about kissing you, touching you, and pretending to want you, oh, about two hundred and forty times since I saw you yesterday. Just in case I needed the scenario for a mission, of course. For the sake of the greater good.'' He smiled at her, his eyes dark, unfathomable—his body way too close. "I must have been training for this mission for a long time, honey, because I've been *pretending* to want you ever since I was fifteen.''

She wasn't just hurting now—she was in anguish. A few sultry words and she had to fight the urge to reach out and touch him, trail her fingers over the hard ridges of muscle, to pull his mouth down to hers for a long, scorching kiss...

Dear God, I'm still pathetic. I can't walk away free if Tal can still keep me bound in the same old chains.

"Mary-Anne?''

The name was soft, husky. Sending flaming arrows of need and hope through her stupid dreamer's heart. She turned away, blinking hard. "I'm Verity." The words were shaking, wobbly in their flickering defiance—and a complete lie. She'd never been Verity, not even to herself. Even after seven years, she still felt a slight shock when anyone called her by her stage name. More often than not, she had to force herself to remember.

"Not to me." The tenderness in his voice showed he saw what was going on beneath the would-be calm surface of her. "Just like I was never the town winner to you. Mary-Anne Poole was the best friend I ever had. I can't call you Verity."

She clenched her fists, willing the tears not to fall. "Okay. Call me Mary-Anne if you want—if it works for the job." Still with her back to him, not daring to show her face, she shrugged. "We both know neither of us would have ever come to the other again, if it hadn't been for this assignment."

"Maybe you wouldn't have come to me," he replied, still quiet, restrained. "I'd have come to you if I'd thought you'd listen to me. I've wanted us to make peace for a long time."

She swiveled back to him, with a glimmering smile of bravado. "Sure. No problem. Peace achieved. Friends again, just like always." And she held out her hand to him.

Instead of taking it, he looked into her eyes for a moment— and she trembled without his even touching her. With a single look she was a stupid schoolgirl, the shy, chubby loser head over heels for the popular, handsome boy next door.

She tried to drop her hand...but he caught it and lifted it to his mouth, palm up, the kiss gentle yet intensely sensual: a slow, tender seduction. "Were we just friends, Mary-Anne? You told me you loved me. You wanted my baby."

She froze, her eyes fixed on his, her body hot and weak and shaking with the neediness she couldn't hide. "I was a silly girl," she whispered. "And like all good fairy tales, the prince rode into the palace with the real princess." She knew her hot, shivering reaction to him was giving her away. "I failed the princess test. I missed the pea under the mattress."

Breathing against her skin, he moved his mouth with infinite tenderness to her wrist. "I guess I'm not your average prince. I liked Cinderella a lot better than Snow White or Sleeping Beauty. And I always preferred Mary Ann to Ginger."

She shook even more, as shooting darts of heat burned up the flesh of her arm to her deepest core. "Y-you did?" Then, without warning, blinding reality hit her, broadsiding her with its careless cruelty. "Of course you did. Well-endowed redheads were never your thing, were they?"

He frowned, his mouth pausing between tiny kisses. "Who fed you that piece of propaganda—or do I even have to ask?"

Snatching her hand from his, she wheeled away. "Does it matter? It's old news. I got over it years ago."

"Obviously." His voice was gentle. He moved closer to her, so close he must be able to feel her intense response to him...like the gullible fool she'd always been with him, her heart and body screamed, *Touch me, Tal, oh, please, touch me...*

Untamed magic surrounded him, an aura of dangerous chemistry ready to combust in her—a catalyst straight to a broken heart. And no Gil waited this time to save her. *Don't look. Don't let him touch you. It's the only way to survive.* "We've made peace—we'll do the mission. Let's leave it at that," she muttered, willing him to follow her lead.

"What if I can't leave it like that, Mary-Anne?" he asked, husky, dark and aching. "What if I want to show you how good I can be at pretending to want you—right here, right now?"

Helpless, mesmerized, she turned her face to his...and she saw that look on his dangerous, beautiful face—the look he always wore before he'd kissed her on those pulsing-hot summer nights by the billabong, when she'd dared to believe the boy she adored really wanted her, really loved her. And her needing body performed a coup d'état on her will. "Oh, Tal," she whispered, and swayed toward him.

Then she noticed a shadow flitting from a shrubbery to the

trees beside the runway. Within the shadow of another bush, she could see the reflecting glint of a lens aimed their way.

He can't see Tal's scars.

Desperately she grabbed his shoulders, pulled him close and pressed her mouth to his, hoping Tal had enough acting skills to make his side of the kiss look passionate—

Yet before she'd even finished the thought her tongue was twined around Tal's so tight it gave a whole new definition to tonsil hockey, her body splatted against his like paint on a wall, and she wriggled and whimpered like an excited puppy going walkies, begging for petting and stroking…and oh, he was petting and stroking, his hands hard on her bare skin beneath her top, sending jolts of heated need from skin to her most feminine core while she purred and moaned in helpless pleasure…

Verity West the Iceberg? An iceberg in the equator, maybe. She was so hot for him steam was curling around her ears. Even though warning bells in her brain screamed at her to back off, she couldn't help it. Her hands found his bare skin and caressed him in ardent eagerness. Her mouth, with a will of its own, remained plastered on his, harder and hotter. She couldn't stop it, couldn't help the languid sexual heaviness of her body, urging her on, urgently demanding more, demanding it all.

Cupping that glorious male butt in her hands—oh, finally, this fantasy had come true—she moved against him, purring in delight at the hard male reaction she felt to the kiss. His kiss grew even harder. His hands were everywhere, caressing her bottom and breasts, sending hot shivers of need through every single nerve ending. The alarm on her lambent hormonal clock shrieked at her—five years, four months and eighteen days since she'd last been loved by a man…and oh, to love Tal, to finally have him touch her body, slowly strip off her clothes and bring her to completion, right here, right now…

"How's the throat infection, Miss West?" A familiar voice: Gary Brooks, from a tabloid not known for its discriminating taste in stories—or their verification of what they printed as "fact." "Did you feel like sharing germs with your lover?"

Tal's whole body jerked. She emulated the movement, not needing to pretend to make it look real, she'd forgotten all about the damn reporter. She gasped and turned away. Oh, no, what had he seen—and photographed? "Tal, close the door!"

"Too late, sweetness," he whispered dryly. "As was your intention, I think, when you grabbed me." With a cynical twist to his smile, he turned toward the eager photojournalist, still snapping off picture after picture.

"No," she whispered urgently, pushing him back. "Don't let him see the scarred side of your face!"

His face cooled with instant comprehension and complete self-control. With a pang, she knew her chance of making a connection to him was gone. He shrugged and moved into the shadows. "Sure. I don't particularly want to be scrutinized as the walking freak show fiancé or husband of the beautiful Verity West. Just as well, I haven't seen my parents since before the accident, and nobody outside the Nighthawks knows about it."

She closed her eyes. She'd foreseen this, but it slammed into her soul—the guilt of a woman who knew too well how it felt to need to hide from ridicule. And she'd done it to him, she'd made him feel not good enough for the person she was now.

Damn you, Nick—you opened the door, then gave him the ammunition to slam it right back in my face.

With all her will, she turned to Gary Brooks, mustering up the haughty, imperious look that had first given her the Iceberg tag, but Tal spoke first from within the shadows, his graveled voice strong and confident. "We'll do you a deal, mate. Take off for now—hold those shots, and we'll give you the announcement of your life, complete with exclusive photos."

Mary-Anne gasped. He'd not only grasped Nick's take, he'd taken full control of the mission in three sentences. Yes, a perfect take on what Nick would want. He and Nick were alike, all right, and in more than just looks.

"Just one photo of you both first, face-on," the man pleaded, who'd obviously already caught on: he wasn't arguing.

"Tomorrow, in Sydney." She jumped in, before Tal could speak. When the journo looked mutinous, she added, "Do you know who this is, Gary? It's the man all the stories were about three years ago. You're going to have the scoop of your life in twenty-four hours. I'm willing to put that in writing, if you go away now. We'll meet you at the Grand Hotel, tomorrow at four."

Gary Brooks's eyes lit with a mingled kind of ecstatic wariness. "I'll release every damn picture by tomorrow if I don't get that contract," he threatened, and left.

"Well, you sure know how to take charge of a situation, don't you, sweetness?" Tal spoke from the superheated half darkness of the wall. "He must have taken about twenty-seven shots of us eating each other alive. Anson will be happy with our progress. We'd better call him to get a real marriage certificate." He shrugged. "We can stay together a year or two, make our families happy, go home for visits, right? I'm not going to risk hurting Mum and Dad, or Aunt Miranda and Uncle Ed—not for any of Anson's save-the-world principles." His eyes glittered with sardonic humor. "And Greg was my best mate for twelve years—we still call each other now and then. I won't dump his little sister, sweetness. You'll have to dump me."

Not knowing what to say, she nodded. Everything he said was right, with the mission and their families in mind—but considering their mind-blowing kiss and its degrading, tacky aftermath, his self-control chilled her soul. "I don't want to get married in Cowinda," she said quietly. The one thing she couldn't face. A real-yet-sham wedding with Tal was bad enough, but she'd never survive the hype and happiness of everyone in Cowinda. She'd break down for sure.

He gave a short laugh, without humor. "Fair enough—it's too personal for us both. We'll do the whole thing in Sydney. We can call our parents when we get there and tell them what's going down. What's the condensed version—that we met again by accident and fell madly in love?''

It took all her self-control to keep the tears in. If he *knew* how she'd dreamed of that since they'd passed each other in the hall at headquarters in Canberra three years ago. How she'd wished she wasn't urgently needed in Nick's office just as he was leaving on assignment... ''That's about the size of it.''

''Okay, done. We'll say problems with your schedule kept us from coming home for the wedding. They'll understand that, and be too busy to think about being hurt, I hope.''

''I think we'd be better off giving it a day or two. We need to orchestrate our romance a bit.''

His mouth twisted. ''Wining and dining, sizzling slow dances, a few kisses. Yeah, a whirlwind society courtship sounds like the perfect end to our decade-old torrid billabong affair. Being in Sydney should maximize the impact. If we hide my face, that is. How does Anson plan to do that, by the way? And why?''

There was no easy way to say it. She took a breath and blurted it out. ''Burstall might not know your real name, but he knows you survived the blast. He knows you're Australian, and he also knows you're a doctor because of the kit you left at the village.'' She heard her own voice, full of quiet despair. ''He knows the extent of your injuries, too—there were several unauthorized hits on your hospital records at the database. You were admitted under a fake name, but we can't take risks. You're relatively safe to go to Amalza if he sees no sign of your injuries or scars, but if we go to the Embassy and you show up with your face as it is now, along with your limp, and being an Australian doctor—all the world knows your profession, thanks to Ginny—it will only take seconds for Burstall to put two and two together, and he'll kill us both.''

The deadly cold look on his face said it all: he already knew what she was going to say before he asked. ''What's the plan?''

Her fists clenched at her sides, knowing that her secret hope of making their "passionate affair" real, was fading with every word she said. "For you to look as much like your old self as possible. Nick had a special set of inserts made to put inside about five different pairs of shoes, to minimize the limp—and you have to wear special cover-up makeup over your scars, so your face looks the way it used to."

The silence was sickening. "*Makeup.* Like a bloody *girl.*" He stared at her as if she'd grown another head. "I'm supposed to put *makeup* on my face. That goop you girls used to wear for school shows that made you look like you'd shoveled dirt on your faces. I'll look like a bloody cross-dresser."

A typical Outback boy's opinion of any kind of makeup. She sighed. "If it helps, this isn't that thick pancake stuff—it's makeup that won't look fake at all. It doesn't look like goop. It will be specially made to suit your skin color, and there's a polysynthetic cover to make it look and feel like skin, so it won't smudge or come off easily. The cream also has vitamins and collagen to actually help lessen the redness. I've used it to soften my freckles. It works. And it's for your protection."

"I don't give a damn if it works. I'm not a bloody actress, and I won't make myself look *pretty* for anyone—not even you." His face was controlled, his fists clenched hard. "I'm not putting any crap on my face. Take me as I am or leave it."

She moved into the shadows beside him. "I can't. If Burstall sees the scars, he'll kill us both. It's not just you taking a risk by going as you are. You'll put me in danger, too, and every operative on the island. I can't marry anyone else without it looking like a setup. Without you, we'll have to send another team in without the cover of being my personal bodyguards or journos covering our honeymoon. Burstall and Falcone will have them killed within an hour of their arrival on the island."

He invoked the name of his savior, but Mary-Anne didn't think he was asking for help. What could she say or do to make this easier? "Tal, I didn't want to do this. Nick ordered it. If it weren't imperative for the mission—and to save your life—''

"I know." He didn't jerk away from her, didn't whiten or show any signs of fury. He simply crossed to the roller door and shut it. "Fine. I might even get to like it, huh? If I learn how to use it right, I can keep it on hand for all social events in the future." He grinned at her, but she could see the gritted teeth, the bleak look of self-hate in his eyes. "That was one hell of a kiss, by the way—but you always were a bloody good actress. Your iceberg rep just got flushed down the toilet. Good work."

She moved farther into the shadows, to cover the shock that drained all the blood from her face.

So despite the obvious signs of male arousal, and the hard passion in his mouth and hands, had Tal only been pretending to want her, just as he'd said? Had he been *acting,* maybe turned on a bit but not enough, while she'd floated three feet above the ground in some love-starved, ecstatic-cloud cuckoo land?

The same old irony. The only man who could tempt her out of her iceberg reputation—who suddenly made her feel as though her fame, success and life with the Nighthawks was some kind of tundra-filled wasteland—was the only one who didn't want her.

His voice, quiet and unemotional, broke into her despair. "What's next, then? What do we do?"

Helpless, not knowing what to say, she shrugged.

He rolled his eyes. "Come on, Mary-Anne. Our cover depends on what you'd do if this were above and beyond the job. What would you do if we were normal lovers? Imagine you'd come here as a tourist, saw me for the first time in ten years and fell for me again so fast you were caught here almost doing the deed with me," he finished with the dark, sardonic smile she'd never seen on his face when they were kids. "What would you do now?"

The cover, the cover! How can he be so clinical? She'd given him the idea of revenge, but he'd taken the bait and swum right into the ocean with it. How could he still be so thoroughly on the mission when all she wanted was another hot, glorious kiss—dragging him inside that plane and…ooooh, yeah…

"Take off in the plane and find somewhere private for us to finish making love for the next day or three," she answered his question, still half locked inside her gorgeous dream.

Tal burst out laughing, hard-edged, ironic, stabbing her heart with its icy control. "Sounds like a good plan to me. Okay then, Miss West—" he added with a swift, mocking bow. "So we go to your place? Sydney's probably the best place to do it."

She blinked up at him. "Um, what?"

His grin twisted. "To start our assignment. Don't worry, *Miss West.* You can safely get in the plane. I'll keep my distance."

Too stunned to do anything else, she obeyed him, climbing up into the cockpit without a word. She sat frozen while he opened the hangar, checked to be sure the journo had gone, limped to the plane, climbed in and prepared for takeoff. She was silent right through takeoff, her mind busy reliving his words.

So Tal was where she'd been ten years ago. Impossible to believe she wanted him. Sure that his accident, and her life now, changed the way she'd once wanted him…

When you lose someone you love so much you want to die, too, you know how they feel—and you'd do anything to stop it.

She closed her eyes, wanting to smack her own forehead for her unthinking stupidity. She should have *known,* should have realized how Tal would take that—just as she'd have taken it if she hadn't met Gil. Verity West, beautiful, curvaceous man-magnet, never needed to hide from the world…but, like Tal, Mary-Anne Poole-West still wanted to.

This assignment would be the hardest of her life—in many more ways than one.

"Where are we heading?" she yelled over the noise of the engine, frowning straight ahead.

He shrugged and handed her a headset similar to his own so that they could speak normally. "Your place would be the most logical place to hide out. We'll tell Anson to meet us there with our kit. I assume you brought backup to the island to bring our stuff to us, and contact that journo?"

He wasn't just with her on the mission, he was light-years ahead of her. She nodded and waited for the rest.

"Good. Then we might as well get going straightaway, and gain some ground on selling the romance of the year. Today's as good as any other day to start. No point in mucking around."

After a moment's stunned silence, she blinked and started laughing—laughing so hard her body jerked and tears streamed down her cheeks.

He turned to her, frowning. "What?"

"You sure know how to shatter a twenty-year dream, Tal." She wiped her face with her hands. "I used to imagine you asking me on a date, or romancing me, or proposing to me almost every day—and my fantasies never included 'no point in mucking around.'"

He gave a slow, reluctant grin. "Sorry about that." He turned back to his controls. "But then, your romantic proposal probably didn't include a few other things it's got, like a banged-up face and leg. I bet I wasn't a has-been, washed-out beach bum, either. I seem to be good at destroying your dreams, *Mary-Anne.*"

"And you?" she asked, hearing the emphasis he'd put on her real name. "What about your dreams? Aren't they ruined, too?"

"I don't have dreams." He thumped his damaged thigh. "Let's leave the past out of this, as far as we can. Your dreams came true years ago—you're everything you ever wanted to be. And I'll bring Burstall down. That's all I ask."

She stared at him, her pain a choking ball in her chest. "Did the accident take so much away from you?"

"Don't, all right?" he all but yelled. "I'm here. I'm in on the mission. Just let me handle this my way."

"Tal—" She remembered her words to Nick a few days before about a shined-up penny, and felt helpless. What could she say? How could she ever make him believe he had so much more than his looks, when she still didn't believe in herself?

They were a pair of cripples, she and Tal: hostages locked in cages so close to identical they could see the other's pain, recognize and understand their fears, yet couldn't reach out to heal. Past and present locked in silent, fruitless battle on opposite sides of the field.

Her empathy was as useless as it was heartfelt.

She blew out a frustrated sigh. Oh, why didn't she *know* what to say or to do to help him, like she used to?

Because back then I knew him like my own soul, and loved him with such blind devotion I'd have walked through fire for him.

But that time was gone, and she couldn't use it. There was nothing left between them to trade on—no certainties, no guarantees. She didn't even know if he wanted her beneath the ice-cold need for vengeance against Burstall.

She was walking in darkness with Tal, not knowing what he thought or felt, and that hurt more than almost anything had since the day Gil told her about the multiple, inoperable benign brain tumors that might leave him with only months to live.

How could Nick ask her to do this? How was she going to get through it?

"Okay." She shrugged, wishing everything didn't always have to hurt with Tal. "Let's get this assignment on the road."

"The shipment of arms is on its way to Dilsemla. I'd appreciate knowing when your end of the bargain is forthcoming."

Burstall pushed a pawn across one square, bored but knowing he had to play a game not of his choosing at present. "I have someone checking out the possibilities at present, Mr. Falcone. With the UN interested in Tumah-ra's future, it's…awkward.''

"For your someone, perhaps. Are they expendable?''

"Not at present. They're my only concrete link to finding the favored name for the oil contract.''

Robert Falcone, a well-built, dark, intensely controlled man in his late forties, moved his knight with precise care. "I see. How many names are up for discussion at present?''

"Seven. The usual big boys, and Haversham.''

Falcone seemed pleased at the news. "Can we persuade the UN representatives toward Haversham in any way?''

"Only by our silence.'' *You idiot.* "Trust me, Mr. Falcone. I was a Federal agent for nine years. They know who we are and all our associates—even vague ones.''

"I'm aware of that,'' Falcone snapped, and Burstall held his breath—but the gentleman gunrunner and drug dealer, well known for ordering a hit on whoever annoyed him, went on smoothly. "I have someone in mind.''

Curious now, Burstall lifted a brow and waited.

Falcone leaned forward, his normally bored eyes glimmering. "I've heard reports that Verity West is coming here incognito for a fortnight's holiday early next week.''

He wanted to yawn. Falcone's well-known sexual appetites left him cold. All he wanted was to get the Nighthawks here, any how, any way. His hunger for revenge on Mitch McCluskey for killing his twin sister—his gnawing need for pretty-mouthed Lissa—grew daily. "How do you know—and what possible influence could she have with the UN delegate?''

Falcone chuckled. "You're not the only one with spies, dear boy. I've had her—shall we say, watched—for years. I have a man on her now.''

Something in Falcone's words chilled Burstall. "And?''

"The delegate, like many men, is a massive fan of hers. If she can get his ear—''

"How do you propose to do that?'' *As if I didn't know.*

Falcone laughed gently. "By getting in her ear. Oh, what a challenge—making the famous Iceberg melt. For years I've thought about getting up close and personal with that beautiful, ice-cold lady and making her melt for me."

He put his hands beneath the table so he could drum them in silence on his legs. His jaw ached from the need to yawn. This man was so boring Burstall even had occasional second thoughts about using his money. "I hear she's not susceptible to any lures of wealth. Or to mixing with the rich and famous."

Falcone only smiled, all his famous polished address back in place, cool and smooth. "Oh, she does—and has. You see, it's not the famous that lure the lovely Miss West, Mr. Burstall—it's the infamous. I met her once, briefly, at a party that was, shall we say, not quite kosher, or government-friendly? The lady has a penchant for walking on the dark side, and flirting with danger. There's more than one way to skin a bankroll, Mr. Burstall—and to make a reluctant woman eager to please you. Knowledge is a useful tool. And if all else fails, there is a man in her past—a man she was extraordinarily fond of…"

Chapter 5

Come on, just do it.

He'd been ready for half an hour, dressed in dark jeans, a leather jacket over a polo shirt and boots—with the special thick, flexible insert that, he had to admit, made walking a hell of a lot easier on his thigh. This was the first official day of their courtship, and Gary Brooks was waiting at Centennial Park, where he'd "find" them sitting by the lake, kissing. They were due there in fifteen minutes.

And he still couldn't make himself dip his fingers—or the special little thing that looked like a mini-shovel—back into the goop sitting on the bathroom vanity in front of him.

He'd already botched it twice, slathering it on because he couldn't stand watching himself in the mirror, putting on *makeup*. Mary-Anne had put it on for him yesterday to meet Brooks at the Grand Hotel, but he was a *man*, damn it, a Nighthawk operative, and he had to do this himself.

"Tal?" A gentle knock on his bathroom door, in the bedroom beside hers in her lovely Sydney waterfront mansion. "Do you need any help?"

He gritted his teeth. "No. Thanks." *Be a man. Do it!* He dragged in a breath, used a towel to blot out the trickling sweat on his cheek, and grabbed the little shovel.

"Protect Mary-Anne. Protect Mary-Anne," he chanted grimly under his breath. That thought alone got him through. He watched every damned movement, as every molecule of the bloody goop landed on his skin like an alien invasion. He forced his fingers to smooth the stuff over the scars, using the special blending sponge to soften the effect, and the ultra-thin layer of artificial skin to cover any lumps, smoothing the edges into his real skin to make him look normal. *Protect Mary-Anne. Protect Mary-Anne...*

He had to blot more sweat off by the time he finally finished—but even under the strong artificial light of the bathroom, he could barely tell that his face had ever been torn to shreds. The evidence of four rounds of plastic surgery was gone. He'd pass muster in the most searching photos...and with his parents.

And yeah, he still felt like a bloody cross-dresser. Normality had too high a price: he was gonna toss that goop in the trash the second this mission was over.

"If Brooks yells 'Miss West' once more, I'm gonna deck him."

From where she moved in Tal's arms, Verity slanted a glance at him. He meant it, all right. Acting wasn't his forte. He'd been stalking around the glitziest locales within the city of Sydney the past three days like a modern-day Heathcliff—tense, brooding, seeming far above all he had to do. In his tux, wearing makeup and the shoe insert, he was every woman's dream man once again, but with a darker, dangerous edge—the true, dark-hearted alpha male.

And he was a Navy doctor again, to boot. In a deal made by Anson he'd re-signed with the Navy before they'd started their campaign, as he called it. They had been more than happy to provide him with a cover, with the added publicity the marriage gave them. "I need to match the woman of my dreams in my career as well as my face,'' he'd murmured as Gary snapped off shot after ecstatic shot of him in his uniform, holding her in his arms. "Not that I could fulfill the demands of either job for long, but the real objective has been attained."

Yes, he was the perfect romantic match for the international darling of the music world…

And she was going silently crazy.

Nick's plan was working without a hitch. Sharing ice cream in the park. Picnics on open boats. They'd been found sharing candle-lit dinners for two, dancing in each other's arms on snug, crowded dance floors and on beautiful, tiled garden balconies under the stars. Impromptu kisses orchestrated by the moment that seemed appropriate for them.

Making her body hunger…but not for the plates of fruit and salad she ordered. She ached with a need so strong she couldn't think, could barely breathe. He slept in the room next to hers in her Sydney Harbourside mansion, and while it strengthened the speculation on their being lovers, it left her tossing and turning, waking over and over after gorgeous, unfulfilled dreams.

And always the flash of cameras accompanied their every move, as well as fans asking her for her autograph, clever journos who found them constantly asking intrusive questions.

Their families were on the way down for the wedding set up for the day after tomorrow. They couldn't keep going like this. They might fool the world that they were happy lovers, but their parents would know straightaway their love affair was false.

She closed her eyes, knowing from long experience what would happen. Mum and Aunt Sheila would start crying. Dad and Uncle Dal would either retreat to the pub or exchange blows. Sensing his little sister's unhappiness, Greg would deck Tal like he had after Tal got Ginny pregnant—and the family free-for-all that followed would shoot the mission to pieces, if Gary Brooks was there to document and photograph it. Falcone and Burstall, on the hunt for Nighthawks to show up in

Amalza, would sniff trouble straightaway, and Burstall would kill them before they even reached the Embassy's gates.

She had to do something to pull Tal out of his inner darkness—or the blackness of everlasting night could fall on them both.

"Miss West! Miss West!"

Tal swore, harsh and guttural. "That's it. He's outta here—right on his arse." He released her and turned to Gary Brooks, murder in his eyes.

"No!" She twisted him back to her and pulled his mouth down on hers, hard and fast, holding him with all her strength until he moved against her, his mouth opening to hers...

Then she forgot everything but the feel of his mouth on her, the taste of him—her aching, pounding *need*, and the pool of heat gathering inside her.

He apparently felt the same. With a lightning movement he had her outside on the balcony. He jammed the doors locked with a chair and moved until they were out of sight of the crowd. "It's time we tried this privately. We've got about two minutes before they find a way out here," he whispered.

She swayed back into his arms. "Tal..."

He cupped her face, looking down into it with an expression she couldn't interpret. His thumbs moved, touching her jaw—and she moaned in anguished ecstasy. His eyes darkened. "Now we're going to do this right." Slowly, so slowly she shook with excited anticipation, he lowered his head to hers.

The simulated kisses were gone: a slow-burning sensuality took their place. And she didn't care if it was deliberate, if he had an agenda or not right now. His kisses had always taken her breath away: now they left her in a little puddle at his feet. "Tal..." Her voice throbbed with aching, pounding need. She arched against him, wrapping her arms hard around his neck. "Oh, Tal, it's been so long since I felt like this," she whispered.

In the moment he resisted her pull, she looked up and saw she'd confused the hell out of him. *Is she acting, or not?* She smiled and closed her eyes, ready for more—

And then the first flash of the camera came again.

"Good work," he whispered against her mouth. Lost in a daze of fiery sensuality, she opened her eyes. His face was a bare half inch from hers, but his eyes glittered in ironic approval. "I could've blown the mission just then. That was a top-class deflection, Songbird. Following my lead looked really natural. Good girl. You work well with your partners, don't you?"

She forced herself to smile up at him, cool and challenging—the exact opposite of how she felt inside. "Well, I must admit that none of my assignments has included this kind of requirement—but did you expect less? I particularly appreciated the way you took it up a notch, bringing us out here. Well done."

He shrugged, kissed her lightly again for the cameras. "I don't like being left behind. You never forget the mission, do you? A top-class operative, Miss West—a real pro."

That broke her. Feeling hot tears sting her eyes behind her contacts, she lowered her gaze a little. "Like you said the other day—I might not look much like I used to, but I'm still a woman," she whispered against his mouth, smiling for the sake of the people inside the restaurant and out here in the garden, watching them with avid interest. "I might be famous, Tal, but I can still *hurt.* So don't punish me for the things we both have to do for the mission. I didn't ask for this any more than you did."

His eyes glinted as he watched her, holding her with deceptive closeness. "You're right. But I'm not punishing you, sweetness—I just don't know you." He shrugged as she flinched. "I could never understand it when the press nicknamed you the Iceberg. But your acting is so perfect it fools even me."

She pressed her lips together. "Is that a good thing or a bad thing?" Her voice came out with a distressing little wobble, an obvious huskiness.

He smiled down at her, but there was a strange, arrested look in his eyes. "I guess it depends on whether we're talking professionally or personally—and whether my opinion matters.''

A tiny sigh escaped her lips. The hot burn of tears unshed, and the constant flash of the cameras, was giving her a headache. ''Of course it matters, Tal. I don't do this job for the kicks.'' Not caring how it looked anymore, she let her head droop to his shoulder. ''I care that so many people depend on us. I care that you hate wearing the makeup, feeling as inferior as I used to. And I care that the person who used to be my best friend in the world is treating me like he can't stand me.'' She shuddered against him, hating that she had to bare her soul under the gaze of a dozen intensely interested strangers. ''And more than anything else, I care that you can't look past the pretense I have to put on for the mission to see who I really am...''

Oh, *no,* she'd let out that stupid little hiccup again.

The silence that hung in the air was grim and tense, shimmering with emotions unspoken. ''Let's get out of here.''

She turned to Gary with her hand upraised as he began reeling off shots. ''Please, we need space. I have a headache. You have a story for tomorrow's edition. We'll see you tomorrow, okay?''

The contract was crystal clear: Miss West had control of how many shots he took and where, or she could break the agreement, and the wedding shots would be open to any member of the press. The journo nodded and reluctantly took off.

They grabbed their stuff and headed for the limo, broken only by a couple of fans wanting her autograph. *Verity*'s autograph.

Finally, in the shadowed privacy of the car, he spoke what was on his mind. ''If I don't know how to act around you, it's because you confuse me,'' he murmured. ''Who are you— Mary-Anne, Songbird or Verity West? Does anyone know what's really inside? I think you've been living a triple life so long, even you don't know anymore.''

Tears stung and burned behind her eyes. ''Spoken like a doctor. You dissected me with all your usual surgical precision.'' She sighed. ''Gil made up the name Verity for me. I told him I couldn't go up on stage, so he said Mary-Anne didn't have to. I could send Verity up there, be someone else. And it works. As Verity West, I can do things Mary-Anne couldn't face. The Iceberg is a creation of the press and fans, but I use that reputation on missions to make men keep their distance from me. Songbird is an exotic cat burglar who goes to the parties of the rich and infamous, using Verity West's name to gather information like no other Nighthawk can.''

She turned on him, her eyes pleading. ''Don't you understand? Gil made Verity West. The press created the Iceberg. Ghost invented Songbird. And though each of them has its purpose, none of them is *me* any more than you are Irish or a beach bum pilot.'' She shrugged helplessly. ''We all wear masks, Tal—and I don't just mean the Nighthawks.''

''I know.'' He spoke in a slow, thoughtful tone, and a tide of hope washed through her. ''Why do you care what I think? You're Verity West. You don't need me now. And given our history…''

Crunch time—she could either keep her pride or she could save the mission and the lives that went with it.

There really wasn't any choice. She closed her eyes, dragged in a breath and said it. ''Verity West, Songbird and the Iceberg are what I *do*. I'm Mary-Anne—and you know what else I am? I'm alone, all the time, because nobody sees me—*me*—not even you, and I'm so *tired* of it, Tal. I've been all alone since Gil died…'' Her voice cracked and broke. ''I just wanted a f-friend—'' *darn* it, there went that pathetic, needy hiccup again ''…someone to talk to, you know?''

The protective warmth of his arms came around her. ''Come here.'' A tender hand smoothed the loosened curls of her chignon. ''The song from the *Blue Straits* album. 'Tearing It Up' is about you.''

She nodded against his chest, feeling at peace. ''And 'Whenever I'm Alone,''' she whispered.

He held her with gentle protectiveness. ''I like *Blue Straits* and *After the Dove*, but *Nobody's Lolita* is my favorite album you put out. The feelings are so raw." She felt the hesitation before he spoke. "I've always wanted to know... 'Farewell Innocence'—"

"You shouldn't have to ask." She smiled up at him. "And for your information, I didn't 'put out.' I released the albums."

"Oops." He chuckled. "Yeah, well, words were always your thing, Ms. Songwriter, not mine."

"Your bedside manner must be appalling." Her smile widened tremulously. She felt timid, almost shy, in this tentative new atmosphere of friendship hovering in the air.

"Gruesome." He kissed her forehead, still laughing. "'Farewell Innocence' has followed me around since it came out."

"I never meant for it to haunt you," she murmured, feeling distressed by his confession. "I wrote it to free us both, to say goodbye. I knew you felt bad about what happened." She laid her head on his chest. "I wrote it before I met Gil, but I only ever sang my songs for him until he entered me in the contest I won."

"Do you ever wish he hadn't?" he asked softly.

A tiny sigh escaped her. "Oh, only about once or twice a day, whenever this crazy life overwhelms me again."

"Mary-Anne."

"Hmm?"

He tipped up her face, looking into her eyes. "Nothing. Just—Mary-Anne."

For the first time the silence was sweet, tender with the unspoken caring of old friendship...and, while she knew she wanted so much more, this moment was enough for now. For the first time since she'd seen him again, the promise of tomorrow wasn't dark. "Yeah," she agreed with another smile. "Just Mary-Anne."

Even when Anson opened the door of her Harbourside mansion for them, in the guise of her butler, Tal didn't lose the mood. He grinned and said cheerfully, "Good evening, Jeeves. And a lovely night was had by all. We'd like hot chocolate, thanks."

Anson frowned as he closed the door. "Did I miss something?"

Tal smiled at Mary-Anne, sharing a memory. "You had to be there, I guess. In Cowinda, that is."

"I'm glad you're in such a good mood, Irish. I have some instructions relating to the arrivals tomorrow—"

"We'll have hot chocolate, thanks," Tal interrupted him without anger or even interest. "Miss West and I want to continue our conversation in private."

"Knock it off, Irish," Anson snapped. "I'm not in the mood for your antics tonight. The families come tomorrow and we need to coordinate our stories on your meeting again."

Tal's brows lifted. "Um, Boss? *You* don't have a story to tell them, unless they're interested in the butler's point of view. And if you seriously think you can give us instruction on our own families, you've been on the job too long." He didn't face their secret chief down or stand up to him. He simply grinned at Anson's blank look. "Come on, Boss. You can't believe we need your help with our own parents. Now if you want to be of any use in our plans, please ask the cook for two mugs of hot chocolate. They're necessary," he added with a perfectly straight face.

Mary-Anne giggled at Anson's narrow-eyed gaze. He wasn't used to being put in his place or to admitting that anyone could know more than he did about any aspect of a mission. "He means it, Nick. We always used to sneak into each other's kitchens at night for hot chocolates when we were kids." She smiled to conciliate him. "Our parents will drive here overnight, taking shifts, and be here in the morning. Unwashed cups from our hot chocolates will do more to reassure them that everything's fine with us than if we're sleeping in the same bed."

"I see." Anson's brow shot up. He glanced at Mary-Anne, whose hand still lay in Tal's. "As you wish," was all he said. He bowed to them both with an ironic inflection and left the room.

"Man, that felt good," Tal murmured in her ear as they

moved to the informal living room at the back of the house, overlooking the pretty rose garden leading to the Sydney Harbour waterfront.

"Yes, it did," she confessed. They sat on the thick comfy sofa, only inches apart. Could he feel her hunger, the physical ache to touch him? "Much as I admire Nick, sometimes he needs his microchip reprogrammed to remind him that he's human."

Tal chuckled. "He is like a robot, isn't he? I've often wondered if he ever lets loose, screams, goes to the movies or the pub, plays football or does some one-on-one on the court…or finds a woman to forget saving the world, if only for an hour."

She slanted a half-mischievous glance at him, covering her intense curiosity. "Is this personal experience speaking? Did you need to forget for an hour, Tal?"

He shrugged. "I'm only human. Sometimes, when it all got to be too much…" He shrugged again when he saw the look on her face. "You don't know what it's like out there. You do the glitz rounds. The things I've seen on SAR, what I've had to do—sometimes a man will do almost anything to be able to leave the memories behind."

"Okay." She bit her lip, trying desperately to hold it in, but the words tumbled out. "Look, I know I have no right to ask, but—promise me you won't do that while we're married? I know we won't be really married, but I…" She dipped her head, ashamed of the hot jealousy spearing her heart, stabbing her soul…but oh, the thought of him touching, kissing, another woman, moving inside her, bringing a stranger to fulfillment while she ached for him—

With a gentle finger he tipped up her face, his mouth a whisper's breadth from hers. "As long as you're in my life, I can guarantee you I won't even think about it." His voice was hot and rough, starkly lush as the red Outback land they loved.

"Not at all?" she whispered, moving closer, her gaze locked on his mouth. "Not even…with me? Not with me, Tal?"

His eyes darkened. "There's no one to see. You don't have to put on a show."

She heard the words, swirling as if through warm, sticky fluid, making no sense. She was gone, her arm wrapping around his neck on its own, her mouth seeking his. She needed this, oh, she wanted him so much…to finally know how it felt to have him on top of her, inside of her, filling her emptiness with his dark magic…

One kiss, two, and she was in his lap, her hands seeking his skin under his shirt while he hitched up her dress, his tongue dancing in her mouth and his moans—or were they hers?—took her away from all the pain, the past—and all she could do was feel *here,* feel *now* and *want*—

The clinking was tiny, a frisson of sound, but it broke the heat like a bucket of ice water. As one they broke the kiss and turned to look at the source of the interruption.

It seemed Nick Anson was human, all right. The Cheshire-cat grin he held inside showed in his eyes, the twitching of his dimples. "Um, I beg your pardon, sir, madam, but it seems your families have arrived a day early."

"She's *what?*"

Burstall looked up from the picture he held—a picture of Lissa in her wedding dress, with McCluskey's face torn from it. Falcone's words, so unlike his supersmooth tones, set him on edge. What the—

Falcone's face was pale, his eyes burning. "Mr. Brooks, if you're lying…yes, yes, I know about him. When is the intended wedding?" His hand gripped the phone so hard Burstall thought it might crack under the strain. "I haven't waited five years for my opportunity with the lady only to have it snatched from me. Kill him." He gave a slow blink as the guy at the other end said something. "I see. Good evening, Mr. Brooks."

Burstall watched in silent fascination as smooth-as-silk Robert Falcone lost it. Swearing viciously, he slammed the phone down and tossed the table it stood on, smashing the fine china.

He picked up the loose receiver and threw it at a collector's print. The glass splintered, tearing the print beneath.

Then, calm and smiling once again, he retrieved the receiver and dialed a number. "Mr. Longley? Mr. Brooks is of no further use to us. Kill him and take his place...follow Miss West as her official reporter, and kill one Dr. Tallan O'Rierdan, once he reaches the island with his bride. That will be all. Thank you."

Chapter 6

Behind Nick, the faces of their parents, and Greg, told it all. They didn't even bother to hide the size of their grins at the passionate encounter they'd just seen.

She scrambled off Tal's lap, pulling down the dress he'd hiked around her thighs. "Um, sorry…we were just, um…" She looked at Tal who shrugged and grinned, busy adjusting his own clothes.

Her mother's smile was misty. "Darling, if the two of you weren't just, um—we'd be worried."

Aunt Sheila rushed over to them, her plump form quivering like her smile. "We're so happy. Oh, Tal, darlin', you've made your mum and dad so happy!" Her arms enfolded them both in a hug. "We've been so worried that you'd marry some city-girl doctor or patient and stay here. But marrying our darlin' Mary-Anne—" she kissed Mary-Anne's cheek "—this is our dream come true. You'll come home one day and bring our grandbabies home to us." Aunt Sheila smiled over at Mum, who joined in the group hug.

As everyone took their turns at hugs and congratulations,

Mary-Anne's eyes met Tal's and saw the same stricken guilt she knew must be hidden deep somewhere in her own. In giving in to a moment of mutual desire, they'd just done far more to reassure their families that they were madly in love than any amount of Nick's forgotten hot chocolates.

But they were living a lie—masks that were more shameful than the makeup covering Tal's scars. Even if they were able to save the whole world, or a vital part of it, it didn't make facing the people they loved most in the world any easier to bear.

"I now pronounce you husband and wife."
Watch what you wish for—you just might get it.
The words floated around and around in her mind. Yes, she'd heard the words she'd always wanted to hear, found herself inside the scene she'd dreamed of for twenty-four years. She was beside Tal, taking the traditional, old-fashioned vows of forever love. She felt him slide his ring onto her hand, and she slid hers onto his. He wore the tux she'd seen in her dreams. She wore a lovely ivory designer silk gown, a garland of flowers in a unity ring style in her hair. Her family and his were here to witness the event, held in the secluded English garden in her yard. A photographer—not Gary Brooks anymore; John Longley from the same tabloid had taken his place—eagerly snapped pictures every few seconds.

Her dream come true, yet she kept waiting for the nightmare landscape to arrive, for some disaster to stop the final words...

"You may kiss your bride."

She looked up at Tal, feeling lost, helpless. He smiled down at her. "Chin up, kid," he whispered, touching her cheek. "We're in this together." He drew her close and kissed her, less in passion than in tender encouragement.

"Congratulations." The marriage celebrant—which Nighthawk's wife, lover, mother or girlfriend the woman was, they would never know—smiled at her.

"Thank you." She burrowed into Tal, desperate for warmth. She felt so cold, shivering yet somehow disembodied, as though an alien being had taken over her body and left her outside, watching in helpless fascination as her life changed forever.

If only…if only she could be *sure*…if only—

Though she knew the lives of many people hinged on this act—though what they'd done was noble and right—she couldn't push aside the sneaking sense of shame. This mockery of a wedding followed the path of their acquaintance, all their lives.

A secretive friendship. A long-hidden talent. A wedding with pomp and ceremony, surrounded by family—even the passion she'd always wanted—but they'd never have made it to this point without the job.

And the scariest part was, deep down inside, she didn't know if she cared…

"Hang in there, Mary-Anne," he whispered in her ear as the family once more crowded them in joyous hugs. "It's almost over."

A shiver of foreboding rippled up her spine. They had only a week of their mission left to go. And that made each moment she'd have alone with him more infinitely precious.

"Booking for Mr. and Mrs. O'Rierdan. Take the bags to Cabin 701, Vincenzo."

"Sí, señor." The cheerful porter nodded and grinned, not seeming to recognize Mary-Anne. He took their luggage to their isolated luxury cabin at the beachside resort on a private, pristine stretch of coast off the Spanish mainland.

Tal had already broken one of Anson's first rules. The Boss had said to use a standard double room, to remain inconspicuous until the news of their marriage broke, but seeing the stress she was trying so hard to hide from him, the smile that trembled, he'd booked the honeymoon suite. He didn't need Nighthawk money. He'd give his wife first-class treatment out of his own wallet.

But the lovely rose-scented suite only reinforced his worst

fears: tonight it was just Tal and Mary-Anne, facing each other in their new life together—with their new bodies.

With the force of sheer bloody-minded will, Tal refrained from tugging at his shirt collar. Cold sweat trickled down his back, his stomach was a ball of burning pain and his heart had spent the day in a frenzied tachycardic-bradycardic arrhythmia, fast and then slow, as though it had gone schizophrenic on him.

If it weren't for that ruthless bloody Ghost, so willing to sacrifice their private past and feelings for the sake of the Nighthawks and faceless masses in danger from Falcone's black market arsenal, she wouldn't even be here. Neither would he.

"Thanks." Mary-Anne's voice startled him. The porter was closing the door behind him. Illogically, Tal felt as though his last defense had just fallen.

She tossed off the big floppy hat she'd all but glued to her head to cover her famous tresses. Her heavy mass of hair tumbled down in rich fire to her waist. "Aaahhh. What a relief." She lifted her arms in a stretching motion filled with slumbering sensuality. "I felt like I had a brick attached to my head."

He closed his eyes to shut off the glorious sight of her breasts lifting with her arms beneath the simple tank top, her long, toned legs revealed by the shorts she'd changed into in the private jet. "Why not cut it?"

She chuckled. "The cover, my dear. Verity West's famous hair. You wouldn't believe the amount of times in the past few years I've looked at women with bob cuts and felt so much jealousy."

"I reckon it'd suit you," he said gruffly. Oh, yeah, she'd look gorgeous with shorter hair. Less glamorous, definitely, but with that sweet, pixie-like face and sleepy, silver-green eyes, she'd look like a wood sprite. More like a woman he could—

Don't go there!

He was a man; of course he went there. He must've thought

of sex at least two hundred and forty times a day since she'd walked back into his life those few days ago.

Hello, Tal. From Mary-Anne, it was all the foreplay he needed.

"No point in thinking about it. I'm stuck with this mess for now." She ran her hands through the sexy disarray, and her body flowed into the movement with sinuous grace.

If he'd seen her do it three years ago—a year and a half ago—he'd have been dead sure it was a sweet, provocative come-on, a signal that she was as ready to finally fulfill their secret love as he was.

But now he couldn't be sure this wasn't Songbird the Spy, playing her part for the sake of world peace, giving to charity like a warped beauty pageant contestant.

But it didn't stop his body screaming its response to her.

"You want a drink?" She smiled at him, but it was shaky, as if she was scared. Of him—or what he wanted to do with her? "I don't know about you, but long flights make me thirsty."

"No. Thanks." He didn't want a drink. He wanted to haul Mary-Anne into his arms and to kiss her senseless. Strip her slowly, lay her on the bed and love her as he'd never been able to before, the girl he couldn't tear out of his heart even if he tried.

If only he could be sure her kisses weren't orchestrated by Anson to make their courtship look bona fide! But the words she'd used on the island taunted him every time he dared to hope her passion wasn't a fake. *I'd do anything to stop it. Anything...*

"How about ordering room service?" She crossed the room to the phone. "We haven't eaten much today, and that isn't good for you, with the physical stuff you might have to do this week—"

She was babbling now. Her hands were shaking—he could see that from the other side of the room. Her nerves were strung as tight as his.

How the hell did they get through this? It felt as though he was balancing on electrical wires over water: aching for her, wanting to lose himself in her, scared stupid that one look at his worst scarring would send her screaming out of the room.

Over and above all that, he had a strange, tingling awareness of being within fifty miles of Burstall and Falcone. Losing concentration equaled heightened danger. Those gut instincts that had saved his butt more than once on SAR ops were already on high alert—far more than they should be right now.

"Okay, we'll eat," he said quietly. "But I don't think we can afford to want anything but food and sleep right now, Mary-Anne. We have a big week ahead of us."

Stark white replaced the soft rose in her cheeks of a moment before, her freckles standing out in sharp contrast against the paleness. She turned away, but he saw her face: as devastated and betrayed as it had looked their last night at the billabong.

At that moment he knew what she'd meant by her fame being her cover: deep down Verity West was still Mary-Anne Poole, the girl who'd taken the gibes of everyone at their school in silence. The girl who'd allowed the barbed insults to impale her soul.

Fat girl, fat girl, they'd taunted her. *Mrs. Ronald McDonald. The walking, talking, red-haired clown.*

He closed his eyes and sighed, rubbing his forehead. "Honey, I didn't mean that the way you took it—"

"Stop it! You don't want me—I know, all right? Just don't *apologize!*" She spat the word out like an epithet, cutting him off before the second word of apology had left his lips.

Before he could move or think of what to say to her, the door slammed. She was gone, bolting from him and the anguish he'd never meant to inflict on her.

Just like last time.

He found her just before sunset, running on the beach, drenched in sweat, her feet pounding on the cooling white sand.

"Mary-Anne!" He waved and limped toward her.

She bolted straight past him, her face set and cold despite

its rosy flush. Her hair flew out behind her like a banner of dangerous fire. Her eyes, like delicate chips of ice, warned him not to come any closer.

But like a fool—or a driven man—he ploughed on. ''Come on, stop and talk to me,'' he yelled. ''You don't understand!''

She didn't even pause, her near-flying feet taking her where she knew he couldn't follow anymore.

He kicked his shoes off and sat on the sand to wait. There was nowhere she could go but back to the resort, unless she wanted to be mobbed at the local pub, less for being Verity West than a scantily clad beautiful woman. What if they—

No need to worry about her on that score. She was a Nighthawk now. She had the training to take on every single one of the drunken fools at the pub and wipe the floor with them without a hassle. It still left him reeling, thinking of his gentle, never-fight-back Mary-Anne, kicking arse…

Full darkness soon surrounded him, warm and close. He sat quiet and unmoving, watching the waves touch the shore, waiting.

Long before he saw her, he heard the slow, uneven pounding of exhausted feet, the high-pitched ragged gasps of exhaustion. She slowed as she got close to where he sat unseen, and came to a stop on the stretch of sand approximately behind their cabin.

He peered through the soft, fragrant velvet darkness. Seeing little at a thirty-foot distance, he moved closer, with all the stealth he'd been taught in training.

She was bent over double, holding her sides. Her face, strange and ethereal in the rising moonlight, turned toward their room, filled with that look of helpless self-hatred she'd always had when she looked in a mirror as a girl or copped abuse from the kids in town for being so different.

A tear trickled gently down her cheek and fell to the sand.

''Stupid, stupid,'' she muttered, and dashed at her face. ''Why do you keep hoping? Don't you ever *learn?*'' Her open hand rose, smacking herself on the temple. ''He doesn't want you. It's never going to happen. You're always going to be alone!''

He almost gasped at her words. Dear God—the press called this woman *The Iceberg?*

Before he'd gathered the words to break the horrifying sense of hopelessness, self-hate and silent anguish he felt radiating from her, she spun on her heel and staggered to the water's edge. A slow, careful look around, then she kicked her shoes and socks off, put them out of the water's way, then stepped clothed into the shimmering dark ocean, the moon playing off soft silver lights on her gilded hair and pale skin.

''Mary-Anne,'' he called, quiet yet commanding. ''Come on—enough's enough. We need to talk.''

Up to her knees in the warm water, she stood frozen, her curly hair falling down her back, her fists clenched. ''How long have you been there?'' Her voice was neutral.

''Since you ran past me.''

She sighed. ''What's to say? I got the message. You made it loud and clear.'' She didn't turn around, wouldn't or couldn't look at him. ''It's old, familiar territory.''

''Even if that was true, nothing about this is familiar,'' he retorted bluntly. ''You're the famous one now, you're the one who's bloody gorgeous—and I couldn't keep my hands off you when you weighed nearly twice what you do now.''

Her head drooped. ''There's no need to lie about it. You're here for revenge. You know I can act. Falcone and Burstall will never know we aren't happily married. So you're off the hook.''

He chuckled wryly, limping over to her. ''Oh, he'll know the difference all right, sweetness. Any man would. When a woman's frustrated, she's cold or tense. When she's satisfied, she glows. It's unmistakable to any guy. Trust me.''

''So I'll rub Vitamin E oil on my face and smile a lot,'' she snapped, still facing outward to the shimmering ocean. ''Now would you please leave me alone?''

''It wasn't about you, Mary-Anne. No, yes, it was—but not how you think. We're in a bloody dangerous assignment and if I start touching you I'll lose control—and neither of us can afford that.'' At her stubborn silence he grabbed her shoulder, twisted her around to face him, his eyes burning. ''You want the whole truth? Fine—I was too bloody scared to take my clothes off in front of you!'' He thrust his face at her, his ugly mess of a cheek. ''This makeup won't be on forever. I look at you, so bloody beautiful you take my breath away, and I look at myself and wonder how a woman who could have any man she wanted could be crazy enough to want to look at my face and leg in bed—even just once—without wanting to throw up.''

If she answered him in words, he wouldn't believe her. If she argued, self-disgust would still conquer reason. But one simple act stunned him: she blushed so furiously her face, throat and shoulders were scorched, visible even in the moon's dim light. She turned away in terrified silence.

Standing up to their knees in warm ocean, hidden in the shadows of soft-lapping water and sensuous night, they froze in time: she couldn't or wouldn't, speak, and he was too speechless to respond, his heart hammering in wild hope. His hand shook as it reached out, turning her face back to his. ''Mary-Anne?''

Tears filled her eyes. She bit her lip, but she looked right into his eyes, letting him see inside her soul to the naked longing, the anguished hope and want. ''You think I'm beautiful?'' she whispered. ''You really want me?''

Holding his breath, half expecting the moment to shatter, he came closer, moving his imperfect body against hers in gentle testing, and her longing became pain, a need so strong and sharp it cut his fears to shreds. Tipping her face up just a touch closer, he whispered, ''Hell, yeah.'' He watched her move her tongue over her lips, her breathing harsh and erratic, her eyes fixed on his mouth as if glued there: a tender, terrible hunger, the need eating her alive. ''I always did,'' he said, his voice hoarse and rough, gravel-edged with sex. ''So don't look at me like that unless you mean it. Be sure, because there's no going back after this.''

"I don't want to go back. I want you." A trembling hand lifted to caress his face. "You're the only man alive who knows who I am. I've dreamed of making love with you for over half my life. I just want Tal, my best friend. However you are." Her voice shook with such heart-deep desire, his white-hot need overrode the faint, far-off screams of his survival instincts, telling him, *This isn't smart, O'Rierdan...* "Please, Tal, give me tonight. Make love to me."

Knocked sideways by her words, he closed his eyes, dragged in a heaving breath. By instinct, his mouth brushed hers.

She made a tiny mewing sound, like an eager kitten. With a harsh groan, he pulled her up hard against him and deepened the kiss, but she was already there before him, making a tiny, guttural sound of pleasure as she ravaged his mouth. Her hands slid beneath his T-shirt, drinking in every inch of skin she could find, with a need for him so absolute, so *voracious,* he gasped for air between consuming kisses and insatiable touch.

He tore his mouth from hers to nibble soft-freckled shoulders and throat. Her head fell back, with gasps of joy. As his hand hesitated on her rib cage, she moaned and pushed it onto her breast, shuddering when his touch brought the peaked nipple to shooting life. Then she uttered magical words, words he'd never thought to hear again from any woman, let alone the beautiful, incredible woman in his arms. "I want to make love *now...*"

The insidious whisper inside his mind made all the fears come back. *Take your clothes off...* "Mary-Anne..." How to say it? He'd always been the shining one with them, the beautiful one, her dream and master. Now, like a twisted Catherine and Heathcliff their lives had reversed and, *damn* it, he didn't want to see her face when he stripped—

"I know. Did you think I wouldn't understand?" Smiling in blatant invitation, she backed off a step deeper, crooking a finger. "Come on." She turned and dived into the warm, swirling waters of the Mediterranean.

Joy burst inside him as he dove in after her. She *did* know.

She understood, and, like the miracle she'd always been to him, she found a way for them to be together. No lights, no facing her with his imperfections.

No comforts, either, yet somehow it seemed *right,* loving her out here instead of in the luxurious suite. Out here he could forget her fame and jets and limos and concert tours and fans—he could forget everything but that tonight, they were just two best friends finally becoming lovers. Tal and Mary-Anne, the two Outback kids who'd always hated boundaries, making love in the exotic yet hauntingly familiar outdoors.

Water being the one place where he lost his athletic disadvantage, he caught up with her easily—and found her in chest-deep water, waiting for him, smiling. "Welcome home, Tal." She opened her arms to him.

With the first touch of their mouths, he was gone. She melted against him, caressing him in a need so frantic that until this night, unable to believe a woman like her could want him at all, let alone with this heated desperation, he'd dismissed it every time as an act for the camera or for their families.

But now there was no audience, and she was undressing him—literally tearing off his clothes—and her own. Kissing every inch of him she could with a fevered intensity that burned him almost to the bone. Grabbing his hands, putting them on her wet, naked body, she muttered sweet, sensual encouragement for him to touch her, kiss her, explore her most secret desires.

This was *amazing*—beyond any experience he'd ever known. It was awkward, glorious, sensuous, terrifying—and sexual reassurance with a vengeance. Why she wanted him so badly, he didn't know or care. Mary-Anne had been his own personal miracle too many years for him to question this new night magic. Untamed love in inky-wet darkness, wild and free, fulfilling frenzied, ravaging need.

He groaned when she arched back to reveal her breasts, glistening pearl-like in the moonlight with a few spirals of her hair falling dark and wet over them. "Touch me…" Her sweet voice was low and husky with sensuality. "Put your hands on me, Tal. I've fantasized about watching you do that so many times."

Slowly, shaking a little, he filled his hands with those lovely, firm breasts. *If this is another dream, God, please don't let me wake up anytime soon.* He'd lived this so many times in his mind, he could barely separate fantasy from reality, but this was so much *more*—so *them,* to be making love out here where only wild creatures and God existed.

When his thumbs moved over her sweet, hard nipples, she moaned and arched against him. "Your mouth, Tal. Oh, kiss me there…"

Lifting her in his hands, he took a wet, salty nipple into his mouth, feeling half dizzy with the joy of yet another fantasy fulfilled. He suckled her, tenderly grazing with his teeth, almost losing it when she gave a low, keening cry of pleasure. "Now!" she cried, writhing against him. "I need you *now!*"

From somewhere close by he heard a boat engine humming…and as the sound quietly cut, his instincts resurfaced. *Protect Mary-Anne.* "Let's go inside and do this right."

Her whole body stilled with his words. "You didn't want to before."

He could hear the uncertainty quiver in her voice, ringing like warning bells in his heart. It seemed surreal to him that the beautiful person in this scenario should be the one to need the reassurance—but if his Mary-Anne still existed beneath the lovely shell of Verity West, it made perfect sense. Her heart held more unhealed scars than his face and leg ever would.

"I won't change my mind. I don't think I could," he said, wishing he had sweeter, more tender words to give her, but he was still an Outback boy, brought up on spare, blunt words and long days of hard work. He swam for the shore. "Come on." He held a hand to her backward, keeping the sight of his worst scars—those on his thigh—from her eyes. "Let's go to bed."

She ran out of the water to him, then suddenly stilled. Her face lifted to his in quick horror. "Uh-oh. Tal…"

He frowned. "What?"

"Our clothes are—out there," she whispered.

"So? What's the problem? We've got plenty of fresh clothes in the room—" Then he got what she hadn't said. "Oh, boy. I think we're in trouble…"

She grinned. "I didn't think you'd found a new and miraculous place to hide room keys."

He laughed again, too happy right now to give a rat's behind that they were locked out of their room. "So you wanna toss to see who climbs in the bathroom window and explains to Anson why he's got to pay damages for the insect screen?"

Her smile turned smug. "No need for that. Breaking into rooms without sound or damage is one of my specialties. Like I told you, I'm the Nighthawks' cat burglar at socialite or political functions. I have to keep my little toy with me 24/7 during any missions. I put it in my shoe before I headed into the water."

"So why'd you freak out about losing the key?"

"I forgot," she admitted, biting her lip on a smile of pure, sweet confusion. "I got sidetracked with, um, other things."

Liking that admission—a lot—he nuzzled her neck. "Let's go to bed. Or maybe we can take a shower to get all this salt water off?"

Her eyes lit and glowed as she moved to pick up her shoes, in danger of going underwater. "Can we do both? I've had so many dreams of us making love in a bed, in the shower, the bath…"

His heart and gut tangled around each other in their mad flip-overs at her words. "Whatever you want."

She led him back to the cabin at a gentle gait he could follow without difficulty, smiling at him every few steps, like every man's fantasy come to life in the light of the creamy moon.

Within a minute they were inside the room, laughing like

kids, brushing sand off as sensual foreplay, kissing, staggering toward the bathroom—

"Hmm, I see you've gone above and beyond orders to fulfill the mission—but you might want to hold off any further attention to detail until you're alone."

Mary-Anne gasped, shrinking against Tal. "Nick?"

Anson sat on their bed, holding the running shoes she'd just tossed, his jeans covered in the sand from the soles.

Tal thrust her behind him, and into the bathroom. "Put on a robe, honey. Bring one for me." He spun back to face his boss, naked and not giving a damn. "I don't care how you got in here—you just crossed the line, Anson. You might think your position gives you personal rights over us, but you will not invade our privacy." He folded his arms, facing his boss down. "Knock on the bloody door from now on, and if we're not here or not answering, wait outside the door. Got it?"

"Absolutely." Anson didn't even blink at his nudity—he'd seen all Tal's injuries more than once, since he'd kept him alive until the chopper had arrived to take him to Darwin. "I beg your pardon, Irish." Anson grinned and scratched his head. "I'm used to unrestricted access to Songbird at almost any time or place. It appears that time's ended."

"Bloody oath it has." Just what the hell did Anson mean by "unrestricted access"? And where did his arrogant boss's sudden burst of humility come from?

Anson got off the enormous king-size bed where he sat. "I see you still blame me."

Mary-Anne emerged from the bathroom, dressed, and handed Tal a robe. He slipped it on, with a brief smile of thanks. "For what happened to me? No. For not telling me Burstall is still alive and still up to his tricks? Hell, yeah."

"Among other things." Anson shrugged. "I wanted to give you time to heal first, without fretting about where he was or getting to him. I wanted to tell you face-to-face once you left the hospital last time, but you wouldn't answer my summons. So I thought it might go down better coming from—Mary-Anne."

The way Anson stumbled over her name showed just how impersonal the guy was. How many years had it been since he'd used a name, not a code? "Yeah. It went down real well."

Mary-Anne spoke from behind Tal. "What are you doing here? You said we could have until we got to Amalza before—"

"Gary Brooks is dead." Anson always railroaded his words when he had something tough to say. "We found his body wedged among the rocks below your house in Sydney this afternoon, just after your jet flew out."

She gasped. Tal laced his fingers through hers in instinctive protection as his mind raced. So that was why his instincts had gone into high alert? "Murdered?" he asked bluntly.

Anson nodded. "Shot in the head. AK-47 assault rifle, range at least two hundred meters. He was hit by a pro."

Mary-Anne's free hand lifted to her mouth, slow and shaking. "Why?" she whispered.

"Hacker got into his bank account half an hour ago. She reported that Brooks has had several sudden very large deposits made to his account from Switzerland in the past few years—over two hundred thousand in total. We think someone's been paying him to follow you for the last few years, Songbird. It makes sense, since he always had stories on you, and he was the only one to find you in the Torres Strait."

"You think it's Falcone?" Tal asked grimly.

Anson shrugged. "Yes, him—or some other rich, obsessed fan, maybe. But why they ordered a hit on Brooks is unknown."

Tal met Anson's eyes for a fleeting second. They both knew why—and he knew Anson would check out Brooks's replacement with all his old CIA tricks. Hell, he probably already knew what time of day Brooks's replacement woke up, what he ate or when he went to the john—but it wasn't enough for Tal's peace of mind. Not nearly enough. "Mary-Anne shouldn't go to the Embassy, Boss. Not until we know what's going down."

Anson paced the room, looking like a wild thing, a caged animal. "I don't think we have a choice in that now. A man answering Burstall's description took a young tourist hostage today—and though we haven't heard anything yet, we believe he'll try to ransom him for Skydancer or Countrygirl, or both. He's got the leverage, too. The tourist happens to be the nineteen-year-old son of the Australian foreign minister."

"Oh, the poor boy." Mary-Anne's eyes filled with the immediate sympathy she always found for any suffering creature. "What's the plan?"

"Mary-Anne, you can't go in there!" Tal whipped her around to face him. "It's obvious what's going on. He's going to take you hostage, and there sure as hell won't be a ransom!"

She looked up into his eyes, flushed and earnest, and so lovely in the simple fluffy white robe, her wet hair hanging down her back, it hurt him to look at her. "As a trained operative, I have a greater chance of getting away than that poor boy. I have the resources to get away, and Nighthawk backup." Her hands gripped his. "Tal, Ghost is right. I don't have a choice here. None of us could live with leaving the boy to die. You know Burstall won't let him live long if he doesn't get what he wants."

He jerked his hands out of her grasp and turned back to their boss. Damn her for being right—and for being too much like him, willing to risk her life to save a stranger...

Anson smiled briefly at Mary-Anne, expecting no less than the decision she'd made. "Orders came from the Australian government via the Virginia branch. We can't leave him there—he's worth too much, both in ransom and in information. Joel St. Bremer's family was staying at the ambassador's residence in Ramiara when the religious war broke out there two years back, and we had to go in and get them out." Anson slanted a glance at him. "Remember the kid? The fighter? He was sixteen then. He's nineteen now."

Oh, yeah, that mission in Ramiara wasn't easily forgettable, on any level—and he'd had to jab the hysterical kid with a

sedative before he'd stop punching and kicking them. He nodded. "Yeah, he kind of sticks in the memory."

"We have to get him out. We can't use Skydancer or Countrygirl as bait—she's eight months' pregnant. The sight of her
could incite Burstall to do something stupid." Still pacing the
floor, he spoke with an irascible kind of self-control. "The
situation is deteriorating fast. Our orders are to get in ASAP.

"If Joel St. Bremer is in the Embassy, only you have a
chance to get us inside, Songbird. Falcone's previous interest
in you guarantees he will send you an invitation as soon as
news spreads of your arrival. So wangle your arrival into the
local newspapers. You know how, just make yourself visible.
Once you're in the Embassy, gather information in your usual
manner while Irish conducts a search for the hostage and
checks out points of entry for a rescue effort. Any questions?"

Yeah—can I finish making love to my wife first?

Mary-Anne kept looking at the floor, shuffling her feet. She
was thinking about it, too—but she didn't ask, either.

Anson got to his feet, brisk and capable. "Get dressed and
pack. We have a jet cat to take us over to Amalza. Hotel's
booked and there's staff on standby for your arrival.
ETA 2245 at the resort jetty."

Tal looked at Mary-Anne again. She looked at him, then
quickly away. Yep, he had to give it to Anson—he sure made
an entrance. The loving mood was completely broken. "Sure
thing, Boss," he drawled. "We're at your service."

Chapter 7

They finally reached the hotel in Lortámacino, Amalza's only town, at 0200. By the time the boys, in the guise of Mary-Anne's bodyguards, had finished sweeping the honeymoon suite in the hotel for illegal surveillance of any kind and had installed their own handy-dandy polytechnics, it was almost 0400. "Right, let's go through the agenda for today, then we can get a few hours' shut-eye," Anson said.

Tal glanced into the living area of the suite, where Mary-Anne was curled up in the high-backed armchair, fast asleep. "She needs to rest."

"Don't think for Songbird, Irish. She won't thank you for treating her as less than the complete professional she is."

Anson crossed the room to her as he spoke—but Tal got there first. "Look at her, Ghost," he growled softly, pointing to the dark smudges under her eyes. "If you can't see that she's on the edge of collapse, you're blind. She's been working nonstop for months on end, and this mission is taking its toll on her. She needs more rest than she's getting."

"Don't worry about Songbird. She's used to sleeping anywhere on missions." Anson's words were a mixture of impatience with Tal and admiration for Mary-Anne. "The floor, a chair, a sofa—it doesn't bother her so long as she can sleep. She's a real trouper on assignment. She never complains, no matter what I ask of her."

Tal frowned at his boss, wondering if Anson had any idea of how bad he made himself look with those words. "She might not complain," he agreed, "but that doesn't excuse your neglect of your operatives' needs."

"Back off, Irish." Anson looked dangerous now, his eyes flashing and his face like thunder. "You're only her husband temporarily—and you're way out of line."

"No, *you* back off." He stood between Anson and Mary-Anne, arms folded, going toe-to-toe with Anson, blocking his approach to her. "You hired me as the Nighthawks's chief medical officer in the Australasian region. I am totally in line when I diagnose an operative—and this particular operative will be unfit for duty if she doesn't get more rest. If you want her to complete this assignment without collapse, I'm telling you to let this woman get some sleep!"

Standing toe-to-toe with him Tal could see his boss's jaw clench, and he curled his fists, ready to fight if need be to protect Mary-Anne's rights. Then Anson, his body rigid, wheeled around and snapped his fingers. "Time to call it a night. Get some sleep, all of you. Meet back here at 1200 sharp."

Without waiting to see if they left, Tal scooped Mary-Anne up into his arms and laid her on the bed. He covered her warmly with the thick white chenille spread, glad one of them would get some sleep tonight—he sure as hell wouldn't. The face-off with Anson had left him too strung out—and crawling into bed beside his beautiful wife wasn't conducive to rest, either. It was more likely to give him a six-hour hard-on and aching hands from being in permanent fists, trying to keep from touching her.

So he was left with two alternatives: take a cold shower or watch a few hours of TV. Yeah, *The Brady Bunch*, *Lost In*

Space and *Leave It To Beaver* would go down real well dubbed in Spanish. *Soy estúpido, Señora Cleaver.*

As he was closing the bedroom door, he heard a soft whisper.

"Mmm…Tal?"

Man, how did she *do* this to him so fast? One word and he was aroused, catapulted back to seven hours before and the loving that would have given him the right to sleep in the bed with her. Maybe wake up in the morning and love her again. "Yeah?"

"Thank you for that," she said softly.

He grinned. "My pleasure. Now follow doctor's orders. Rest."

"Yes, Doctor." She sighed, almost three-quarters back to sleep already. "But I'd sleep better if you were with me."

Oh, boy. The mate inside his jeans was rock-hard, screaming at him for release, and she wanted him to *sleep* beside her? If he believed in reincarnation, he'd ask what he'd done in a former life to deserve the torture of this night. Yet his mouth spoke the words, "If you promise to sleep."

Great, now he was in league against himself!

She sighed as he crawled in beside her and wriggled back until her sweet little ass snuggled against him. A tiny catching sound came from her lips, the closest she'd ever get to a snore. A spiral of hair tickled his nose.

Yep, and a great night of sleep will be had by all. He groaned under his breath. *Don't touch her, don't touch her…* But his arm moved by itself, draping over her waist. He laid his chin on her hair and relived the almost-loving they'd had tonight. A living miracle in itself, whether they'd completed the loving or not. *She wants me. She really does want me.*

Man, was he trying to *kill* himself?

As the sun crept over the horizon, his eyes finally closed.

And the dream came again.

"Three kids left. The line's swinging like crazy with the force of the typhoon… God help us, I'm not going to make it…hang on, kids, hang on!"

Mary-Anne, half awake from the urgent muttering in her ear, came to life with a shock as a viselike grip held her wrist, almost cutting off her circulation. "Tal?" She blinked, trying to orient herself in the gentle light of dawn.

Tal swore viciously, hanging on to her as if a fall from the bed would kill her. "If I don't get these kids into the bird now, they'll die. My Achilles tendon's stuffed, but I can still make the sixty-foot free-fall to the cliff shelf. Go, go!"

Mary-Anne listened in horrified silence. Something told her this dream was the incident Braveheart had told her about, when he'd saved the kids on the cliff. Knowing Tal as she did, he wouldn't be having this dream, unless—

Unless something about it still haunted him.

She lay still, allowing him to hold on to her for security— or had she become one of the kids?—as he muttered on, finding the only form of release his taciturn nature would allow.

"Aaaargh!" He panted for a few moments, then he spoke, as if to someone else. "Come on, kids, we're all going this time. Come on, sweetie, up on my shoulders—no? You're too scared, baby? Okay, I'll hold you. Yeah, good one, mate— you're a big boy, you're not scared to hang on. Crap, the line isn't strong enough for us all. Typhoon's closing in... Alpha Delta one-two-five, send down a reinforcing line. Bringing remaining survivors up now!"

Mary-Anne gasped, reliving the story in vivid, horrifying detail. Dear God, is that what SAR units had to face on every mission? *Sometimes a man will do almost anything to forget…*

"I don't give a damn, Flipper—the typhoon's here!" he yelled. "Now give me the bloody line!"

He made frantic scrabbling motions. "Good girl, wrap it 'round you. Good boy. Now we're set. Go!" he called, obviously to those in the chopper. "Oh, God help us—steady the chopper, Braveheart! The kids are panicking and I don't know how to calm them down…oh my God! God, *no!*" His voice rang with anguish so sharp it left her heart bleeding. Oh,

God…baby girl…she was only about six… Baby, I'm sorry I couldn't hold you…'' A dry, racking sob escaped him. "I'm sorry, Kathy," he muttered hoarsely. "I can't save them all. I want to, but I can't…''

The horror gelled—the scene was so real Mary-Anne felt the sobs wrenching from her gut, and her eyes ached from the tears.

"Tal." The word barely registered through the rocks lodged inside her throat. She twisted around to sit up, and shook him. "Tal, wake up. It's over. It's over…''

"Bastards." Tal half sat up on the bed, soaked in sweat, his scars standing out in sharp contrast to the stark whiteness of his skin. Whether he was awake now or still sleeping, she didn't know. "Miserable bastards, dumping helpless kids to die, so they won't talk about what they've done. Is it worth it?''

"No," she whispered. "No, it's not worth it." She was beyond tears—and she now understood why Tal said what he did the first day, about his injuries rendering him useless. She knew about his exploits: Irish was the one who took more risks than anyone to save others on Search And Rescue—especially kids. And, as much as he wanted to be there—to save other kids like those on that fateful cliff shelf, kids who were dying around the world every day, he wasn't physically strong enough to perform the amazing feats he used to. It wasn't his life being over he fretted about, or his looks. It was the kids, the men and women—the innocent victims of war—he mourned for most.

And she'd accused him of self-pity. She'd accused him of being afraid to take risks—but that was all he'd ever done.

"I'm sorry, Tal," she whispered, tenderly kissing his mouth, the lips still making silent pleas for forgiveness from the children who hadn't made it. "I didn't understand. I didn't know. But I do now. I'm so sorry I wasn't there for you." With her free hand, she caressed his drenched hair. Her tears fell onto his face like touches of healing. "But I'm here now,

Tal. I'm here.'' She kissed him again, willing his pain to subside.

''Mary-Anne. Mary-Anne...'' The name barely made it from his tortured throat as he fell back on his soaked pillow, lying in the total quiet of exhaustion.

She smiled down at him, finally understanding the soul inside the man her beloved boy had become. ''Yes, Tal. I'm here.''

''No...another—damn—dream,'' he muttered, frowning. ''You—never come. Miss you—like hell—like a great big goddamn hole inside me...and you never come.''

An ache bloomed in her chest, making it hard to breathe. With a trembling hand, she caressed his scarred cheek. ''I should have come,'' she whispered. ''I should have come. But I'm here now.''

He sighed with the touch of her palm. His eyes blinked, then shut, in the slow wakening that comes after a dream. ''Wish—I could say...all I feel. Can't...so stupid.'' He sighed again, pulled her close and slipped back into sleep.

With her head on his shoulder and her body lying half across his, she should be half crazy with wanting, but all she felt was a strange, aching peace. She felt alive, glowing with newfound joy, and totally content. As the soft, fuzzy morning light filled the room through the windows, she closed her eyes and joined him in the deep slumber that knows no dreaming.

''I'm telling you, sir, I've had no chance to kill the guy. He and the lady are never apart, and they haven't left the hotel room since they got in it.''

Burstall grinned as he took turns viewing and listening in on the conversation through the hole he'd painstakingly drilled in silence through his bedroom floor last night. Hell, if he had a woman like Verity West in his bed, he wouldn't get out of it, either.

''Surely there has been one opportunity to kill the man?''

The edge in Falcone's voice got stronger with every sentence he spoke. Falcone had it as badly for Verity West as it was rumored he'd once loved the wife who'd run from him years ago, supermodel Delia de Souza Falcone.

"Not at the distance I have to keep to divert suspicion, sir," Longley answered, respectfully enough while standing before Falcone like a kid called to see his teacher. Through the hole Burstall noticed the man's clenched fists. Longley was as itchy to lay into the smiling bastard as he was. "If the other journalists here identify me it would lead to you."

Falcone tapped his foot on the floor and a pencil on his cherrywood desk. "Fine. Fine. Just do it soon, Mr. Longley."

"Sir, there isn't much I can do until they leave the hotel—and even then, they have several bodyguards."

"Then get to him when they're alone," Falcone said softly, his chilling eyes and fine mouth smiling once again. "I am sure they won't have bodyguards in their suite. Break in some-how, Mr. Longley—and kill O'Rierdan. Do it now."

Longley gave a curt nod. "Consider it done." He turned and stalked out of the luxuriously appointed room.

"Well, surely you have an opinion, Mr. Burstall? Consid-ering the trouble you endured to create your peephole last night, you must have some thoughts on this? Why don't you come down here and express them?"

Burstall cursed to himself. Damn the man for always being a step ahead! He got to his feet and walked downstairs and into the study, taking his time. "If you want my opinion, you need a backup plan, sir. The men surrounding O'Rierdan and Miss West are professionals who could take Longley down when he makes his attempt. Get the happy couple in here, out of their depth and away from their support systems. On your turf, you can easily kill him and take her."

"So crude, Mr. Burstall—I shall *persuade* her to stay. But though vulgarly expressed, your thoughts are sound. Yes, we'll execute that plan, but we'll leave aside yours for now."

Burstall started. "Mine, sir?" He looked in the eyes of the man who sheltered him, and he saw—*Falcone knew about Lissa.*

Falcone nodded, smiling. "Of course I know your plans to

ransom young St. Bremer for the lovely Mrs. McCluskey. We
will leave that out of our reckoning for now. It interferes with
my plans—both personal and professional—and that I do not
tolerate, Mr. Burstall. I do not want Interpol breathing down
my neck while my shipments change countries, or investigat-
ing possible links between myself and Haversham, Inc., until
the oil contract is in my hands. And a woman taken hostage,
or a spy murdered, is bound to bring the wrath of the above-
the-government groups down on us.''

Damn it to hell! It took all his self-control to remain calm
and quiet and to say the expected words. ''Yes, of course, sir.
As you wish, sir.''

''Good.'' Falcone lifted a brow. ''Oh, and you do know
that Mrs. McCluskey is rather heavily pregnant?''

Shock froze him, sickened him. Cruel devil, he got enjoyment out of torturing others. ''Yeah, well, Mrs. O'Rierdan
might be pregnant, too, by now, sir.''

The amusement fled. His eyes grew cold, reptilian. ''The
only children Miss West will ever give birth to will be mine.''
He spoke without his usual polished purr.

Burstall made the mistake of smirking before Falcone had
left the room…and he knew that he'd better get out of here
soon. Or he'd pay for talking back to Robert Falcone—with
his life.

Chapter 8

Two hundred and thirty-two...two hundred and thirty-three...
two hundred and thirty-four...

Mary-Anne lay on the floor of the honeymoon suite of
Amalza's ritziest hotel, heading toward her daily goal in sit-
ups. She was almost done. She'd finished a ten-kilometer
treadmill run and a dance routine workout in an outfit designed
to please the eager photographer snapping at her through the
enormous plate-glass window. Her presence here would be
known in hours...and hopefully they'd get an invitation soon
from the target. Falcone had sent her so many invitations in
the past, she had no doubt he'd send one today, and the mission would be on in earnest.

She quashed the spurt of regret. She knew she'd had only
one real chance to make love with Tal. The cabin on the Spanish coast was the only true private time they would have during the mission, without cameras and listening devices surrounding her. So close to attaining her lifelong dream... But
Anson, who never thought of his own or any operative's personal needs on a mission, had snatched their time without hes-

itation. There would be no chance for them now until after the mission.

If he stayed with her.

"Are you going for the women's world record for crunches?"

His voice held no irritation, no anger—just concern. As she'd had for him this morning, during the dream he apparently didn't remember when they'd awakened an hour later. Two-fifty-six...fifty-seven...fifty-eight... "I do this...every day," she panted between sit-ups. "Three hundred and I'm done for today."

"You'll make yourself sick. You won't be able to move tonight."

"It keeps me fit and healthy. I don't overdo." Stopping for a moment, she said, "I know some singers and actresses who do what I do, plus five hundred or more crunches every day. You get a gorgeous four pack, but I'm not into muscles, just keeping fit and trim." She grinned. "See, I'm not as excessive as some."

He hesitated, then spoke the worry that was obviously preying on his mind. "But you don't eat enough to support this level of exercise. And you're already too thin for your height. You'd be lucky to hit the scales at one-twenty, and you're five-eight."

"I'm one-twenty-three." She grinned in delight. "And thank you—nobody else has ever told me I'm too thin before."

"You are," he said, with all his usual bluntness. "You should be at least one-fifty at five-eight." He shook his head, frowning. "Do you do this much of a workout every day?"

"Sure. I have to keep superfit to get through my concert schedule." She spoke in panting puffs between cross-training elbow-to-knee crunches. "They're pretty rigorous, you know. All that singing, strutting and dancing demands a level of exertion you wouldn't believe. And my missions include a lot of wall-climbing, running and jumping. This program is the

Nighthawks' advanced fitness stage.'' She frowned at him. ''You do it, right?''

''Yes.'' He did his classic hesitation, then said, ''But you're already too small, and you don't take in enough calories to keep up with the levels of fitness you follow. Your body will suffer later for what you're putting it through now for your shows and the Nighthawks. And you don't sleep enough, either. When's the last time you had a week off?''

Two-seventy-nine…she blinked, startled, and looked at him, frowning. ''I'm having two weeks off now.''

His face was grim. ''No, Mary-Anne—I mean total time off. No singing, no writing, no recording, and no missions.'' When she didn't answer he took her hands and hauled her to her feet, his eyes searching hers with uncomfortable depth. ''How long have you been jumping from one job to another without rest? How long have you been falling asleep on chairs and on the floor? When did you last think of your own needs and not those of your fans, your missions or saving some part of the world that's in crisis?''

She felt more heat creep into her cheeks than even the exercise warranted. She tried to shrug it off. ''It's no big deal. I'm used to it now.''

''Which is even more dangerous for you. Not enough rest, too much work and working out will take a toll on your body you won't even know has come until you collapse.'' He used a finger to brush away a bead of sweat. ''When did you last have your period?''

She gave an involuntary glance up at the camera hidden inside a wedding photo of the two of them. There were operatives there, strangers watching, listening in on her private business…she felt stripped naked emotionally, raw and vulnerable. The concern in his tone did little to ease her embarrassment at strangers hearing her admit that the regimen she followed was excessive.

When *was* her last period? As a former nurse she should know, but she couldn't remember. She turned away. ''I don't remember coming to you for a checkup, Doctor,'' she joked.

"And, honestly, my cycle is none of your business unless I ask you for advice."

He neither stiffened nor smiled at her attempt to deflect his questions. "If you still have a cycle at all, I'd be surprised."

She frowned and looked at the floor. "Please, just leave it, all right? I don't want to talk about this."

"You helped me last night. Let me help you now. Please."

She looked up, startled. He shrugged and gave that slow-to-be-born smile of his, showing his dimples. "Yeah, I do remember some of it now. How much gut-spilling did I do in my sleep?"

The look in his eyes was unashamed vulnerability—and even if it was a trick to gain her trust, she melted. "I'm so sorry about the little girl, Tal."

"Me, too." Stark anguish mixed with the concern in his eyes.

"You apologized to Kathy for not saving her," she dared to add, and watched him flinch at the name. "I always knew her illness was why you became a doctor, but I didn't know you felt so personally responsible for her death."

He shrugged, trying to smile but making a dismal failure of it. "Yeah, well, I know it's not a logical thing to feel, okay? No need to sic a shrink on me over it."

"You don't let go of those you love, do you?" she said softly. "She's been gone seventeen years and she's still always in your thoughts and dreams."

"Yeah…along with some others I never forgot." He tipped up her chin, looking deeply into her eyes.

In wonder, she whispered, "You, too?"

That made him smile. "We're two of a kind, aren't we? Nice to know I wasn't forgotten…even if it was because you haven't found anyone else you're comfortable talking with since Gil died." He turned her face up with a finger, making her look at him. "Come on, talk to me," he said softly, his eyes so caring. "I'm here. I'm not just a doctor, I'm your friend…and right now those six babies you want are in danger of never being conceived."

The deep worry in his chocolate eyes undid her. She trembled under his hands. No one else knew her as Tal did—no one could break through her barriers to find her long-buried yearnings and hidden wishes. And no man could hurt her more with just a few simple words…but then, he still didn't know that the only man she wanted as her children's father was planning to divorce her. "How about I book an appointment to see you another time—when there's no one listening in would be good for me."

"Somehow I doubt you'll ever make that appointment." His words were grim, his gaze fixed on hers with the unerring accuracy of his long-term knowledge of her.

Oh, God help me—I can't cry now! "Look, I'll rest more if it will make you happy, and I'll be sensible about exercise. But this has been a pretty intense twenty-four hours. I need a shower." She walked into the bathroom—the only place in the suite without any kind of surveillance beyond infrared detectors at the entry points—and closed the door before he could argue. She stripped fast, turned the shower on hard and stood under it before she let the tears fall.

Good work, O'Rierdan, he thought ironically, standing outside the bathroom. *You finally start gaining her trust, then you pull this stunt when you know how tired she is.*

But damn it, she had only slept until 0830—and she'd worked out enough for the entire Olympic team after eating less than an average six-year-old did for breakfast.

At first he'd joined her regime. He'd done special weights to strengthen his leg as she walked, and he'd been beside her on the upper body workout. He did two hundred cross-training crunches before he called it quits…and she'd hit two-thirty when he started to realize what she was doing to herself. Yeah, he'd been spot-on in his assessment of her to Ghost last night. When did she stop, rest, kick back and have a day or two off?

He should have taken her outside, away from the Nighthawk cameras and bugs installed to protect them at all times. He *knew* how she hated anyone but him knowing her vulnerabil-

ity, her fears and hopes. Trouble was, he wasn't used to this
level of secrecy unless he was in his fatigues and paint. Being
on guard 24/7 was new to him, if not to her.

He'd realized that when he'd seen her smile fade and her
eyes blank out, haunting him with the hollowness locked inside the gorgeous green depths, just before she walked into
the bathroom.

Moments later, beneath the sounds of the shower running
hard, he could still hear the muffled yet unmistakable sounds
he hadn't heard in over ten years. Opening the door too quietly
for her to hear, he saw a huddled-up ball of humanity in the
corner of the shower, curled over herself, a clenched fist covering her mouth. Letting the hot rain fall on her as soft, hack-
ing sobs wrenched out of her gut.

He'd never heard a sadder, lonelier sound in his life.

She'd come in here to cry—the only place she wouldn't be
followed or overheard. She didn't want him here, that much
was obvious—but he obeyed the gut-deep instinct that she
needed him. Had she leaned on anyone since Gil West's
death? Whether she wanted him or not, he was here. He strode
to the shower, walked right in wearing his sweats and T-shirt,
and hauled her up in his arms, absorbing her startled gasp with
his mouth. "I'm sorry. I'm sorry." He kissed her swollen
eyes, her nose, her mouth. "You've had a rough week, and I
put that on you."

She lay limp in his arms, like a rag doll. "It's all right,"
she said, so soft and sad he could barely hear her under the
shower's hot spray. "I'm fine. It's okay."

"No, it's not. I know you, and I still pushed. I was trying
to help, but all I did was hurt you."

"You didn't mean to." Slow, hesitant—so timidly it
shocked him—she put her hands on his shoulders and looked
at him, her face flushed, wet and so beautiful beneath the
steaming water—as lovely as the body he was trying like hell
not to look at right now.

"I want babies, Tal, but it's not going to happen," she said,
her sweet voice strong and sad with loss. "After Gil died, I

decided that I'd never have babies without a father who's going to stay the distance—and that man has to love me. Me, not Verity West, not wanting to show the world he can melt the Iceberg. Me. But that hasn't happened since Gil died— and I don't think it's going to now. All I have is my career and the Nighthawks." She smiled bravely at him, but it wobbled. "I may not get babies, but at least I help the world, right?"

Seeing the shattered expression in her eyes she covered with that trembling smile of bravado, his heart and defenses shredded. He kissed her over and over, willing the pain to fade. "That's not true. You have me. I'm here."

If anything, the sadness grew worse, tearing at his very soul. "For how long after this week?" That wobbly little hiccup came from her throat, an unwilling witness to her distress.

He'd do anything right now to make it go away, say anything, give any promise. "For as long as you want me—as long as you can stand having me here. We'll have those babies if you want."

She gasped and buried her face in his neck. "*Want* you? Have your baby? Oh, *Tal…*"

The longing in her voice drove him over the edge. He lifted her face and kissed her, hot, deep, with the jagged-edged hunger he couldn't hold in anymore—and she was with him all the way. She moaned, wrapping her arms tight around his neck, her tongue twining with his. He pulled her up against him, filling his hands with her bottom, pushing her against his hardness. "Good…that's so good. Oh, yeah, do that," he muttered in hoarse encouragement as she yanked his T-shirt up and over his head, and filled her hands with his skin.

"Don't stop this time," she whispered between nibbling kisses, her eyes alight with sensual discovery. "I've been going crazy, pretending to be glowing when I'm *dying* of the pain of being near you, having you near me day and night, touching you but not the way I want to—need to—or having it interrupted, like last night. I can't do it anymore. Even if it's just for this week, or whatever time we have, I've got to have you, Tal…''

She pushed down his track pants—and he stilled. He couldn't help it. That ugly, mangled flesh, pink and puckered where the bone had burst through the flesh and remained infected for months, made him sick. And she was looking right at it…

And then she was touching it, touching the mess Burstall's grenade had made of his leg. Deep, fevered, drugging kisses on every inch of his skin, including his thigh. Hot, needing kisses right on his mangled flesh, without the slightest change in her hungry desire.

He kicked the tracks away and leaned against the shower wall, feeling weak, dazed—burning alive. Oh, it was so damn good, so erotic, with her fingers and mouth trailing over the intensely sensitive nerves of his scars. "How can you want me like this? How can you touch me there?"

She smiled up at him, drenched and gorgeous. "I used to think that, when you kissed me," she said softly. "I couldn't believe you wanted to kiss me, either. But you did. You did…"

"You were chubby, not ugly." His voice was dark with the disgust he felt whenever he looked at the mangled remains of his thigh. "*That* looks like a living explosion."

"It looks like what it is—a badge of honor for a brave and courageous man injured in the line of duty," she retorted fiercely. "It's just one part of you, Tal—the man I'm aching to make love with." She trailed her fingers over the scars again, and the exquisite rush of sensation hit him all over—and when she kissed him again, it felt like a healing touch to his soul as much as his injured body. "The man you are is the man I want."

The emotional impact of her words socked him in the solar plexus and rocked his world. "Just don't write a song about it, okay?" he managed to say through his stark longing for her.

She kissed his scars once again, laughing softly. "Promise."

Her eyes burned silver-bright with sudden urgency as he slid down the wall to her. "Will this hurt?"

"I don't *care*." He met her mouth in a tender kiss that soon turned hot, filled with need and connecting urgency and gratitude slamming each other for top place inside him. Urgency won. "I've waited so long for this. I don't think I can hold on anymore."

With a smile filled with joyful sensuality at his words, Mary-Anne straddled him, her breasts sliding against his chest, slick with water, and he groaned aloud, filling his hands with the round, full firmness of her. "Now, honey, now..."

"Yes, oh yes!" No preliminaries, no sweet foreplay—this was need as hot and raw as the land they came from, gravel-edged and bodies hurting with long denial. She lowered herself on to him.

Her head fell back as he filled her, her mouth open, the hot water running in rivulets over her face and breasts. She arched back, wild and exotic, a lovely nymph riding him in a waterfall with a cascade of wet curls falling down her back. Her eyes closed. "Oh, Tal, now—please, now..."

What followed was the wildest, most intense ride of his life. In all his imaginings of them together, he'd never once thought their first time would be this. Precariously balanced in a slippery supersize shower stall, leaning back on his elbows while hot water rained over him and she, his shy girl, took total control of his body. It was more magnificent than he'd dreamed, hotter than the fires of hell, as infinitely beautiful and unforgettable as the gates of heaven. Loving that would burn in his memory until he drew his final breath.

In the end, he didn't know if the cries of pleasure were hers or his. He was so focused on her, lost in *feeling* her delicious friction, making her moan and cry his name every time he filled her again and again. He groaned when the sweet wet gush all around him told him she'd reached climax, not once, but twice.

He couldn't breathe, couldn't think as he followed her final strangled cry of satisfaction with his own. A hoarse sound ripped from his throat. He pulled her down to him, kissing her mouth, loving the feel of her soft breasts against his wet skin.

"Are you okay?" she whispered, her eyes shining as she smiled down at him. Yeah, she was glowing now, her tension and sadness gone. She looked happier than he'd ever seen her. A one hundred percent satisfied woman…and like no iceberg he'd ever seen.

He chuckled and kissed her again. "Isn't that supposed to be my line? Checking for regrets or something?"

Leaning into the kiss, she took it a level higher…and it grew hot and intense a hell of a lot faster than he'd have believed in all his sexual experience. "You know you don't need to ask." She reached up and turned off the shower. "Am I hurting you?"

"Honey, I've got no complaints at all." He cupped the breast that moved in front of him as she twisted the taps. "How can your breasts be so full when the rest of you is so tiny?"

Purring with his touch, she murmured huskily, "You know my mother and grandmother, and you can't figure that out?"

"Mmm. Thank heaven for Aunt Miranda and Grandma Rickard's genetics." He filled his mouth, gently suckling. "Coral-colored nipples. Freckles on your belly. Can I play connect-the-dots?"

She purred, "Using what to connect?"

"Chocolate sauce? My hands and mouth?"

"Any or all, welcome," she whispered, smiling as she moved off his body, "and I wish we had time now…but Ghost and the team are due in at 1200."

He checked his watch. "You're right. Time to reapply the face goop, I guess. I'd better get up." With a groan of regret, he started hauling himself to his feet.

Mary-Anne's brow quirked, checking him out. "You're already up. It seems Irish is always ready for action."

Grateful that she'd diverted him instead of offering to help him with his precarious balance, staring at his arousal instead of his scars, he grinned at her. "When you're around, I am."

A strange expression flitted across her face. Then she smiled so sweetly he could almost believe he'd imagined it. "Good, because I'm ready to make the most of that state this week."

This week—this week. The words kept pounding at him like a relentless prizefighter, reminding him that soon she'd be gone, back to her concert tours, jets and limos and all the luxury her star status lifestyle demanded, and he'd stay behind to whatever he made of his life after he took Burstall down. He was too damaged physically to handle the rigors of being married to a star, and it would kill him to be a husband to Mary-Anne in name only. He couldn't live her life. If he ever got enough strength to go back to work, he'd want to be where he was needed somewhere, not following her around from place to place, being the "and husband." No. He couldn't do it. He'd just have to get his fill of her this week, and walk away after the mission a free man, then.

Would a week be enough?

But deep down, beneath all the old betrayals and the disgust for his face and body, the hate of an empty life that he couldn't change, he knew he was kidding himself.

If the Verity West juggernaut didn't exist around her, if he could stand and walk and run beside her as a full-bodied Nighthawk operative and doctor—or if by some miracle she could be Mary-Anne Poole again, just an ordinary woman he could keep as his wife, the question would be—

Would a lifetime with her be enough?

Chapter 9

The invitation came an hour later.

Under the guise of bodyguards, the team of Nighthawks finished the latest sweep of the room and checked out security and all points of entrance and exit of the entire hotel.

Looking as though he was itching to open the envelope himself, Anson handed it to her. Mary-Anne opened the envelope marked "Miss Verity West." "Falcone. An invitation to a party, plus an offer for accommodation for the length of our honeymoon, should we need or desire the added privacy he can provide for us."

Tal took the note from her outstretched hand. "It's for tonight, and you're the guest of honor? He didn't waste time."

"All the better for the mission, isn't it? The quicker we get in, the quicker we get Joel St. Bremer out of there and safe."

But Tal continued to frown. "How did he find out we were here and organize a party in your honor this quickly? Even with all his money and connections, it seems wrong."

Startled by Tal's spot-on assessment, she blinked. "The reporter this morning talked to him?"

"Why would the reporter tell him before the morning edition is out? He doesn't own the paper here."

Anson looked at Tal with sudden, intense attention. "You got a hunch, Irish?"

Tal frowned. "None of it's sitting right with me, Boss. It's too quick, like he knew we were coming here—like he keeps tabs on Songbird's life and whereabouts beyond her press releases. I think he had this all set up and ready for her arrival. I don't like it. This could be a test—and if we jump to accept too fast, it puts us all in danger, but especially Songbird."

After a moment Nick nodded. "Excellent reasoning. What's your take, then?"

Mary-Anne almost tripped over her jaw. Had the world started spinning backward, or was their control-freak Area 4 Head of Security deferring to Tal—Tal, who might be an SAR expert but had never been part of an op like this?

It didn't appear to faze Tal. "Let's wait a few days before we go in. If we go to the Embassy tonight or even tomorrow, it'll look pretty suspicious. We're on our honeymoon after what the world knows was a whirlwind courtship. A bona fide couple would want a few days alone."

"You're not a honeymoon couple," Nick barked, "And the orders are to get that boy out and take Burstall down, ASAP!"

"And how can we do that if we arouse suspicion? You said it yourself—the Embassy has tighter security than the White House. If we go now, we put the whole team at risk, all of whom know a lot more about our operations than a kid like Joel St. Bremer."

Anson nodded with obvious reluctance. "Okay, you have a point—but what do we do with ourselves in the interim?"

Tal only grinned at the impatient question. "Well, I don't know what you feel like doing, Boss, but I'm all for having a honeymoon with my wife…without electronic surveillance." He turned to smile at her, the look in his eyes warm and relaxed—like a man who'd just been thoroughly loved…and she felt herself blushing under the amused, interested glances of Braveheart and Wildman. "A couple of days on a yacht, just the two of us."

Anson sighed. "How bona fide would Verity West and her husband look going out on a boat alone, without protection?" he demanded irritably. "You'll have the paparazzi after you within hours. Can you think without your gonads on this, Irish, and act like the operative I trained you to be?"

"That's the point," Tal shot back. "You want bona fide? If I'd married Songbird without the assignment, I *would* be thinking like a horny kid. I *would* take her on the yacht for peace and quiet, because she hasn't had any form of rest in over a year. Let the hounds fly over, take shots—it only helps the mission, plus it strengthens our reasons for accepting the full invite to the Embassy. After a couple of days, we get sick of the intrusions and accept Falcone's offer of accommodation. Anything for peace and quiet before her next tour in America."

By the time he'd finished everyone in the room was nodding, including Nick. "Excellent planning, Irish. You think well on your feet. Okay, we'll hire three yachts, one for you two, and three of us will be in each of the others. I'll check it out with Virginia, but I'd say this plan will get the green light. Enjoy your honeymoon, Songbird and Irish." His grin was wry. Obviously he was still irritable, but even he knew when he couldn't change the flow of the river.

"You bet, Boss." Tal grinned right back. "Every second you don't annoy the hell out of us."

She felt a blush staining her cheeks, but to her surprise, Nick laughed. "I'll be sure to knock from now on." He snapped his fingers. "Let's go."

With smothered grins, the men filed out of the room.

As soon as they'd gone, Tal pulled her into his arms, kissing her ear. "You happy with the yacht idea?"

She wrapped her arms around his neck. "What do you think?"

The kiss was long, hard, intensely passionate. "I meant what I said about rest, though," he murmured mock sternly against her mouth. "Stop kissing me, woman, I'm serious. I'm going to make sure you sleep. You've pushed yourself too hard for too long. You're on the edge of exhaustion, even if you won't admit it."

She twinkled up at him. "So keep me in bed, day and night. I promise, I won't complain at all. Doctor's orders and all that."

"And don't you forget it." He nuzzled her lips. "There's no way I'll spend half of our time on the yacht cramped in the bath or shower, hiding out from the guys. I want to make love in the comfort of a bed...or maybe the ocean at night, finish what we started last night," he whispered between slow, hot kisses.

Her body fired, but her heart constricted. Could she make love with him and still hold back her heart? She had to protect herself. When their time was up—dear God, could she face being alone again, playing the part of the Iceberg to the world, being Verity West because Mary-Anne didn't have a life of her own?

Could she make him want to stay with her?

I couldn't handle this life for long...

She faced it squarely. Well, damn, if she only had a week or a year with him, then she'd make it a week or a year to remember. "Perfect," she whispered back.

A loud knock interrupted the kiss they were about to share. "Sir? Madam?"

Anson again. Tal sighed. Every single damn time he started to break down her barriers, made her start to think of herself rather than the mission, their ruthless Ghost returned to haunt them. Reminding them both that they'd never be here, would never be together again, but for the mission.

"Come in," he called, but kept a tight hold of Mary-Anne. Would she object if he super-glued her to him for, say, a few weeks...or maybe months...oh, heck, make it a few years?

Anson strode in, either not noticing or not perturbed by the fact that two of his operatives were locked in each other's arms, obviously in the middle of a steamy intramarital affair.

"Virginia says go. I've rented the yachts, but we can't get them until 1100 tomorrow. So we'll follow your plan, Irish. I've booked us into Amalza's most exclusive restaurant tonight, where the press is bound to find and annoy you. They'll be camped outside the hotel 24/7 by morning. I've doubled the amount of operatives on this in line with that inevitability. They'll be here by 0400, and after a morning exposing yourselves to more publicity overkill, we'll do a fifty-one—"

Okay, now Tal was way out of his depth. "What's a 'fifty-one'? I've only ever done a job as high as a forty."

"That's as high as SAR op numbers go." Mary-Anne rolled her eyes as she grinned. "Fifty-one is a glitz round 'celebrity escape.' Our surrounding bodyguards yell *no comment* while the press shoves their microphones and cameras at us, trying to take pictures, and we look stressed, angry, scared—whatever works. Our guards push us toward a limo, where we make our escape."

He blinked. "Ah, right."

"I hate it, too, if that helps," she whispered, hugging him.

Anson was too deep in thought to notice. "Flipper's qualified to sail a boat, so he'll be your skipper. On the fifty-one— we can't let the journalists get to Irish. Even leaving aside the fact that any one of them could be in Falcone's pay as Brooks seemed to be, if even one of them sees the makeup, inadvertently touches his cheek or wrecks his shoe insert the mission's shot."

Tal nodded, feeling out of control with this part of the mission—a feeling as unfamiliar as it was unwelcome. "Right. I'll call Falcone." He released Mary-Anne, picked up the phone and dialed the RSVP number. "Hello? This is Verity West's husband," he told the feminine voice that answered. "I'm calling to decline the kind invitation by Mr. Falcone for the party tonight as we're on our honeymoon. I'm sure he'll understand."

"Please hold," the woman said softly.

A moment, a click, and another voice spoke. An English voice, smooth like clotted cream compared to his own flinty

Outback twang. "This is Robert Falcone. How may I help you?"

"Hello, Mr. Falcone. This is Verity West's husband—"

"My deepest congratulations," the smooth voice interrupted him, rich with gentle male laughter and something more sinister beneath. "You have a real jewel. I presume that I'm speaking to Dr. Tallan O'Rierdan?"

Tal felt a small, icy chill creep up his spine. "You presume correctly. We can't make it."

"A handsome couple, indeed," Falcone went on as if he hadn't spoken. "You will have many lovely children—six was the number your wife once said she wanted, if I'm correct. But on your honeymoon, I can empathize with your reluctance to share your exquisite wife with the world any more than you have to. May I ask if you will be socially unavailable the whole tenure of your time in Amalza?"

"My wife is getting over a throat infection." How the hell did Falcone know about Mary-Anne's most private wish for half a dozen kids, which he damn well *knew* she hadn't spoken about publicly? Oh, this guy was good—too good, and the chill snaking back down his spine began spreading up and outward. "She's worked too hard the past few months. I want her to have a complete rest."

Mary-Anne's eyes widened. "Tal, what are you doing?" she whispered urgently, but Anson nodded his approval.

Falcone asked gently, "So is there no chance that she—that you both, I mean—will be able to visit my home while you're here? That's terribly disappointing. I had hoped for a day or two's visit, to get to know you both—"

"I don't think that will be possible. It's our honeymoon. I'm sure you understand."

"Yes. Of course." The patent platitude rolled off Falcone's tongue as polite as it was insincere. He still wasn't resigned, and Tal drew a silent breath of relief. "Do you think, perhaps—just one dinner before you leave…?"

"Maybe we can manage that. I'll ask her. Honey?" He

spoke just loud enough for Falcone to hear. "Mr. Falcone wants to know if we can make it next week sometime."

"I think that sounds all right," she answered after a moment's pause. "I wanted a week together, just you and me," she said, making it loud enough for Falcone to hear.

"Me, too." He leaned forward and kissed her, soft and gentle, yet loud enough for effect. "We'll have it, I promise." He said to Falcone, "Maybe we can make it one night. Can we call you?"

"Wonderful," the insidious voice purred. "I will change the party to any evening of your choice. As guest of honor, dare I hope that your wife will honor us with her superlative voice?"

"If she's well enough," he answered, all but shivering with the effect of this man's gentle, cultured tone on his nervous system. "I'll call you."

"Of course. And Dr. O'Rierdan, take care of your lovely wife. You're a very blessed man. There are thousands of men around the world who would be more than eager to take your place."

"I know," he said—and decided to push the envelope to see how Falcone would take it. "But I don't feel threatened by them, Mr. Falcone, because I love my wife—and she loves me."

Mary-Anne pulled back from him as if stung, her eyes dark and filled with shadows, an effective eclipse of her mind and emotions. She crossed to the window, where the sun's morning light danced over the glowing turquoise waters of the Mediterranean and the town itself, seen through the glass, blazed in washed whites, colorful banners streaming in the breeze. She edged in until she stood half hidden in the curtains, lost inside and amid a glorious riot of color that for once outshone her.

Never had she looked so small, or so lonely.

Terrific going. I might've jerked Falcone's chain with what I said, but I definitely alienated my wife.

"Again, congratulations." Falcone's words were quiet now,

no less charming, yet infinitely more chilling. "To be the chosen lover of the beautiful and extraordinarily talented Verity West—pardon me for using her former husband's name, Dr. O'Rierdan—would indeed be a rare and precious privilege for any man."

Out of the serpent's twisted mouth came truth—more truth than a piece of dirty laundry like Falcone, appreciating only Mary-Anne's flame-haired beauty, iceberg reputation and incredible talent, could ever know. "Goodbye, Mr. Falcone."

"I'll look forward to meeting."

He replied in polite kind, keeping his tone bland until he hung up. "Yeah, I'll look forward to meeting you—and taking you down, you scum," he muttered. "You and Burstall both."

"Do you really think the lovely Miss West is your spy?"

Burstall frowned. "Yes, I do. Her job gives her the perfect cover, and she hangs out with the black market set, as you told me. This honeymoon's a front."

"Yet I had to persuade her husband to even consider a dinner party. So unless you believe O'Rierdan is a complete fool, you must believe him a spy for your fabled Mission Impossible group? And if Miss West is a spy, wouldn't she have had something to say to O'Rierdan about his peremptory refusals?"

"She is a spy. And he's an Australian doctor like the spy I injured in Tumah-ra," Burstall said bluntly. "This is a set-up."

"Suspicious, perhaps—but he is surely one of many thousands of doctors in Australia, Mr. Burstall. We can't suspect every doctor who turns up just because he's Australian. Or is it only when they marry lovely, famous women that you suspect them?"

Burstall only just refrained from rolling his eyes. "It's too convenient, their coming here now."

Falcone shrugged. "Rather a whirlwind romance and marriage, perhaps, but surely in keeping with celebrity tradition." He spoke with slow caution, yet Burstall knew how quick he could be. "Coming here at this exact time is…shall we say 'coincidental.' I'd double check to be sure it's legal. And you do realize that perhaps it is our good doctor who is the spy. Check to see what he's been doing the past few years."

"I'm already on it." He sighed. "These Nighthawks seem extraordinarily loyal to their cause."

"As are you, Mr. Burstall—as is evidenced by your telephone call to Mrs. McCluskey this morning from the shiny new cell phone hidden in your room. You offered her young St. Bremer for her, I believe—something I did warn you against."

Damn his rotting soul, how did Falcone know so much? Whatever moves he made, Falcone always seemed a step ahead of his game. "Mr. Falcone, it shouldn't make a difference to your plans—"

Falcone tilted his head: smooth and smiling, thin and darkly handsome. "I'm afraid it does. You see, I don't *want* my home invaded by your Mission Impossible friends, looking to, uh, 'take you down,' I believe is the expression. Your presence here is causing too much interest in me by reflection. Your obsession with the lovely Mrs. McCluskey is taking your mind from the tasks I hired you to complete. And you most inconsiderately drilled a hole in my home. Apart from the obvious fact that .you were spying on me, you made a mess of my carpet and ceiling. And that I do find most hard to forgive."

Seeing the gentle smile on Falcone's face, Burstall broke out into a cold sweat. Then two men were at his side, grabbing him.

Falcone nodded. "I did warn you—you must admit that I took the trouble to warn you."

I'm going to die…

He must have said it aloud, for Falcone smiled even more. "No, Mr. Burstall, you will not die—not today at least, and not while you are still somewhat useful to me. But you have been…shall we say, insubordinate? Learning to whom you answer will be a most needed lesson in your survival skills."

The first punch winded him, the second he felt crack a rib.

And still the hits came, knocking him down until he curled in a ball, begging them to stop, that he'd learned who was boss.

"That's good news, dear boy." Falcone was gently amused as ever. As if his voice conjured magic, the pounding stopped—but the goons left him on the floor, gasping, trying desperately not to heave. "Wonderful news. I am certain we won't need to have this conversation again, will we, Mr. Burstall?"

"No," he gasped.

"Excellent." Falcone walked over him toward the doors. "Oh, and do try not to throw up on the carpet."

The doors shut behind Falcone, clicking quietly into place, of course. Robert Falcone was always the gentleman, who never needed to yell, to threaten or slam doors. Nothing so dramatic.

Next time he crossed the line, he'd be dead.

Chapter 10

"Mmm...mmm," Mary-Anne sighed as she swallowed a piece of some succulent fruit Tal had never seen or heard of in Australia—the only food she'd eaten all evening, except for one piece of chicken and a few mouthfuls of salad. "This is glorious." She picked up a tiny ball of fruit between her fingers and lifted it to his mouth across the candlelit table. "Taste it, darling."

Tal opened his mouth, holding in a groan when her fingers deliberately brushed his lower lip. "Delicious."

Her eyes gleamed soft and sultry. "I knew you'd like it." She leaned forward and kissed him, long, lingering—

And carefully controlled...because everything they did tonight was an act for the avid cameras snapping at them outside the enormous plate-glass window. Her eyes and luscious body promised pure heaven—and flames of desire were licking at him, even though he was in on the performance. Verity West the Star was showing the world her superb talent.

Now he knew why so many men were obsessed with her. The Iceberg had proven her ability to turn a man into a shivering wreck of frustrated desire. Heaven knew he was a wreck already, and yet he knew he'd soon be gettin' lucky again… and now he'd made love to her, he knew *lucky* was a massive understatement.

But—looking beneath the veneer her beauty and talent presented, he still saw the shy girl who would once almost rather have left one of her beloved animals to its fate than kiss and touch a man in public—even him.

She hated every second of this.

He leaned forward and whispered against her mouth. "Hang in there, honey. It's almost over."

Her smile widened, as if he'd said something wonderful, but her eyes revealed more. Beneath the self-satisfied expression of Verity West, Mary-Anne's need to run had only grown. "It was hard enough when the whole thing was only for the mission and I thought you were acting," she muttered, "but now—"

"Now that we're lovers, you mean?" he asked to distract her.

Soft hands reached out to his, playing the game. "I don't want the world knowing about us. I don't want them hounding us for pictures and questions. What we have should be ours alone."

His kiss this time was real, a tender reassurance. "It will be while we're on the yacht."

Her face, shimmering incandescent in the candlelight, took his breath away—but her words haunted his soul. "Every day is me belonging to my fans, and tabloid journos thinking it's their right to invade my life…"

He clamped down the words hovering on his tongue. *Then walk away.* If that time ever came, it had to be her decision alone. "I don't know how you do it. I couldn't handle your life."

That flash of pain came and went again, followed by a smile of bravado—the one that grabbed him by the throat and wouldn't let go. "I guess our lives have reversed, huh? I could never handle all the attention you got when we were kids."

Willing to follow her lead, he grinned. "I didn't handle it too well, either. Why do you think I loved hanging out with you so much?" His fingers moved, caressing her palm, willing her to smile. "You were too busy shoving your injured animals at me to care about my latest score on the football or cricket field, or whether I'd put Murrumbooee High on the map with my test marks."

That made the pain fade, because she laughed, that lovely silver and golden ripple of sound he loved so much. Her hand turned, she laced her fingers through his, and from her wrist, the scent of rose and lavender floated up to him, filling his head. How could such a soft smell seem so completely sexy? "I guess you must have felt like you went from the sublime to the ridiculous."

"I loved it. When I was with you and your animals, I could just be myself." He felt the corner of his mouth quirk up; he rolled his eyes, trying to ignore what just the simple act of holding her hand did to him. "Yeah, I really was myself when you made me muck out that hell on earth you called a hospital. The farmer's kid, doing what he did best—shoveling muck and dirt."

"Hey, bud, I was right beside you on that job—even if you had to remind me to do it most of the time." Her eyes lit warm and soft with the memory. "I think Mum forced Dad and Greg to build me the shed for my hospital, just so she could have her laundry room without animal droppings or slipping in the blood I'd forget to clean up."

Remembering some of Aunt Miranda's choice cusswords when she'd find her laundry a disaster again, he chuckled. "Forget? Yeah, right. You always hated cleaning anything. Leaving the blood was your way of getting your own shed, if you ask me. If your mother screamed or fell over in the mess enough—"

She pressed her lips together, trying hard not to laugh. "I didn't do it *deliberately*."

His brow lifted. "So you gave poor Aunt Miranda a few real Freudian slips?"

Laughter bubbled out of her then, rich and true, its joyous beauty making him laugh, too. "I guess it's just as well I can afford a housekeeper these days. I still hate picking up after myself, and as for cleaning or mopping…" She gave a dramatic shudder. "Cooking, I can handle. I even like it, much to my cook's disgust when I invade his kitchen. But there's only so much fancy food this Outback girl can handle. I like spaghetti or lasagna or just a steak and salad now and then."

A shaft of some deep emotion sliced through him at the unconscious reminder of how far apart their worlds were now. He had to face the truth: if she was so far above him now, it was his own fault. He'd had the chance to keep her with him forever, and he'd blown it with his own naiveté. If he'd demanded to see the results of Ginny's so-called blood test—

Yeah, well, you never asked, did you, Tal? He could still hear Ginny's taunt that day, ringing clear with all the contempt and hate she felt for him. *You didn't ask because you wanted to show the world a poor farmer's son could marry someone like me!*

Even ten years on, he honestly didn't know if Ginny had it right. Maybe she did—he'd only been twenty-one and still locked in that boy's insecure need to prove himself to those he loved. But it was a habit he'd outgrown. The hell on earth that was his marriage to Ginny, and living with Max, had cured him of any need to prove anything to anyone but himself.

"Yeah, just as well," he answered her, and even he heard the hollowness in his words.

"Miss West!"

In automatic mode Mary-Anne turned to face the call from a table near the doorway, with her trademark smile—but with one glance and no hesitation, Tal dived out of his chair and on top of her. "Get down!" he yelled, taking her in his arms and rolling under the table in one smooth motion.

As if by magic, the Nighthawks sitting at the other tables went into action, tackling the would-be shooter, others closed and locked the doors and curtains on the flashing cameras that lit the dark intimacy of the room like the sudden fury of an Outback lightning storm.

And still he held her beneath the shelter of their dining table. Mary-Anne felt trapped, pinned down by arms that felt like bands of steel. "I think you can let me up now," she said, more shaken than she'd show.

He looked into her eyes for a long moment, and she realized—oh, *no,* she was trembling. But to her surprise, he said softly, "Sorry about that. Overkill," giving her the dignity she deserved as a fellow operative. "Clear?" he called aloud.

"Yes, sir," Nick's voice spoke, low and respectful: a bodyguard's tone. "Is Miss West safe? You, sir?"

"We're both fine." Tal loosened his hold on her.

Mary-Anne rolled out from under the table, needing space—needing him to keep holding her—oh, heck, she didn't know *what* she needed right now, except maybe to slug the stupid jerk who'd ruined their dinner.

The stupid, gangly, pimple-faced little jerk currently lying facedown beneath a splay-legged Braveheart, whose massive form dwarfed him and knocked the breath and fight from him. "Let me up," he whined in a Spanish accent. "I didn't mean any harm, madame. I did not mean to frighten you, madame, or your husband…" the young man gabbled, his strained, red face paling in sudden and obvious panic. "I am no threat, I have only my tape recorder! I am a great fan of madame. I am a songwriter!"

At that, anyone who'd ever been on assignment with Mary-Anne groaned. Grumbling, Braveheart let the kid up.

"I just wish to play my song for her," he went on earnestly. "I have written, oh, so wonderful a love song, just for Miss West's glorious voice. It will take the whole world by storm, but her agent would not show her my work!"

The boy then rushed to the piano in the corner of the room and started singing in a thin, reedy voice about the impossible love of a boy for a girl too high for him to touch.

Wildman shook his head. "Loser alert," he rumbled, shoving his weapon back in its holster.

"And before dessert, that's just plain inconsiderate." Braveheart rolled his eyes. "I wanted that *bavaroise.*"

Mary-Anne lifted a hand, listening intently to the words and music. Slowly she walked over to where the boy played, looked at the score sitting on the music desk and began singing along, hearing the gentle poignancy in this, a tragic sweetness that surely arrested everyone in the room.

The boy looked as if he'd die from joy any moment.

"She'll take it," Braveheart predicted to Wildman.

Wildman shrugged. "It's pretty good—and at least we'll get dessert while we're waiting."

Mary-Anne grinned. They'd spoken loud enough for her to hear even as she sang. They were right: for the first time with this kind of interruption, she'd take a song. If this boy had more songs like this, he had a magnificent career in front of him.

When she finished, she leaned over the boy and took up the score. "It's a lovely song—what did you say your name was?"

"Miguel, madame," the boy breathed, his eyes glowing.

She smiled down at him. "Well, Miguel, I'm going to send your name and phone number to my manager, and my record label. Once my husband and I are home from my honeymoon, of course." She looked down at the score in her hand. "My personal assistant, Rhonda, will contact you. Now, I'm on my honeymoon, and my bodyguards get unhappy if they don't get their sugar fix. They may punish you in a way that would relieve their feelings, but your fingers wouldn't be good for the guitar for a few days."

"But I have three more songs, and I would so love to hear you sing my—" The kid gulped, even his enthusiasm tamped by the sight of Braveheart and Wildman moving in on him. The kid was obviously no match for two big, hulking guys in the absolute peak of condition. He backed away toward the exit. "Good night. Thank you, Miss West. You are a beautiful and gracious lady."

Anson unlocked the door and the kid bolted through it, past the multitude of flashing cameras and into the night.

Wildman's dark, handsome face twisted with deep long-suffering. "Why do you always let 'em get away with it? If you'd do your Iceberg number on them, it wouldn't get around that Verity West's only soft spot is for desperate kids with tragic songs."

She shrugged, feeling the flush creep up her cheeks. "I know how it feels. I was that kid once, writing songs I never thought anyone but my family or Gil would ever hear. I got my break."

"You made your own break happen. Gil knew you'd win, or he wouldn't have entered you." The voice came from a darkened corner of the restaurant. "So this happens to you a lot?"

Turning around, she saw Tal sitting quietly at a table. With his face lost in the shadows, she couldn't read his expression—but she shivered. "It happens to all celebrities, Tal."

"Shall we go back to the hotel, Miss West?" Anson asked. "I feel every day of my fifty-one years right now."

In one smooth movement the Nighthawks surrounded her in a fifty-one, ready to follow Nick's hidden command. Tal moved into the inner circle, both for appearances and to protect his face and shoe from detection. "Okay. Let's do it."

Nick paid the bill, then they crowded around her as the doors opened, cameras flashed and journos screamed questions, asking for anything from wedding photos to intimate details of their marriage.

Pushed and shoved one way and the other, staggering and almost falling but for Tal's steadying hands on her arms, she moved forward, holding on to the moment she and Tal would be safe in the waiting car.

Sighing with relief when the doors locked behind them and Braveheart took off, she glanced at Tal. His face still had that unreadable look...and stress bloomed along her nerve endings like wildflowers on Cowinda's dirt roads in spring. "It's hard to cope with all this the first time. These people are in serious need of a life—and it seems it's my life they want." She tried to make a joke of it as Gil used to, but somehow it fell flat.

Maybe it was the look on Tal's face. He seemed so cold and remote in the warm darkness, his face tense and brooding.

Stupid. Gil took a year to get used to this life enough to make jokes about it...and you're still not comfortable with it. Sometimes she got scared that she never would be...that even the thrill of singing to thousands of people at once, and the joy of knowing people loved her songs, would become overshadowed by the constant intrusions into her life.

Tal spoke from where he sat half-sprawled in the corner of the limo, his voice as deep and quiet as the dark surrounding him. "How often do you let kids like Miguel get away with that?"

She jumped, startled out of her reverie, and sighed. "I don't know." Helplessly, she shrugged. "What do you do, Tal? They're kids with stars in their eyes. They're desperate to make it, and I think to myself, if the receptionist for my record label hadn't been in the audience at the contest Gil entered me in—"

"Would it have been so bad?" he asked, still quiet. "Was your life so unhappy when you were a nurse? It was all you ever wanted once." After his classic hesitation, he plunged in. "Are you happy with the life you have now? Does the smell of leather in these seats, the dresses and diamonds you wear, the jets and limos and all the adulation give you what you need? Because except when we're alone together, I never see you smile with your eyes. I don't hear you laugh from the heart."

Damn that surgical knife of his, cutting away self-delusion to the truth beneath—reality with a cutting edge. "I was happy nursing, but winning the contest and recording *Nobody's Lolita* changed my life. My career provides a cover that gives me access to inner circles. It allows me to perform covert ops for the Nighthawks that no one else can," she said, her voice suddenly filled with intensity. "I play my part for regional peace, and I live a life most people only dream of. Why shouldn't I be happy?''

Was it a trick of the night or did he move farther into the darkness? He was slipping away from her in more ways than just the physical… ''You tell me, Mary-Anne. Do you ever play 'what if it never happened?' Do you like being Verity West? Do you feel happy—I mean, on a personal level—being a Nighthawk?''

The limo pulled up in front of the hotel and the unanswered questions hovered between them, underscored by the crowd of journalists waiting outside and the Nighthawks standing at the ready to escort them inside.

Tears rushed to her eyes. She turned her head away from the scene in front of her and Tal's eyes probing her face in the dark. Maybe he was right, her life was all about other people—but wasn't that a good thing? Why shouldn't she be happy?

Are you? a little voice whispered. She tasted the vile metallic tang of blood in her mouth from where she'd clamped down on her lip too hard.

''So what's the number for a celebrity in-scape?'' Tal asked wryly. ''Or are we inventing new numbers for this assignment?''

Taken off guard, she laughed and turned to him. ''Want to make up a number for it? I think we're up to seventy-five.''

''Seventy-five sounds good.'' He touched her jaw, his eyes looking deep into hers. ''Chin up, kid. We're in this together.''

As always, his use of ''kid''—the careless nickname he'd given her when someone had hurt or embarrassed her when they were children—warmed her. ''Are we, still?'' she whispered.

''You haven't lost me yet.'' He cupped her chin in his hand. ''Just takes a little getting used to, this kind of mission…but man, it has its perks.'' Leaning forward, he kissed her, a quick, hard thing that left her flushed and aching. ''If Ghost thinks he's putting surveillance in the bedroom, he'll have a fight on his hands,'' he muttered. ''We're not spending the whole time in the shower, hiding out from him. I want a bed, and the right to make love whenever and wherever we want to.''

"Within the bounds of decorum, of course," she added, smiling up at him. Oh, how she was looking forward to their time on the yacht. She had a feeling that "whenever and wherever" would be constant, exciting and inventive... "Flipper may object to our using the engine room, or the cook might want the galley."

"Yes, of course, dear," he agreed, his eyes hot with promise. "Since Ghost threw his rules out the window on this, he'll have to accept that we're lovers for as long as this mission lasts."

She felt her heart thud and boom against her chest at the stark pain his final four words invoked, but before she could answer, Braveheart had opened the passenger's door and the unofficially numbered "celebrity in-scape" swung into motion.

Chapter 11

"Do you mind if I run for a while?" Mary-Anne asked the next day, as they walked along a blooming cliff path—Nick insisted the more exposure to the press right now, the better.

"Sorry," Tal returned bluntly. "We're on our honeymoon. It'll look suspicious to anyone watching us if I don't run with you."

Stupid! She almost smacked her forehead. "I'm sorry, Tal. That was a dumb question."

He shrugged. "No, I'm the one who's sorry."

The look on his face said it all. Making love added a layer of cosmetic work to his battered sense of self, but the self-disgust was still strong. The shoe insert and makeup he had to don each day were constant reminders that he'd never be the man he was two years ago.

"It's only a run, Tal," she said quietly. "There are more important things to worry about in the world than that."

"Yeah." His voice was stark. "Like saving people in need. Like hunting murderers on the run."

"What part of that aren't you doing? Joel St. Bremer is a

boy in need. The men we're hunting are murderers." Feeling
as if she was hitting her head against barricades of bricks, she
went on doggedly. "You're performing a vital work right
now."

"Yeah, with Nighthawks to protect me because I can't protect myself." He swept a hand at the men forming a barrier
around them at a discreet distance. "I used to be one of them.
One of the protectors. Now I need bodyguards."

"You still are. What if that kid had had a real gun last
night? You'd have saved my life."

"But he didn't. I panicked over a stupid tape recorder."

"You panicked for me," she said softly, "and you don't
know how much that means to me." She held her breath,
hoping that her words would penetrate the wall surrounding
him.

He turned to her with sudden fierceness, gripping her hands,
his eyes burning. "Next time I may not be fit or fast enough.
I can't run or carry you more than a few steps if you're hurt.
If my leg packs it in, you'd be the one carrying me. I'm a
liability here. I'm putting you in danger by being here."

Her eyes stung, but sympathy was useless: it would only
cause his barriers to lift even higher. "We wouldn't even be
here but for you. Joel St. Bremer wouldn't even have a chance
but for you. You're central to the whole assignment, and
you're taking bigger risks than the rest of us because of your
injuries."

"My risks are taken by all of us. You know none of the
guys would leave me to die or get taken," he muttered, his
face dark. "I can't carry my weight on any assignment, and
you know that, too. I'm just window dressing to streamline
your job, thanks to Ginny's tabloid lies three years ago."

"You're the one who'll be finding and saving the hostage,"
she replied, feeling adrift in a turbulent sea of emotions.
"And—is it so bad, being with me again, Tal? Even if it came
about thanks to Ginny's lies?"

"Bad?" He swore softly. The others melted into the background to give them space. He dragged her into his arms,

holding her fiercely. His whole body was taut, wired. "Not you. Never you…''

She closed her eyes and leaned against him, and right now, it was enough. A memory to hold when he was gone again.

"I wasn't talking about us," he murmured, caressing her hair. "Three years after I got free, her revenge still affects what I do. Will she never stop manipulating my life with her lies?''

She gasped and blinked. Did he mean…? What was he saying…? Her stomach churned in time with the pounding of her heart. "She got away with lies before the tabloid stories?''

He wheeled away, looking over the knife-edged cliff to the brilliantine dapples of sunlight on the Mediterranean. "Yeah, and she got paid for it, too. Got paid real well.'' He shoved his fists into his jeans' pockets, every line of him tense, brooding.

Hesitantly she touched his shoulder. "Tal—"

"Dumb-arse jerk.'' He leaned against a tree beside him, plucking off leaves and tearing them up. "I knew she was a liar. I knew she'd stop at nothing to get what she wanted— me on a platter—and still I believed her. I gave up my life for five bloody miserable years so she could play doctor's wife, and it was just another one of her lies, orchestrated by Max to bring the poor farmer's son to heel.''

The world suddenly spun slower, making her stagger. "She…she wasn't pregnant?''

His laugh held no humor, a short bark of sound. "Well, if she was, it sure wasn't mine.''

Putting a steadying hand out onto the tree trunk—for she'd swear later that the earth beneath her had just rocked—she frowned. "It…wasn't yours?''

"Couldn't have been, is the more correct term." He threw a dark, intense glance over his shoulder at her. "She taunted me with it years later. She thought it was hilarious that a medical student not only didn't ask to see the blood test results, but didn't know when he'd done the deed or not. She climbed into bed with me when I'd passed out.''

Oh, dear God… She blinked, trying to reorient her mind. "So—you're saying…you didn't—"

"Not for want of trying, apparently, but no. I was out of it, dead drunk, and she couldn't wake me. So she set the scene. I couldn't remember anything the next morning but waking up with a massive hangover and her beside me in bed. And I fell for it."

"You never slept with her?"

"Well, not until after we were married," he replied dryly. "I kinda kept out of her way until the wedding, staying at college and studying for exams, but after that I couldn't avoid her. I might not have liked her, sweetness, but I was a twenty-one-year-old with limited experience, and she was eager and available."

"And beautiful," she added softly.

He shrugged. "I never went for the dark-haired Barbie doll type—she always looked like one of those girls in those meaningless teen flicks. Too perfect, too much makeup and not enough inside. And after a so-called 'miscarriage' three weeks after the wedding, I got the picture. We had a massive fight, and I told her that liars turn me off. Our sexual encounters were pretty much hit-and-miss after that—I missed her whenever I could and she hit on any guy who'd have her."

Taking the step that separated them she wrapped her arms around his waist from behind. "Why didn't you leave her?"

"I tried, after I found her in bed with Brett, my old college roomie." He turned in her arms and laid his chin on her hair. "Max came to me. He said he'd been the one who'd really paid my scholarship to medical school, and if I didn't go back to his little girl pronto, he'd recall every cent of it. Mum and Dad would lose Eden. And with Kathy buried there—"

He didn't have to say any more. If Tal had been the shining boy, his little sister had been the life, the heart and soul of the O'Rierdan family. Her diagnosis with leukemia had torn them to shreds…and had been the catalyst for Tal's decision to become a doctor—to fix the unfixable, to heal those in desperate need. All the chemo had done was make Kathy even frailer.

She'd lost weight, and the energy to play, but her sunny nature remained right up to the end. Aunt Sheila and Uncle Dal doted on Kathy. Her grave was almost a shrine to them—and to Tal.

And for all these years, she'd blamed him for getting Ginny pregnant! "How did you finally leave her?"

He chuckled. "I joined the Navy, and volunteered for any posting out of state. Even Max couldn't argue with the Australian Defence Force—and I'd paid off Eden's debt by then. He couldn't make me come back...and within two months Ginny shacked up with some guy and sent me divorce papers. Max didn't care by then, since she was pregnant, and the guy was willing to take Max's name for his son. After two years in the Navy with not much to do, and fully trained, I joined the Nighthawks."

Suddenly, Mary-Anne wanted to throw up. What a *fool!* She'd spent a decade believing he'd betrayed her—but she'd tried and condemned him on hearsay and humiliation. She'd run off without giving her best friend a single chance to defend himself.

"Oh, Tal," she choked, and held him tight. "I'm so sorry."

"It's not your fault," he murmured into her hair.

She shook her head against his chest. "I just ran away. I didn't ask what happened, I just took Ginny's word for it."

"So did I. If I didn't doubt her story, why should you?"

"I let you down, Tal," she cried, hating herself. "I should have been there for you...should have stayed friends—"

"But that was the point of it—to get you out of my life."

Arrested, she lifted her head. He nodded. "She saw us together. She knew. So she set out to make you want to run away from Cowinda and not come back, or ever want to see me again."

A lump the size of the boulder behind them on the cliff edge filled her throat. Her voice came out scraped as raw as her emotions felt right now. "She said the thought of making love to me made you sick. And I believed her. I listened when she described what you were like in bed. And I did just what she wanted—I ran away. I am so sorry…so many years, wasted…''

"You believed that?'' He held her against his thumping heart. "I called you every day from college, took you out when I could. We were together all the time when I was home. I even mucked out your animal hospital and painted the thing to make you happy.''

"We were best friends.'' Lost in sadness, she sighed. "What Ginny said—the way she put it to me—made sense. You didn't want to lose your best friend, but you knew I was head over heels in love with you. Well, everyone knew that,'' she added wryly. "So you kissed me, did things to make me happy, then went to Ginny and did what you couldn't make yourself do with me.''

The harsh condemnation that ripped from his throat was guttural, foul and completely deserved. "She knew where to hit. I could kill her for that. All those years, fighting to keep my hands off you—''

"And I never noticed. So blind!'' With a gentle sigh, she laid her head on his shoulder. "But, Tal, you *really* need to work on your communication skills.''

He chuckled, his fingers brushing her neck in a gentle tickle. "I only hung out with *you*, kid. I only took *you* home to Mum and Dad. I only called *you* from college. I only kissed *you*.''

"I didn't know,'' she muttered, her throat scratchy.

"I don't get it,'' he said quietly. "I thought I'd shown you.''

She couldn't speak for the shame washing through her. Tal was right. She'd known him like her own heart and soul back then, yet when Ginny told her that Tal had been her lover for months, and she was pregnant, she'd believed every word. "Tal—''

"Knock, knock.'' With a rueful look on his cheerful, handsome face, Braveheart stepped closer to them. "Sorry to interrupt your deep and meaningful moment here, guys, but the boss says the yachts are available now. He's getting itchy to get going so the mission can swing into gear.''

Embarrassed, she jumped out of Tal's arms. "Oh. Sorry. We lost track of time."

Braveheart grinned. "Understandable. Ghost may not believe it, but we can have lives outside of work."

"Yeah," Tal said, his voice mock sour. "We're trying to." He captured her hand in his, leading her away from her "bodyguards" again. "Let's go pack our things."

One peek at him confirmed it. He was thinking about it, too. Touching each other, exploring each other with soft, erotic kisses…slowly stripping off, falling onto that big, beautiful bed and coming together as one to find blinding release…

Can I handle a week's affair and walk away? He obviously has no problems with it.

As they came near to the hotel, she drew a deep breath for courage. "Tal, I—"

A car careered off the road and onto the path, coming right toward them.

With a quick, hard shove, Tal sent her sprawling. She stumbled off the sidewalk, ripping her jeans, skinning knees and palms as she fell. His body cannoned into her legs, knocking her farther out of the car's path. She landed facedown, half on the cement, half on a grassy verge, trying to remember how to breathe.

"Get up!" He lurched to his feet, dragging her with him, pushing her behind so the car would hit him first.

She rolled around and up, pulling the gun she carried at all times on a mission from her jeans pocket. Tal faced the car as it came toward him. He covered her, his own gun between his hands, refusing to shoot until the last possible second in case this was an unbelievable accident.

But the car kept coming. She locked her gun—

Two shots rang in the quiet of the empty street; a violent hiss following one bullet as it shattered the windscreen. The other bullet lodged in the engine. The car, shrieking a tinny protest, skidded off the sidewalk and out of sight down the road.

Tal dragged her into his arms and the smoke from his gun

curled around them like an aura of acrid protection. "Thank God. He could have killed you, Mary-Anne."

She wrapped her arms around his waist, feeling the same. If she lost Tal—but, thanks to his quick thinking and action, she wasn't dead and neither was he. Thank God, oh, thank God…

"Are you all right, Miss West, Dr. O'Rierdan?" a growling voice yelled. Braveheart's bearlike form bolted toward them, his bronzed skin, bright blue eyes and twitching dimples showed up to advantage even now, even in stress.

"We're fine, John," she replied, using his Nighthawk cover name as she rubbed at the scrapes on her hands. "Thank you."

He came right up to them. "I'm so sorry I wasn't quicker," he said quietly—unlike his usual teasing self. "I can't believe that anyone would try this stunt on the main road."

"It's all right. We're fine." She kept the sigh of relief in as Nick, panting, motioned with a hand and three "onlookers"—operatives she hadn't worked with—hopped into a car and chased the would-be assassin. The protective ring was around her, as always. She looked up at Tal. "Are you all right, darling?"

Tal stiffened with the endearment, used for the small pack of people gathering as onlookers. Even his attempt at relaxing his body was stiff and forced as he put the still-smoking gun in his jacket pocket. "A sore knee, that's all."

"You should have left it to us to stop the car, sir," Braveheart said respectfully for the sake of the onlookers.

Tal threw Braveheart a quick, sour glance, which could be the look of any new husband who resented the intrusion into his honeymoon—but Mary-Anne knew it wasn't. "Yeah, sure. Come on, honey, let's go inside and count the damage. Alone," he added, giving her one of his old "signal" looks. He needed to say something and she was half afraid to find out what it was.

He limped toward the hotel, the depth of the limp indicating that his shoe insert had burst in the fall. He had to get inside fast, or blow their cover.

With a swift glance around and a click of his fingers, Nick sent four Nighthawks right behind him, covering his back.

A series of flashes followed him inside the hotel.

She sighed, held up her sore palms to indicate the attack—and after two minutes of photos and questions, she pleaded the excuse of needing to tend to her injuries and followed Tal inside, surrounded by the remaining four of her bodyguards. "We should call the police, or it'll look suspicious," she whispered to Nick. "Who do you think that was?"

"Not Falcone," he murmured. "He doesn't want you to die. Why would he risk your life to take out Irish? It was probably a Burstall trick, designed to see how you two would react."

"And?" she asked quietly.

"If they didn't suspect before, they definitely will now," he said dryly. "You both reacted as operatives. Your training came to the fore without hesitation."

She sighed. "Can I scotch it? What if we put out a story that makes it reasonable, like we'd gotten professional training because somebody had threatened our lives?"

"I'll message that to Virginia. Sounds good to me. It won't fool Burstall, but Falcone will want to believe the best with you."

"The rest of the pack will arrive anytime now, after that interview," she murmured. "The story, and photos of the attack, will go around the world. We should be prepared."

"Some Fleet Street boys flew in this morning. Expect some fun," Nick muttered. "Start playing the game. This will be the most dangerous one we'll face. It's going to be very public from now on. We should get it done, fast."

She nodded. "Turn off the cameras and sound surveillance, Nick. Just switch on the infrareds on points of entry. I need to talk to Tal about what's going on here and what we'll need to do to keep things looking right."

"Again?" he asked sourly. "Seems to me you two talk too much. Maybe it'd be better if you both accept you have a history and get over it."

"We only met again a week ago and most of that time has been working. We've been complete professionals all the way." Her slanted glance held all the hot anger she felt for the boss she'd never let down, not once in three years, even if it affected her career and left her with no private life. "You ordered us on this, knowing we have a history and baggage to work through. We have lives and needs apart from your mission. Live with it, or get over it. Take your pick."

Nick's eyes flared with brief surprise. Then, with obvious reluctance, he nodded. "How long do you need?"

She didn't thank him. Braveheart was right, Nick needed to know that his operatives had lives outside the job. "Ten minutes should be enough." She slipped into the elevator, fending off anxious questions by members of staff with a smile. Once on her floor, she ran into the honeymoon suite to find Tal.

Chapter 12

An arrangement of blood roses covered the coffee table. Tal sat sprawled in an armchair, his face dark, lost in the shadows inside his soul. "Looks like an admirer found you already."

Why did the mission have to rev up right now? She glanced at the roses and shrugged. "Thank you for what you did just then." She spoke softly, testing the waters. "You saved my life."

He shrugged. "So I didn't feel like becoming a widower two days into the marriage."

"You're so romantic," she teased, knowing Tal wouldn't talk about it; he hated attention and kudos of any sort—and he hated the reminder that for a whole of ten seconds he'd had a strong emotional reaction to the threat of losing her.

Just get on with it. "Nick's turned off all the surveillance except the infrareds for ten minutes. We need to talk."

He lost his smile, his eyes darkened. "What's there to say?" His voice was flat, like the expression on his face. "We're worlds apart. I can't live your life, and there's no way you could live mine. So why don't we just focus on the mission?"

A hot shiver of pain sliced through her. "All right," she said very quietly. She moved into the bedroom, her head clogged as if with soaked-wet cotton wool, heavy and clouded. She'd barely slept last night—or any of the nights since Nick had told her she'd be on this mission with Tal.

Making love with him had been the fulfillment of a dream, but it resolved nothing. They wanted each other like hell, but their love was too many years ago and too far away. As he'd said, their lives were too different now. How she yearned to turn back time to ten years before and have her choices over again…

But she couldn't. All she could do was what he'd said: take this week together and pray she could store up enough memories to last the rest of her life—because forgetting Tal was never going to be an option.

Tal's voice came to her from the bedroom door. "We might have a problem here."

She spun around, wearing only a bra and panties. He stood in the doorway, stripped to the waist, exposing the golden-brown skin of his chest. He was holding out a note to her. "This fell out when I was throwing out the flowers. Somebody's threatening my life if I don't leave you now. Probably just an obsessed fan, but we need to take it into account—"

Then his gaze locked on her half-dressed body.

Oh, help—she was gone. Tall and golden-fair with deep, dark eyes blazing with need, lithe and brown and muscular, but it wasn't the sight of him alone that started the pounding tom-toms in her treacherous body. He was Tal, and she couldn't help it, couldn't stop it, couldn't remember the reasons why this was a bad idea, or why he'd wanted or needed to back away last night, or even five minutes ago. Still and always, Tal unlocked her volcanic sexuality without a word— and, oh, he made her *forget* all that hurt so much to remember. One look at him, and she was hot and wet and needing, craving his touch—

"I can't play games anymore." His voice was hot and as rough as the land they loved, harsh and gravel-edged with sex.

"I'm already hard and I'm too tired to dance around the fact and pretend I'm not. So if you think it's a bad idea to do this again—if you don't want this, you'd better stop looking at me like that. You got three seconds."

With a tiny sound she barely recognized coming from her own throat, she took three steps, in time to the unheard count, and filled her fingers and palms with the rock-hard, sweaty skin of his chest and shoulders.

The note fell to the floor unheeded as Tal picked her up and tossed her onto the bed.

She unhooked her bra and threw it to the ground. Wanting, *needing,* so badly to celebrate being alive after what happened outside. "Come here. I can't wait…"

He shucked his track pants and briefs and fell beside her on the bed, his eyes smoldering. "You drive me crazy, woman."

Beyond words, she kissed him hard and fast, caressing his body with jolting movements. He rolled her on top of him, taking her breast in his mouth, suckling so deep it sent fiery shots of pleasure through her. "Now, Tal! I need you…"

Something crossed his face. "Um, Mary-Anne?"

Dazed, she stared down at him. "Huh…? What?"

"Sorry, honey." With a wry grin he helped her to her feet, and handed her the fallen bra. "The official peep show will be reinstated in—" he checked his watch "—three minutes and twelve seconds." He slanted a half smile at her, hot with promise. "We still have those two days in the yacht."

The yank of pain in her heart made it hard to breathe—and whether it was the physical pain of not making love now, or the anguish of knowing how soon they'd be over, she wasn't sure. She might not know exactly what she wanted, but losing him this time would make last time look like a picnic, a kids' tiff at a party. Now that she knew how it felt to make love with him…

Once she had her bra on again, she gathered her courage to speak—but the door to the suite burst open and a short, dark-haired man staggered in. "I've been shot," he said hoarsely in a harsh German accent.

In seconds she had her T-shirt and sweats on and bolted to the man. "Stomach wound, Tal!" she cried, seeing the blood all over the center of his shirt.

Tal swore beneath his breath. This was complete crap. How the hell did he pass through the infrareds—unless Anson let him through? It felt scripted, and whether he was a spy or a journo, they had to allow the play to run its course.

He dragged on his track pants and crossed the room to the man, carrying the black bag he still took everywhere with him. After a ten-second examination he knew by the smell, or lack of it, that this guy's only problem was a moral one. "Call the hospital. I won't be able to hold this for long if it's hit the celiac artery. Go, honey!"

She frowned, scenting his act—maybe from the way he yelled, but more likely from the extreme lack of blood in the room. If his celiac artery had perforated, there'd be blood all over the floor. If the infrared detectors were still on, Nighthawks would burst into the room any second—and if this guy was scoping them out for Falcone, he had to get him out fast before they blew the mission. Much as it galled him, this guy had to get away safe, or his absence would tell everyone exactly what Verity West and her husband were, unless celebs had resorted to infrareds and cameras in hotel suites for safety and privacy.

Hell, what did he know? Maybe they did.

When Mary-Anne left for the other room he took a good look at the guy's face—surely the fair hair was a dye…but yeah, otherwise he was the image of the journo who'd taken Brooks's place—and snarled, "Can the act, Longley. What the hell are you after? My wife's bodyguards will be here any moment and you'll be arrested for trespass."

"Smile, Mr. West!" With a quick laugh, the man pulled out a digital camera from his jacket. He reeled off some shots before Tal, torn between white-hot fury and sick relief that he hadn't pulled a gun, grabbed the camera and slammed it on the ground. He yanked the guy up by his shirt collar and stagger-walked him to a wall by the window. "I warned you."

He clipped him under the jaw, hard enough to seem like a furious groom, not a pro.

But to his amazement the guy stared, blinked and crumpled down. Tal released him and let him fall to the floor behind the door, watching, waiting—hoping like hell the guy didn't wake up and pull a gun this time.

"Tal! Tal!" Mary-Anne screamed through the door, her panic a clear warning. Damn, the reinforcements had arrived.

Thank God, within a second the man jumped to his feet, bolted across the room, yanked open the window and vaulted through it—making it out just as the door flung open, knocking Tal off his feet as six armed Nighthawks burst into the room.

Tal bolted to the window to make it look good, but the guy was gone, slithering down the back of the roof to the alley behind. And he couldn't do a damn thing about it. Leaping over roofs might suit James Bond, but not the persona of blissfully ignorant honeymooning husband that Falcone, Burstall or any rogue Nighthawk should assume him to be.

Then a blasting tide of weakness hit his leg, reminding him yet again that he couldn't have chased the guy far, anyway. That part of his life was over.

"Tal?"

Pivoting on his good leg, he turned back to the nine people watching him in silence, and held a finger to his lips. "He only took photos of me. I think he was paid to get close-ups of the man you married, honey." He pointed to the floor.

As one, all the Nighthawks fell to their knees. "What do we do?" Mary-Anne cried as she searched the floor for bugs.

Even if he had to damn well sit, he'd hunt with them…he slid down the wall and began combing through the expensive carpet with thorough fingers, praying only the weakness would stay and not the pain that normally followed—but it was inevitable after diving in front of the car this morning. "What do we do? Sue his sleazy tabloid into nonexistence, that's what."

"But that won't stop half the world seeing the pictures of us on our honeymoon first!"

He pointed across the room. "The camera stayed here, honey."

"Thank God!" She shook her head, indicating her search had brought up nothing. Every other Nighthawk shook their heads in silence. No bugs—not anywhere the guy had been, anyway.

Where did they go from here?

He looked around and noticed what he hadn't before.

This room had been searched by a pro. Whoever turned over the place had good stealth work skills—the room looked almost untouched, but they didn't know their target. Tal had a thing for numbers and angles. Leaving things in precisely arranged mess, with articles sitting on a certain angle when he was on a mission was his way of laying a strategic hair on his things.

A three-degree difference in the way his pen lay on the desk. Five degrees on the way his shirt was tossed. His shoes, minus the inserts he had to reinsert every time, about five, as well.

Almost good enough, my friends—but not quite.

With a quick hand motion, he got everyone's attention. *Nine,* he mouthed, letting everyone know the search had to resume.

Aloud, Anson said, "Miss West, after an invasion of this kind, I hope you realize that we need to search your room for any kind of electronic surveillance? These tabloids will stop at nothing to get an exclusive story."

"Of course," Mary-Anne sighed.

Anson left the room to turn off the Nighthawks' equipment.

A minute later, turning on the electronic detection sweeper, they got confirmation of Tal's suspicion: there was some type of electronic device hidden somewhere in the room.

The beep wasn't strong enough to be anything big. Couldn't be a hidden camera. Maybe a bug or something he'd never heard of.

He cocked an eyebrow at Anson, who sighed, shrugged and started searching. "We have to check the room thoroughly for hidden cameras, Miss West," he said. "Some desperate member of the paparazzi could make a fortune with unauthorized photos of you and your husband in bed."

"Nice thought," Tal said wryly, checking the curtains, the tables and drawers beside him as he spoke.

She stripped the bed, checking beneath the mattress and under blankets. "Sorry, darling. I did tell you I'd need bodyguards with us and electronic surveillance in the suite."

He made his voice sound incredulous. "You mean, some newshounds break into rooms illegally to get shots of stars?"

"Of course they do. Especially wanna-be journalists desperate to break in." She sighed to make it sound good to any listener. "Do you think those different shots every week of Julia Roberts or Meg Ryan are authorized releases, or Fergie or Princess Diana wanted those less-than-flattering shots sent around the world? If famous people don't have protection, they don't have a private life—the press harasses them wherever they go, shopping, swimming, spending time with family—even at funerals. Fans feel it's their right to know all about our lives. It comes with the territory, darling. You'll get used to it."

"And the car attack this morning? No wonder you wanted me to be prepared for anything and you insisted that I learn how to defend myself and use a gun. Do you think the driver was the press, a fan, or is it some other part of the downside of fame I don't know about? Will your more rabid fans try to kill me so they can keep fantasizing you'll be with them one day?"

Her head snapped up, her gaze held a deep respect bordering on awe at his cover story for their response to the attack this morning. It must match the story she'd cooked up with Anson. "I'll tell you as soon as I can, Tal—but not with a possible hidden camera or listening device here. My private life would go straight to Fleet Street."

"Found one." Braveheart lifted up a tiny device from beneath the leg of the desk where the roses stood, and disabled it.

Tal checked the monitor. Still beeping. He nodded, wishing he could get on his feet to help. *Go.* The search resumed. He kept checking the drawers, piece by piece.

Even to a man who'd been a spy the past three years, this still felt surreal—downright weird. What happened to his quiet, boring existence in the Torres Strait, believing he could never lead a full, useful life again?

Within a week he was married to the only woman he'd ever wanted or loved, yet they'd never have met again, let alone married, if it hadn't been necessary for international security. And just when he'd got his head around that, she'd changed the game by actually wanting him—wanting him so bad she'd risked her pride to convince him.

Now operatives were openly searching for bugs and cameras in his damned honeymoon suite in a game of bluff-and-double-bluff, talk-and-double-talk.

Keeping secrets, telling halftruths. Living with a woman he should know better than he knew himself, yet she was a stranger. Something weird was going on, like a frightening undercurrent of the mission above.

Was it the journo, or a member of the hotel staff who planted the bug—or someone else? He had a feeling Falcone and Burstall wouldn't be as obvious as this, but what the real game was in this crazy circus surrounding them, he had no idea. Yet.

He found the second bug in his middle drawer, inside a pair of rolled-up socks. Once he disabled it, the monitor stopped beeping, but it resumed in seconds—with a different kind of beep, a long, drooping sound he didn't know.

Anson pulled out a little toy Tal had never seen before and scrutinized it. "It's an outside circuit," Anson said, his voice loud and aggressive as he read the face of his gadget. "About fifty yards due east, I'd say, heading toward the 'Beverly Hills' area of the island, where the rich people live. I'll call the police now and get in the full regalia. We'll find who these clowns are, where they're from, and we'll take them down."

Within seconds the signal slowed, softened and died.

"Thought they'd run. Now we can talk in peace." Anson passed the electronic devices to Braveheart. "You like this kind of fun. Find out where these came from and when."

Braveheart gave a mocking salute. "Certainly, O fearless leader," he replied with the same cheeky irreverence he used on everyone. From experience, Tal knew that kind of talk was part of the camaraderie of an emergency service worker—a way of getting through the tragedies they all had to face on a daily basis. Sort of like when the doctors and nurses in the ER ordered beer and pizza after another death.

So Braveheart's in the services outside the Nighthawks? Wonder which part of the game he works in?

He waited for Anson to snap at Braveheart, but Ghost grinned in response, a sort of *yeah, yeah,* good-natured long-suffering he'd never shown any other operative as far as he knew.

"Right," he said briskly. "We have to get out of here. I'll call the manager now. We can storm out and onto the yachts. That should keep the hounds happy for a day."

Braveheart grinned at Mary-Anne. "It's time to give the world a show, Miss West. I believe the fifty-seven—the royal tantrum, yes?—may be called for at this stage of the game."

She grinned back and gave a little salute. "Certainly. I can manage that, O fearless sometime partner."

Braveheart burst out laughing. "I shall retaliate in similar kind, in my own way and time for that, Lady Songbird."

Anson lifted a hand, silencing the camaraderie. "Now we're clean, we have a real problem on our hands, folks." He made sure the outer door was safely locked, then he ushered everyone into the bedroom, shutting that door, too. "Whoever this guy was, he's seen Irish with smudged makeup, and I'd say he's seen the limp, too."

As one, everyone turned to look at Tal, still sitting on the floor. After feeling his cheek, he felt like crawling into a hole.

If he'd been acting like a professional, he'd constantly think about keeping his disguise in place—but by thinking with his heart and gonads, he'd put everyone in danger.

Anson went on, speaking aloud the dread in Tal's mind. "We have to face facts. If Longley's a Falcone plant, Burstall will soon know who Irish is. Even if he's a legit journo, Burstall will know by tomorrow. Which means our rogue in the organization will know we're here and after Burstall. We have to get Burstall safely in custody before the rogue can silence him. The rogue knows he—or she—will have to kill him, because if we take Burstall he's gonna squeal like a stuck pig. He'll give the names of everyone in on his dirty deals, to deal down a treason charge."

The room fell completely silent. Everyone stood totally still, absorbing the ramifications.

"Those of us going into the Embassy will be targets from the first moment we arrive," Anson said quietly. "We can't go in wearing flak jackets and helmets. But we must take down Falcone before that shipment of arms can go out to Dilsemla in Tumah-ra, or to the upper Slovakian or African rebel militia groups. We have to take Burstall and get a positive ID on our rogue, if at all possible. And there's an innocent kid in there, as well. We can't leave him to die." As Tal got to his feet, slowly and painfully, Anson looked around the room at them all, one by one. "There's too much at stake to walk away, no other team to send in that they won't immediately find suspicious—but if we go, there's a strong chance some of us won't come out alive. So if any of you have doubts, a reason to go home, or someone you need to go home to, say so now. No one will think the worse of you."

Silence filled the room once again. Every back was straight, every head held high—every eye met that of their secret boss.

"Good." For once Anson's face held more than acceptance. "I will say here and now that there isn't a team I'd rather have at my back. I've made some preparations to get people inside the Embassy, so we should have a few allies in there." He waved a hand. "Now let's pack up, set up the tantrum scene and get out of here. We may as well enjoy the two days enforced R and R we have, compliments of Irish. We're going to need them.''

Wildman spoke the thought in all their minds. ''Sir? If they suspect us now, wouldn't it be best to go in tonight?''

Anson shrugged. ''He doesn't have photographic evidence, thanks to Irish. Burstall was a cop—he'll want proof. If we go in now, right after this incident, it gives him all the proof he needs. We want him off balance. Irish and Songbird must play the honeymoon to the hilt. And we have to wait until Flipper's team arrives, anyway. Virginia wants a three-team component to go in.'' He snapped his fingers. ''Let's go.''

As the rest of the team filed out of their bedroom in silence, Mary-Anne's hand slipped into Tal's, lacing her fingers through his, squeezing hard.

''You okay?'' He squeezed back gently.

After a moment she nodded but said nothing, worrying the side of her mouth with her front teeth.

''You don't have to do this, Mary-Anne.''

She turned to him, looking up into his face with fear in her eyes—and resolve. ''No. I won't leave. I can't say I'm not scared, Tal—but if I have to die, like Ghost said, there's no other people on earth I'd rather have with me.''

He released her hand to cradle her face. ''I want you to stay safe, but I know it's useless to ask.''

''I'm done running.'' She smiled at him, with a quirky, misty kind of ruefulness that made her look like a vivid, fiery Mona Lisa. ''When I was a girl, I'd dream I was an old lady, dying with you by my side, being your wife. Looks like I just might get my childhood fantasy of being buried as Mary-Anne O'Rierdan—just a few decades earlier than I'd dreamed of.''

Why the hell did she have to have such a gift with words, making him feel warm and fuzzy and scared to death at the same time? ''Imagine that.'' The words sounded as flat as he felt. He'd rather she lived another sixty years as Verity West than have to bury her within the next week as Mary-Anne O'Rierdan.

But neither of them, it seemed, had a choice in that.

* * *

Half an hour later the manager arrived, making sounds of distress about the paparazzi break-in, on top of what already happened this morning in the street. "I cannot believe this. Our guests disturbed, molested and robbed! Their privacy invaded! I do not know what you people have brought upon us—"

Mary-Anne's imperious voice halted whatever else he had been about to say. "Mr. Vasquez, do you know who I am?"

The manager blinked. *"¡Madre de Dios!"* he suddenly gasped. "Miss West! I am so sorry! Forgive me, I have suffered the flu, and I did not know that you had come to our island, our hotel—"

She looked at him, head high, hair and eyes aflame. "Frankly, Mr. Vasquez, I find the security arrangements at this hotel appalling. We'd hoped for peace and quiet before I go to London and New York, which is why I registered under my husband's name. Obviously we won't find any peace here with journalists lying in wait to take shots of us even if we double lock the door! Darling, you were saying something about a yacht?"

As a queenly performance, it took the prize. Tal barely recognized the shy, half-stuttering girl he knew in the arrogant woman lording it over the half-groveling man in front of her. He hadn't seen her act this well since she'd starred as Dorothy in her high-school production of *The Wiz* sixteen years ago.

She'd done what she could to save the mission. Few people would doubt her veracity at least, after this prima-donna stunt. Verity West's royal tantrum would be news around the hotel in minutes and across the world by tomorrow.

He just prayed it was enough to deflect suspicion from her. He could handle going in as a target, but Mary-Anne—

The poor man's face almost touched the floor in humble acceptance of her words. "Of course, Miss West. I am sorry."

It looked the right time for him to smooth things over. "Mr. Vasquez, my wife's naturally upset. This isn't your fault. We should have told you in advance of our plans, so you could increase security for our visit. I think we've caused you enough worries. I've booked a yacht for the rest of our stay in Amalza.'' He turned to Mary-Anne. ''Let's pack our things, honey. The sooner we get our privacy, the better.''

Mary-Anne, her tender heart unable to stand the act, added, ''I know this isn't your fault, Mr. Vasquez. I assure you my version of events won't hit the tabloids.'' She turned to the writing table, pulled out a CD, and wrote on the cover insert. ''I don't know if anyone in your family is interested in my music, but here's a signed copy of my latest album. My agent will send you two front-row tickets to my next show in Paris— with flights, full accommodation and all meals, with my apologies for my temper.'' She pulled a little face. ''I'm sorry. I don't have the best reaction to fear,'' she confessed.

''Neither do I,'' Mr. Vasquez said, smiling back. ''My wife loves your songs, Miss West. She will be most grateful.'' He hesitated. ''If I may just ask—''

Mary-Anne gave him a gracious smile. ''A signed photo taken in the lobby, to show we honeymooned here?'' The little man nodded, his face absurdly hopeful. ''Of course—if that's all right with you, darling?'' she asked, turning to Tal.

What a crazy day—and it was only half over. Feeling as though he'd stepped into an alternate universe where his life-long dream had taken on the features of a nightmare, he managed a nod and followed Mary-Anne and her entourage out the door.

''It's confirmed, sir,'' one of Falcone's guards reported to Burstall within half an hour of the car incident. ''Both the man and the lady pulled guns like a reflex action, within seconds of my driving at them. They held automatics like pros. The man took out the radiator with one shot.'' He grinned. ''I'm glad you thought of sending backup as tourists and journalists—and had another car waiting. I could have been in trouble.''

''Good job.'' Burstall handed the man a wad of notes. ''Mr.

Falcone won't appreciate his lady being a spy, so to keep this to yourself for now.'' He nodded, and the man left quickly.

So they were not the simple honeymooners they appeared—but many celebs were gun-trained in these days of stalkers and terrorists. Hmm. He had to know who he was dealing with. Falcone would not be forgiving if he blew his lady love away without proof that she was a spy trying to take him down.

Ten minutes later he listened to Longley, and he smiled. Verity West's husband had a faded, jagged pink line down his left cheek, and a definite limp. Bingo. Confirmation complete, and for more reasons than Robert Falcone's obsession with the guy's wife, Tallan O'Rierdan had to die.

Eventually. He had other uses for him first.

Chapter 13

Despite her years of fame, Mary-Anne had never been on a yacht—and it was so exotic to the woman who was still an Outback girl at heart. Cruising a yacht in the Mediterranean. Wide-eyed, she stepped from the speedboat onto almost two hundred feet of sheer, unadulterated luxury. "Wow." She had to squelch the need to tiptoe and whisper. "It looks like a museum."

Anson shrugged. "The public expects you to honeymoon in luxury, as would Falcone. You must live up to that—we have to go into damage control now, do what we can to disarm suspicion."

"If this doesn't do that, nothing will. It's fit for a queen," Tal remarked, surveying the opulently appointed saloon. "The settee alone would be worth a fortune with all that tapestry and carved oak. The decor is like a mini *Titanic*."

Braveheart elbowed Tal. "It's very bad form to mention that ship on a boat, Irish. If you had real sailors aboard, they'd bolt. You're lucky I'm not superstitious, like most of my—"

"Braveheart," Nick barked, interrupting whatever Braveheart had been about to say with emphasis bordering on aggression.

Braveheart's bow was mocking, his bright eyes flashed and he spoke through gritted teeth. "I beg your pardon, sir. I forgot for a moment that we can't talk like normal people, or give information about our real lives to our fellow—"

"If you don't like the rules, Braveheart, the door is over there." Nick cut into the words, clear and cold. "I tolerate your occasional impertinence because of your usefulness, and I empathize with your impatience to be out there doing something—but this assignment is too damn important to blow."

"Yes, sir." Braveheart's magnificent, bearlike form, usually so loose and relaxed, seemed carved in ice. "I apologize, sir." There wasn't a trace of apology in his voice.

"Give it a rest, buddy," Flipper snapped at Braveheart, his rugged Gypsy looks almost alabaster with fatigue. He'd arrived at 0500 after flying his team in himself. They'd trekked across the uninhabited north of the island and into a neighboring cove to Lortámacino to avoid Falcone's men. "We're all wired here. If you want to let off steam, swim back to your boat."

"This *is* my boat," Braveheart retorted icily. "I'm Songbird's official bodyguard. Get up to speed, will you?"

Wildman stepped between the two men as they squared up to each other. "Come on, guys, this is bloody stupid. We're not the enemy here. We're supposed to work together on this mission. Burstall and Falcone are the enemy."

Within seconds the American guys and Flipper's team had also joined in, snapping and snarling like dogs that faced a juicy slab of meat just out of reach.

"Sorry to interrupt you, but shouldn't we check the boat before we discuss any of this aloud?" Mary-Anne asked loudly to dispel the rampant levels of testosterone in the room.

Enforced inactivity drove these guys nuts. Serious adrenaline junkies and compartmentalists—she suspected as much in their day-to-day lives and occupations as their secret life—when they worked, it was all-out; when they played, it was hard. There wasn't time to kick back and party in two days, and they couldn't drink in case they had to swing into action. There were no football fields or basketball courts here, the rooms weren't set up for martial arts—they couldn't even swim far from the boat in case they ended up as shark bait, and they sure weren't guys who'd settle for chess or shuffleboard.

There was only one other time-honored method of relaxation—and she was the only woman here. As both a married woman and a fellow operative, she was strictly off limits to all of them—except Tal, who was leaning against the door post of the saloon, arms folded, watching the budding fight with the grin of pure male enjoyment guys wore at spectator sports.

The unseen tempest of male frustration and impatience roared in her ears already—and without access to more traditional methods of male release, testosterone-laden fistfights would abound until they got the nod to infiltrate the Embassy.

She made herself yawn. "Come on, guys, quit it and get the job done. You can prove who the biggest he-man is when you're on your own boats and I'm not around to get bored by it, okay?"

In a slow motion that was almost comical, the men all turned to her, legs still splayed, fists clenched and teeth gritted. Refusing to show any signs of intimidation—she'd never wanted to find out if giving in to fear or feminine softness gained any sympathy, since it sure as eggs wouldn't get her any respect—she gave them all a cheeky grin. "Well? Am I right or am I right?"

"Get to work, men," Nick snapped. "None of this should have been said before we completed recon of the yacht!"

The operatives took over the strung-out men, swinging into action almost without thought. They'd searched the yacht from one end to the other within fifteen minutes, while she and Tal took to the saloon—and from his frequent hot glances her way, he was thinking the same thoughts as she was. *How long until we get rid of all these guys and can be alone?* "All clean, sir," Braveheart reported to Nick, his face and voice subdued.

Nick nodded, having already relegated Braveheart's outburst to the emotional trash bin. "Good. Take an hour to walk Irish through the techno toys you're taking into the Embassy. You'll need the knowledge, Irish—then we'll have to leave you two alone for a few hours, or it will look suspicious."

Tal raised his brows. "Sure, Ghost. It might be difficult, but I think I can handle it."

Nick gave Tal a crooked grin. "I'm sure you can. No details necessary, though, unless you want the rest of us to spend the rest of the next few days all revved up with no place to go."

Mary-Anne gave a stifled giggle at the unexpected joke—but Nick was right. The testosterone levels had definitely kicked up another notch at Tal's words...

To her surprise all the men joined in the laughter, albeit with reluctance at first. "Yeah, it's a tough life, eh, Irish?" Wildman's grin was almost wolfish. "Poor guy—what a mission. Stuck with Songbird, spending hours alone with her for the sake of world peace. I mean, it's not like she's a world-famous hottie or anything, hey, guys?"

Then the male-bonding harassment started in earnest. "Yeah—you'll suffer the rest of your life, being known as the guy who melted the Iceberg," Tapper, one of the American guys, chuckled.

"You'll be a chick magnet for the rest of your days. What a problem to have."

"Yeah, yeah, it's a hard life," Tal agreed with a wry glance at her. "Would you guys mind taking off so I can get through Braveheart's toy selection?"

Nick waved a hand. "All of you, out. Braveheart or Flipper will radio when I need the speedboat."

With a few not-quite-off-color jokes—in deference to her presence—the men filed out of the room and off the yacht. Flipper—obviously a sailor of some sort, by his code name— had already left the saloon and started the yacht's engine to sail them to a secluded cove to the far east of the island.

"I've been checking on your friend," Nick remarked to her while Tal moved to the twelve-seating dining table. Braveheart opened an enormous case filled with electronic wizardry, his eyes alight with eagerness as he displayed toy after toy. "Hacker's working on his bank accounts—she should let me know in a couple of hours. If he's legit, one call from someone from MI5 should scare the hell out of the owner and have Longley sacked for his illegal antics. If he's on the take, we take him down." He glanced at Mary-Anne with a half smile. "I wouldn't take chances with your safety or reputation on a mission."

"Yeah, yeah," she returned, laughing. "I'm irreplaceable. A cat burglar operative with a fan club in the black market."

Anson gave her a reluctant grin. "Whatever works—and, darlin', you work harder than any operative I've got."

Tal watched her sharing a grin of easy camaraderie with their secret boss, and needlepoint blades sliced through him: the same fury that had blinded him when he'd seen the same look on her face nine years ago when Gil West had come home with her. For then, as now, he saw the one thing she'd never given him. He still burned up inside when he thought of the total trust he'd seen in her eyes…

Why did he care? He had her passion, something he suspected Gil West had never known with her.

But—because she wouldn't talk about West—he'd never known. And it killed him, thinking of her crying out West's name, her body writhing in passion as it had above his own.

Faith was the life within desire, the power within love— and Mary-Anne didn't believe in him. Without that, her passion was hollow: a pretty ornament, a shell on the beach to collect and put away on a shelf to gather dust.

And for all that she called herself Mary-Anne still, he burned with the knowledge that Gil West had created the legend of Verity West—and five years after West's death, he was still sure Gil had done it to take her away from him forever.

And he had. Gil West's ghost hovered between them like a living entity, a silent monster trapping him in a one-way street that blocked his way to the girl, the woman he'd never stop hoping would come back to him.

It would take a miracle now. Though shades of Mary-Anne still lingered in her personality, Verity dominated her life in a way only she could conquer…and only if she wanted to. How could he ask her to give up everything for him, so that he could have both *his* career and love? But he couldn't stop aching for what he knew was the impossible.

The word never stopped burning his heart and gut when he was with her. *Impossible.* If she'd only talk to him, admit to the unhappiness he strongly suspected, he could at least try to make her the girl she'd been; but as things stood, Verity West was a fact of life he could do nothing to change.

"I hear Falcone has a marvelous party planned in honor of our dear diva and yourself," Braveheart told him in his favored style of convoluted English, his startling blue eyes twinkling in a male camaraderie free of envy. "You're getting quite the royal welcome, if all I hear via the local catering firms is true."

"Yeah—eat and drink, for tonight we die," he muttered. "What's the precautions on this recon? What do I take into the Embassy—and how will it escape Falcone's detection?"

Braveheart's eyes twinkled. "Oh, you get to test out some great little toys—and we're talking distinctly serious techno crap here. A scrambler so sophisticated they won't know who to blame when security breaks down. Lip and ear mikes so tiny they'll pass for a freckle, and so strong you barely have to whisper, both in sending and receiving. A heat detector so sensitive you'll find the hostage before you look, and image it back to us in seconds." His brows lifted. "But as to Falcone, I believe getting us and the toys in will require all your own ingenuity, my friend."

His interest flamed, Tal grinned. "Sounds like fun."

"Yeah." Braveheart's gaze wandered to where Mary-Anne and Anson talked in subdued voices. "You get all the fun this time."

Tal's eyes flashed to Braveheart—but the other man's bright

blue gaze was gentle as it rested on Mary-Anne's face. "She's one lovely lady, Irish," Braveheart said quietly, "gutsy and smart, and one hell of a good friend in a tight corner—and not the type of woman to play around or even flirt if she doesn't mean it. You're a bloody lucky guy."

"For as long as it lasts," he muttered.

"She asked about you when we worked together. She asked Flipper and Wildman. She asked others. Everyone she worked with, in fact. Just like you did with her." Braveheart tapped him on the shoulder with his fist. "Hell, nearly the whole Nighthawk team knew the score with you two years ago."

That's more than I knew. He wanted to put his fist through a wall. Three years wasted, and all for Anson's stupid rules...

I could have asked Aunt Miranda for her address and phone number, but I was a bloody coward, scared witless Mary-Anne would kick me out on my arse—or, worse, that she was over me and would laugh at my showing up like a lovesick fan.

The truth of the unwanted self-revelation broadsided him. Damn it all to hell, he was as trapped now as a decade ago. He'd fooled himself that all he'd wanted was to make peace, to be friends again—even this week, he'd stupidly believed he could have his fill of her and move on. But he wouldn't, he *couldn't.* She still held the key to those chains around his heart—a key she'd never use because she didn't know she had it. And he, trapped inside his inarticulate nature, hiding all he felt without conscious choice, would probably never tell her.

Sudden agony hit him like a kung fu kick to the groin. The internal scarring he'd yet to learn to live with, and the cut and torn muscles on his inner thigh seized up. He'd been waiting for it since he'd dived in front of the car this morning.

But with the self-control he depended on like a druggie's fix, he managed not to show Braveheart how bad he needed to curl into a ball on that magnificent king-size-and-more bed until the anguish dwindled to the manageable pain he lived with every day. "Is that everything? Maybe we should go through them again to be sure I've got it all down."

From ten feet away, Mary-Anne knew something was

wrong—the strain in Tal's voice gave him away—but she also knew that, for some reason, he'd shut her out. He wasn't including her in the toy hunt, even though they both knew she knew far more about this kind of weaponry than he ever would.

"He's closed off because he's in pain with his thigh, and he doesn't want to admit it," Nick murmured near her ear. "The attacks come regularly, but he won't take anything for it while we're here. He's in agony now, by the looks of him. He's limping, even with the shoe insert. He needs his medication—and he needs you. Go to him."

With a startled blink at Nick's insight—she'd never have believed until now that he'd even noticed them apart from their skills for the cause, or cared what they needed—she crossed the room to where Tal stood almost desperately straight, his smile fixed, eyes too bright. Tiny dots of sweat beaded his brow as he showed Braveheart he could work all the deadly little toys they'd have to take with them to the Embassy.

Nick was right. Tal needed her now, and somehow that made it all right. She slipped under his arm, levering his weight with her shoulder. "Hi," she said softly, moving with subtle strength to take the weight off his leg under the guise of a hug.

After a narrow-eyed glance, Tal leaned into her, kissing her brow. She could feel the sigh of relief he kept inside.

Braveheart, misreading the intimacy, grinned and packed up the kit. "We've been through everything twice. I believe it's time we left the newlyweds alone to their devices, O fearless leader. We can go through everything again tomorrow."

Nick nodded, again accepting Braveheart's teasing without comment. "All clean here. There's no way for anyone to reach this cove, except by speedboat or chopper, and we'll be watching constantly for that. And there's lead lining in every wall in this yacht. No outside device will hear anything inside this room." Nick passed her on his way to picking up part of the kit. "We'll be back at 0900 to go through the kit thoroughly."

He pressed something cold into her hand as he passed her, heading for the doors and the little speedboat awaiting them outside.

As soon as the doors shut behind them, she opened her hand to find a small jar in her palm.

"Thanks."

His voice was quiet but stiff, filled with reserve and a touch of resentment for needing her support. She smiled up at him, refusing to be offended. She'd been there hundreds of times with male patients, waging the battle of need against pride. "What's a wife for—even a pretend wife?"

A trickle of sweat rolled down his temple. "I don't *care* how long it lasts, it's—real now, damn it! Can you help me to the bed—please?"

He could barely move. She didn't have time to think about what he'd said; he needed her now. She used a semi-fireman's lift to get him down the passage to the bed, but her knees nearly buckled under his weight by the time they reached the bed. Still she wouldn't let him twist around and tumble down. She gently turned him and laid him on the covers, lifting both legs at once.

"Muscle…relaxant in my case. Intramuscular shot straight into my quadricep. Do it fast or I'll puke or pass out with the pain."

She nodded and ran for the bag. Within two minutes of her injecting him, the arched stiffness of his body softened a little and color began to creep back into his face. "This is why I don't go on Search And Rescue anymore." He spoke through gritted teeth. "They might have to rescue me."

Her throat thickened with tears, but she swallowed it back. "It will get less and less frequent as time goes on."

He sighed. "I didn't just break a leg, Mary-Anne. The femur broke through in three places and the infection was so bad they had to take some bone out and cut muscle when it threatened gangrene. The damage to the ligaments is permanent. The medical team went in and replaced everything, but with the high-use area the wound's in, the operations will be never-ending, repeated every few years for the rest of my life. They had to shave part of my hip, near the joint. I'll have arthritis later in life. The pain will always be there. The problems will never go away. I can never be on a Search And Rescue team again—even working in an ER or on a surgical team is out of the question.''

''Oh, but surely you can—''

''Trust me, I can't.'' He looked in her eyes. ''Also on the 'out' list would be the rigors of following my wife around the world on tour—or protecting her from obsessed fans on a regular basis.'' He closed his eyes, his face white and tense with strain. ''Honey, Verity West hasn't got the time or energy for a husband like me. She'd always have to leave me behind.''

An ache blossomed all through her chest, realizing how right he was. Mary-Anne could handle the demands of living with him, and she'd cherish every moment; but Verity West didn't have time to deal with the needs of a husband in constant pain, or needing repeat operations every year. Songbird couldn't always be beside a husband like this, either, she'd be on assignment three and four times a year, absorbing every day off she'd earned from her famous work, leaving him behind and waiting for her to come home.

Their differences grew more glaring every moment.

There was nothing as useless as crying at the wrong time. So she winked the tears away and smiled with forced cheerfulness. ''Then let's do something about the symptoms today, at least.'' With gentle care, she pulled his jeans right down.

''Hey, nursie, I doubt I can manage what you're contemplating just now,'' he said with a weak laugh.

Her heart full to bursting with his suffering bravado, she leaned forward and kissed him. ''Trust me, Doc, I'll make you all better,'' she whispered into his mouth, then she unscrewed the jar and inhaled deeply. ''Arnica, comfrey and lavender in an unguent, with Chinese herbs for muscle relaxation and aloe vera and honey for skin healing,'' she said in a quiet, soothing tone. ''Close your eyes, Tal. Rest, and let me help you.''

Through the dark depths of his agony, Tal managed a smile. "Can't rest. Damn goop on my face is making me itchy."

"Then wipe it off," she said softly and, using the cream as a cleanser, she rubbed off the makeup, wiped it with a sponge and rubbed in more cream, working it into his cheek with gentle tenderness. "To soften the irritation and promote healing."

"At least I look decent with the goop and my clothes on. I still don't know how you can stand to look at this mess, let alone touch it," he muttered.

She gasped. "How can you think that? You got the scars trying to save people who needed your help! How can you be ashamed of how you look?" She caressed his cheek, leaving a scent of indignation, unguent and caring. "Don't you get it, Tal? Your scars make you far more beautiful than you ever were as a boy. They tell me and the world that you're a man who cares, who will take any risk—even give his life—to save others."

The simplicity of her belief, the way she saw him—even more of a hero now to her than he'd been when they were kids—left Tal floundering in inarticulate silence.

"Think about it." With gentle circular motions, she massaged the twisted, puckered scars of his thigh, giving him time to absorb what she was saying. "You were always a good person, Tal, but now—what you did in SAR shows what a wonderful man you are. So much more caring, a deeper empathy—more heart and giving. You're a strong man, a fighter for others. Even now. Most men with your injuries wouldn't have come here, or done half the things you've done. But you never hesitated. Just like I hear you didn't hesitate to join the Nighthawks."

He couldn't let her think that, it hurt too much. "I joined the Nighthawks because I was bored in the Navy, Mary-Anne."

"I don't believe it. You chose the Nighthawks," she said gently. "You chose Search And Rescue to combine your flying and medical skills to help people without help."

Damn it, he could *feel* the flush on his face. She knew him too well. How could he deny exactly what he'd thought when Anson outlined the job description to him? "I'm no hero."

Her eyes softened even more, tender emeralds in velvet skin. "You are to me. You're the man I always knew you could be, brave and caring…and a husband I'm proud to have beside me."

He gulped and stared at her. "Mary-Anne—honey—"

She held up a hand, with a gentle smile. "Just go to sleep, Tal. Let the painkiller do its work on your pain and let the unguent heal your body." She gave him a wicked little grin. "I have plans for that body when you wake up."

The smile he gave her was genuine, tender, humble. "Thanks."

She tilted her head. "For what?"

"For still seeing me," he said quietly. "For leaving Song-bird and Verity West behind when you're with me…both Verity Wests. For still being Mary-Anne, deep inside."

Both Verity Wests. The coldhearted star and the grieving widow, two totally different halves of one role, both protecting her from all she was still running from. Only Tal could know her well enough to guess that she wore masks of her own.

Tal blew out a relieved sigh. "The pain's almost gone now. You have healing hands, honey. You're a born nurse."

A shaft of sorrow pierced her soul, forced away only by dogged will. "Private nursing for special patients only."

He looked up at her. "Lucky me." But he wasn't fooled by her joke. He knew she'd gone into retreat, running scared from his insight, from the emotions and ghosts she didn't want to face.

And she'd accused him of cowardice the first day.

Slowly, as she kept up her soothing, rhythmic strokes, his eyes drifted shut. His even breathing told her he slept. She sat back on her knees over him, watching him, looking at the scars on his face and leg that so changed his life.

He couldn't run from his pain. He'd become a man by force

of accident. Even hiding from the world as he'd been when they met again, he'd stopped running from his past.

She was still running, hiding from her past. What she did in the Nighthawks made a difference to the world, and she was proud of it—but if she looked honestly at herself, she took on every mission because she didn't know if she had anywhere else to go.

But something inside her whispered that if she wanted them to have any chance at all of making it, she'd have to relearn all that she'd once chosen to forget about her past—and herself.

"Complete confirmation," Burstall said in a barking undertone to Falcone's "royal guard." The men, all burly in strength, fast, intelligent and lacking in scruples, watched keenly as he paced in front of them—they knew it meant money, big money, to obey him. "Miss West and Dr. O'Rierdan are the spies after Mr. Falcone. They must not leave with any evidence." He smiled, with all the satisfaction in his soul. "Neither one of them are to be allowed to leave once they arrive here, gentlemen. Miss West is to remain alive, and Mr. Falcone would prefer her unmolested—but have fun, be inventive with O'Rierdan, so long as you leave him alive." The smile grew, catlike and happy—the fulfillment of his plans was imminent, whether Falcone wanted it or not. "He's mine."

Chapter 14

For the first time after an attack of leg pain, Tal woke refreshed. His leg wasn't throbbing in pounding agony, forcing him to stretch out the kinks with an hour of full-on workout. The gentle scents of the herbs she'd used on him drifted in the air, filling him with quiet and peace.

It had been worth relinquishing his pride to feel this good. Besides, what was the point in hiding his pain from her? If she could kiss those damn ugly scars like she had—and caress them without losing her hot-blooded need for his body—then she could obviously massage him without feeling revolted.

They make you far more beautiful than you ever were as a boy. They tell me, and the world, you're a man who will take risks, even give his life to save others.

He'd never thought of it like that. Not until Mary-Anne walked back into his life, with her fame and her baggage and her tenderness, her caring and her deep, unspoken need for him. She'd made him a man again...in every sense of the word.

Right now she curled her back into his chest spoon-fashion,

her sweet behind snuggled intimately into him. Her wild curls tumbled all over the pillow and his skin. Her gentle breathing, her funny little catching sounds that weren't quite snores, sent a shaft of tenderness through him.

Uh-oh—his body was reacting just as it did every time he got close to her since he'd been about fourteen. She was so beautiful—just as she'd always been to him, inside and out. But he couldn't afford to take the risk. He only fell in deeper every time he touched her. She had the power to break him heart, body and soul, her destructive potential all the stronger because she still didn't know how damn much she could hurt him.

Then she stirred right against his rebellious hard-on, and made a sound somewhere halfway between a moan and a whimper, and so totally sexual he knew he was a goner if she woke up.

She rolled over and gave her sleepy, sexy smile… Yep, he was going under, hanging on in stormy seas with a leaky life preserver. "Yes, please…" She pulled him down to her.

"Mary-Anne," he groaned in half-protesting pleasure as her lips brushed his. "We have to talk, honey."

"No," she moaned, hanging on to him. "Don't ask me to stop. I can't. I waited so long for you. We'll talk soon… later…" Her lips moved on his in a slow-burning, clinging kiss, and she moved her near-naked body in sinuous promise against him.

He made his voice gentle as he detached himself. "We have to talk now. Or *you* have to talk." He rolled over and sat up. "From the day you came to me, it's all been about me—my injuries, my problems and healing me." He swore softly and tapped his good thigh with a fist as he tried to think. "That sounds ungrateful, but something's missing. I'm doing all the talking, all the sharing…and we both know you're the talker." He twisted around to smile at her—and shock filled him at her white, stricken face. "I don't know anything about you now except what I see on the mission. I don't know anything about the years you were gone, except you're famous, hounded by the press and your fans, and somehow you joined the Night-hawks.''

"That last is easy," she answered. "Nick read the tabloids and scoped me out. The famous singer with a worldwide fan base in the black market becomes a cat burglar for the good of the world. And a possible partner for you one day should a mission call for a famous married couple." She shrugged. "Nick hit me with that last bit the day he told me about this mission."

She was shaking, but Tal suspected it wasn't because of the obvious insult to her dignity and pride in Anson's decisions to recruit her. He wiped his brow. Man, he'd never had to work this hard to get Mary-Anne to talk to him!

"If you don't trust me enough to open up to me, I can't make you." He got to his feet, slipped on his shoes with an insert. "Thanks for the massage. My leg's much better. I think I'll go walk on deck for a while. The sunset looks pretty spectacular over the cove." He headed to the main deck with a heavy heart.

And, inexplicably, Mary-Anne panicked. He was gentle and kind, but he was still shutting her out, just as he had when he was in pain a few hours before...

Like you're shutting him out?

But she couldn't say the words she barely understood herself. How did a woman who'd made the world's Most Beautiful People list explain the terror that came over her whenever he withdrew from her? It sounded so selfish—if he accepted her as Verity West, recording star. But when she looked in the mirror, she only saw the person who'd lost him to a walking, talking Barbie doll. The girl so madly and deeply in love with this man, she'd never thought she'd recover from losing him.

The woman whose marriage, like her life, wasn't quite the perfect dream she presented to the world.

"What's wrong with me?" It was only then she realized what she was doing—and why he was holding back from her. He wasn't breaking her heart—she was doing it all by herself.

Almost the last words Gil ever spoke to her came whispering into her soul. *He loves you, babe. A guy knows these things. If you get another chance with him, go for it. You deserve it, Mary-Anne, for all the happiness you've given me.*

Thank you, Gil, her heart whispered back. And she pulled on a pair of shorts and walked out on deck.

She must have been lost in thought for a long time. Evening had come to the cove on quiet feet. A soft, warm, fuzzy half darkness filled the air, lit by pretty, hook-shaped lights on the top deck and tiny tufts of fog on the ocean, like tender, fallen clouds. Tal stood leaning against the rail between lights, lost inside the misty half shadows, his hair glowing silver-gold like a halo, his sadness and isolation making him look like a fallen angel.

She moved toward him as quietly as she could. The time had come; finally it was time for the truth, but she didn't know how he'd take it, even though he'd asked her.

"Tal?"

"Yeah?" His voice was part of the dusk and silhouettes slowly falling all around them, dark and still.

Her eyes fluttered shut. She couldn't face him as she said this. It was too hard…too humiliating.

Within a moment, she felt him beside her at the rail, watching her—waiting.

"You were right. I do need to talk." She bit her lip, prayed for courage and said it. "Every time you turn me down, or say we need to talk, I panic—I become the girl I was ten years ago. Thinking it's over. And that terrifies me—because my marriage to Gil wasn't the perfect match you think it was."

"Ah, honey." Gently he turned her around.

She backed off a step; her hand flung up between them. "No, please don't touch me. I think I'd break down if you do."

Silence filled the phantoms of the night. "Go on."

She sighed and leaned against the rail, looking out into the gloaming, wanting to fade into the darkness, become one with it. "When Gil started asking me out, I felt flattered. And I liked him a lot. He was a carefree kind of guy, cheerful—he always made me laugh, made me feel special. 'Beautiful' or 'babe' were his nicknames for me. I wasn't in love with him, but I loved him—and he understood when I told him about you. He said we'd take our time, go slow. Then one night, when we'd been dating a few months, he told me about the brain tumors.'' She took in a shuddering breath, remembering that awful night. ''They were a rare kind of slow-growing benign tumor, but inoperable because they were clustered around and inside his medulla. He said he might have six months or six years, he didn't know, but he wanted to spend the time he had left with me.''

Even with her head lowered, she could feel his frowning look down at her. ''You married him, knowing he was dying? But Aunt Miranda said—''

''I didn't tell them,'' she said quietly. ''We only let everyone know when it was obvious he didn't have much time left.''

His eyes searched hers. ''But I saw you together. You loved him. I know you did.''

''Yes.'' She swiped at her eyes. ''When he died, it left a hole inside me I've never been able to fill. He'd become my world in too many ways to explain…he created my new life, he managed me, he was with me all the time. He knew I didn't cope well with fame, and he helped me survive it. He loved me so much, and I cared deeply for him. He was an incredible person.'' She closed her eyes as she got to the point. ''Making love for us was sweet, so tender—it created a strong bond between us. I felt so loved. But he didn't.'' Tears squeezed out of her closed eyes and trickled down. ''Not the way he wanted to. Making love wasn't like it is with you and me. He wanted the uncontrollable passion he sensed in me, he wanted me to give him the love of a woman for a man, a-and I couldn't. He was dying, Tal. Gil was dying, and I tried so hard, but I couldn't give it to him…''

He didn't touch her, but she felt his hand, like the softness of moth wings, hovering above her hair. ''Ah, honey.'' He sounded as choked up as she felt. "That must have hurt you so bad."

"Hurt me? *Hurt me?*" Without warning, a pathetic kind of fury filled her and words tumbled from her mouth like a broken floodgate, all she'd held in for so long. "You know the worst thing? I made myself *not* think about you, or compare—it wasn't fair to Gil—but after he died it all came back. Those dreams of you came back, and I *hated* you, be…because the dreams of us were amazing, so erotic, and they made me think, just your kisses were more intense than making love with Gil." She gripped the rail so hard her knuckles gleamed softly in the night. "Then I saw you again that day in Canberra, and I thought, *He's come to me.* I was so happy. But you never did. I had to come to you for the mission, begging you to come back into my life…and then you treated me like Verity West while I was *dying* from wanting you, needing you to see me, to touch me."

Turning to him, she flailed him with a fist, weak and tired. "When we finally made love, I was burning alive with joy and yet it *hurt*… I only have to look at you and all that uncontrollable passion fills me. When we make love, even when we kiss, I forget Gil completely and I feel so disloyal because he was so *good* to me, he *loved* me and you're going to walk away from me soon, and it's all going to be a sham for our parents. I know our lives are different and we can't work it out, but it will hurt so much to go home, to be near you and touch you, knowing you'll divorce me soon. And still I wouldn't change this time if it's all I'm going to get with you, because it was always you, Tal, it always *was* you and it always will be!"

The stunned silence that followed physically hurt her. She leaned against the rail and closed her eyes, had to restrain herself from whacking her forehead. Oh, heaven help her, she'd gone too far. She should have kept her mouth closed, even if it meant letting him walk…losing him with pride intact was better than making him want to run from her and her stupid emotional outbursts, like the one ten years ago…

Then, tender as an unexpected miracle, he lifted her face and caressed her cheek and down her jaw with his knuckles, the backs of his fingers. She drank in the touch in a dazed kind of wonder and whisper-soft gasps. Her eyes fluttered shut, feeling the essence of him seep in through her pores, loving it—loving *him* as much as she always had. He roamed her face with his lips over and over, caressing her arms and hands with butterfly touches, a memory walking inside her soul unseen.

"Come on, honey," he whispered into her ear, holding her in his arms like delicate porcelain that could shatter any moment. "Let's go to bed."

"Bed?" she whispered, feeling dazed and wonderful and *loved*.

"Yeah," he murmured between kisses. "And if you want to make love, we will. If you need to sleep, that's fine. We'll sneak to the galley and make hot chocolate and snacks and eat them in bed. We have twelve hours before Anson descends on us again. I'm going to look after you, like you did for me when Kathy died."

Her eyes opened, knowing her tears shimmered like the night water below them—because his looked the same. "Oh, Tal," she choked, and clung to him.

"It's okay," he said gruffly. "It's just you and me. You can be scared of being alone. You can cry all you want." He grinned. "Hell, I'm so used to you crying I've even missed it. You haven't cried all over me since you were seventeen and Flopsy gave birth to that dead kitten."

"Well, one more time after that," she whispered, sniffling, rubbing her nose on his chest.

He lifted her face again, smiling down at her: her own personal hero, her guardian angel standing before her, holding back the force of the night. "Yeah, but we're going to forget about that one, right?"

Light and warmth filled her, the poignant joy of being with the man she loved. "Right." She smiled up at him.

With another tender smile and gentle kiss, he took her hand

and walked her back into the stateroom. He made love to her all night, tender and wild by turns, and she fell just a bit deeper in love with him every time.

From a distance, standing on the deck of the yacht floating fifty feet off, Nick Anson, taking his turn at the watch, saw his operatives walk slowly back to their temporary refuge.

He couldn't hear the words, but he didn't have to. Their faces said it all. No matter how hard he'd tried to keep them emotionally apart—and he had no choice with that, it was orders, and for their safety—they just kept on connecting.

Now he understood why no other man had broken through Verity West's icy barriers, and he no longer felt stunned by the pair of them acting like frolicking kids in that untamed, trusting sexuality that had left him near speechless on their wedding night.

Not after seeing them just now.

Something in Verity West and Tal O'Rierdan created a luminous wild beauty beyond magic, deeper than perfection. Like her words and music, the two of them were harmony and symphony, heart and soul and fiery, joyous life…and they were young, so young.

Was he ever that young? Would he ever know a healing like he'd just witnessed? Or would he forever remain the unwanted lurker in the dark, the nameless face watching others as they intertwined their souls?

He sighed and turned away. God, he felt a hundred tonight, and he couldn't remember the time when he'd looked or felt like those kids had tonight. Probably during the only time since early childhood he hadn't been alone.

This night, he'd give back all his years of service for one moment like the rare sweetness he'd just seen…to see that one beautiful smile from the girl who'd given his life warmth and joy since the moment he'd first seen her.

He couldn't have it, but he still recognized the miracle in others. No other operative or criminal could have brought Irish back into the fold. *He* sure couldn't, under any request, order or threat. Irish had resented him like hell since he'd caught him in Songbird's files, and he'd gagged his questions, and his injuries left him feeling unworthy. Small blame to him, for Irish had been the best damn operative he'd ever had, the finest, most caring doctor, and a man who would risk his life and soul to help others.

There'd been only one way to bring him back: to work *with* Songbird to bring Burstall down. Irresistible bait.

If the two of them could bring each other back to the joy in life they'd shared together once upon a time, it was more than he'd been able to do. Despite his best efforts, the glamour and excitement, and even the life-saving work the Nighthawk life gave to her, Songbird hadn't derived any personal happiness, and he'd been too late to save Irish from his horrific injuries.

Just as he'd been too late to save Annie.

Chapter 15

Another chopper flew over where they'd been frolicking in the water. The guy took reel after reel of film, shouting to them to kiss or touch. The Nighthawks had just come back from chasing off the tenth speedboat with a journo since their first night here when some clever guy found their secluded spot.

"I'm glad I married Gil before I was famous," she sighed as she climbed back into the yacht. "This is a nightmare."

Despite his body's utter satisfaction—they'd made love so many times in the past forty hours, he'd lost count—Tal had to agree with her. They couldn't eat on the upper deck, sunbathe, swim or dangle a fishing line off the back of the boat without some tabloid Johnny trying to record the event for posterity. He was just grateful his long-board shorts covered his scars on his thigh. "You wouldn't think there'd be so many journos wasting time here, with so much real news around the world to cover."

"Real news?" She paused halfway up the ladder, grinning

at him over her shoulder. "I'll have you know, mate, that I am a very newsworthy item."

With a world-class butt like the one right above him, so perfectly toned, she'd sure as hell make his top story any day. His hands itched to explore it again, to plant soft, nibbling kisses all over the sweet roundness, making her purr, writhe, demanding to flip over and take him inside her...

A lifetime wasn't going to be enough—he was completely insatiable, totally addicted to the way she made him feel—and he was tired of his pitiful attempts to fight it. He'd take what he could get of her while she was with him.

"Yeah? You rank yourself with real news items like wars, invasions, murders, prison escapes, archeological and scientific discoveries that change the world?" As he reached the top of the ladder, keeping his head down in case his disguise had smudged, sliding his feet into espadrilles with an insert, he added, deadpan, "Pop princesses like you are more like *surreal* news."

She gave him a playful shove backward. "A *pop* princess? A *pop princess!* I'll give you a—"

"Sorry, guys, but there's a desperado alert at five o'clock. They're even coming here on leaky canoes now."

Braveheart's quiet voice spoke from above them. He sat on the upper deck cross-legged, half hidden by a canopy—staying out of their sight most of the time, but watching out for them. The lens of his binoculars glinted in the bright reflections of the shimmering, warm turquoise waters.

Mary-Anne peered over his shoulder as he spun around one-sixty to check it out. He let out a short, humorless laugh and shook his head. "This is pitiful. That canoe's so deep in the water it will barely make it back, and—" His eyes narrowed, and he swore. "That's a bloody kid out there!"

"A kid—yeah, right," Braveheart retorted, but he lifted the binoculars again. "You're right—he's got a fishing pole. The canoe's taking water in pretty fast, and he's jumping around trying to bail out. He's not going to make it—"

Before he'd finished the words, Tal was down the ladder

and into the speedboat moored to the yacht. "Mary-Anne!" he yelled as he frantically untied the ropes.

"Drive the boat," he told her when she jumped in beside him. Within seconds she was revving the engine as Flipper taught her yesterday before the paparazzi found them. "Call the others in, in case it's a trick," he called to Braveheart. "Bring all medical equipment, including splints, bandages and a stretcher."

"You two shouldn't be going together—" Braveheart yelled, scaling the ladder to the main deck.

"We're the trained medical professionals. Just follow us when the others get here," Tal snapped, and Braveheart bolted to the communications room without further argument.

Mary-Anne released the throttle. The boat took off flying, skimming over semicalm waters toward the floundering boy in the canoe. "I'm not very good at this," she yelled over the screaming sounds of the abused engine.

Tal, pulling on fins to help balance his legs' inequality in power, and strapping on a small high-oxygen air tank with breathing equipment, said briefly, "It doesn't matter. Just go!" He watched the kid scrabbling around as the little boat took on more and more water. "Hang on, matey, we're on our way!"

"He's a native, Tal. This part of Amalza has few tourists. He probably can't speak English," Mary-Anne screamed over the start-stop whine of the engine as the boat leaped over waves.

The kid, grasping the sides too hard with shaking arms, rocked the one-man canoe back and forward—and under the weight of water rushing in from all sides, it sank deeper.

Adrenaline shot through Tal as his heart pounded a sickening rhythm, like the rat-tat-tat of gunfire. Oh, God help him, this was East Timor all over again—a panicking kid facing death, and he couldn't speak the language…

Mary-Anne slowed the speedboat as they neared the canoe. "I can't go any closer. The waves will—"

A helpless scream tore from the kid's throat as the canoe

toppled, the boy fell in the water, wild and churning from the boat's sudden skidding halt too close by.

Mary-Anne touched his hand as he wound rope around his waist, ready to tie the kid to him if necessary. "I'll get the preserver and the first-aid kit. Just go!"

He dived over the side of the boat, using sure, swift strokes, kicking as hard as he could. The fins helped. Within seconds he was at the capsized canoe bobbing above the waterline, floating better now than it had right side up.

The kid was gone.

Tal plunged down under the canoe, blessing the diving equipment on the speedboat. He could see a pair of legs kicking less madly than they ought to be, beneath the canoe—too far down for him to have air to breathe. A rivulet of something dark wound itself around the boy's body like an aura of evil.

Blood. The kid was bleeding...*God help us both if there are sharks here!* He dived down, knowing if he came straight at the boy he'd drag them both down trying to use his body to reach the surface. Floating up from beneath the boy, who wasn't thrashing in the instinctive fight-or-flight response, as he ought to be—*Please, God, let it be because the kid's smart*—he dragged in a deep breath and spread his body star-shaped, turning light-headed with oxygen saturation as they lifted steadily higher.

The lack of movement above him told Tal the poor kid hadn't been playing smart.

By the time they broke surface, the boy wasn't breathing or conscious. Tal ripped off his mask and yelled, "Mary-Anne! Head wound! Unconscious and nil expiration!" There wasn't enough he could do here, and panicking now would ensure the kid lost brain function while he floundered around administering awkward CPR and hoping like hell the sharks didn't come for dinner.

He tipped up the kid's chin and towed him toward the slow-approaching boat, swimming as hard as he could—but going backward and upside down, it felt as if he was flailing through cold molasses. Up and down, up and down, and still the kid wasn't coughing, barfing up water or breathing, and for the life of him Tal couldn't find a pulse...

"Tal!"

He grunted as a sudden weight thudded onto the back of his shoulder. He twisted and threaded his arm through it, holding tight. "Go!"

She wound in the preserver until they reached the tiny ladder at the boat's side. He tossed the ring on deck. "Take him!"

With an enormous heave he handed the boy's limp body up to her, holding his feet until she'd dragged him aboard. "No pulse or respiration. Full CPR," he gasped.

Her nonanswer indicated she was already on the job.

He slithered on board while she was on cardiac compressions. "One to five!" he barked. She nodded and stopped pushing at the boy's sternum with the heels of her palms.

He tilted the kid's head back, pinched his nostrils and breathed—*Come on, mate, come on, mate*—one—

Mary-Anne was on compressions almost before he'd lifted his mouth. One, two three, four—*Come on, mate, breathe!*—five—

Tal took a lungful of sea water on his next breath in, and he'd never been so happy to choke in his life. The kid spluttered and vomited whatever he'd had for lunch all over himself. He cleaned the boy's face and covered it with the mask, letting him breathe in the fifty-percent oxygen. Tal noted that, despite breathing and tossing his gut, he hadn't woken up. His pulse was steady, though, and his respirations unlabored: all good signs. No other spot on his body showed evidence of injury.

The roaring of the other two speedboats came to their ears, a moment before the boat rocked hard. "Dr. O'Rierdan, Miss West, are you both all right?" Anson yelled.

"We're fine," Mary-Anne called back, cleaning the boy's head wound with gentle efficiency while Tal prepared the suture kit. "How's your leg?" she asked, her tone saturated with concern. "That can't have been easy on you."

He shrugged. "I just hope I got to him in time to prevent permanent damage."

If she noticed his brush-off—principally because he could feel the stress starting, just by kneeling—she didn't say anything. "Wound site clean."

"Thanks," he said briefly, and, using the bottle of drinking water on board and a tiny bottle of antiseptic to clean his hands of salt, he stitched up the boy's wound.

The boat rocked again and Flipper came aboard, his dark, moody face like thunder. "With all due respect, sir, why didn't you ask me to take the dive?" His darting gaze to the kid and back showed that his mind was still on the job. "I've got combat swimming training and full rescue under my belt. I could have saved you the exertion—sir!"

Tal sighed. All this concern for his health made his jaw clench. "I'm fine—and I didn't know if you could dive or not."

"With a co—nickname of Flipper, you didn't know?"

Flipper sounded really ticked by missing out on the rescue. Yep, Flipper was as bad a rush junkie and control freak as he was, and Anson. Came with the Nighthawk territory—and if he hadn't suspected before that Flipper was ex-SEAL, he knew now.

He finished the final close on the sutures, and twisted his face around to grin at the other man. "You could make funny noises when you see your master, for all I know."

Mary-Anne choked on laughter, and even Flipper gave a reluctant chuckle. "Don't leave me out next time. I'm not a Team Commander for nothing."

"I'm the doctor," Tal retorted blandly. "Or was. Since you're here, make yourself useful and head to the beach. He needs to lay down somewhere calm and stable where we can check him out thoroughly. His parents are probably worried about him, too. Take it easy—he's got possible head trauma. Go slow."

They were on the beach five minutes later, lifting the boy out on a stretcher. He and Flipper laid him down on the sand at the back of the beach, under some trees. "Let's rig up a cover, as well. Keep the heat off him until we can find his family."

Anson said quietly to the others, "Spread out, and find the home or village this kid's from. Flipper, you speak Spanish— you lead. Go in teams of two each."

The men checked their weapons, hid them well, and scattered.

Tal checked the boy over again, with gentle, probing fingers. "He'll be fine, I think, after a long sleep. No evidence of internal injury—but he's been out a long while."

Mary-Anne touched the boy's face, so pale and peaceful it worried Tal. "He could just be in a deep sleep to recover."

He smiled at her. "Yeah, you're right, that happens a lot. Why didn't I think of that?"

She smiled at him. "Because you're too busy guilt-tripping yourself. You did all you could, Tal. You saved his life."

"You played your part in that, Sister," he said quietly.

A small smile crossed her face. "I haven't heard that in years—Sister Poole. Sister West. It feels good."

A light tap on his shoulder made Tal turn. Anson stood behind him, his hands full. "Sorry to do this to you now, but somebody could fly over any minute, or be waiting for us at the village."

With a short nod, Tal took the mirror and makeup from Anson's hands and sat against a tree to reapply his disguise, flicking occasional glances at his boss. He saw no change on his face—but it was obvious to him now that Anson's interruptions to their emotional connections were deliberate, done to keep their minds on the job at hand and off each other.

And damn Anson's single-mindedness and his own hot-blooded blindness, the Boss was right. If their feelings for each other got in the way at the wrong moment, they could die. They had to reach some kind of emotional distance to survive.

By instinct he turned to her and saw the look on her face. As bad as he looked now after the rescue, hot and dripping wet, applying the stupid face goop, her gaze drank him in, her eyes the shade of dew on grass in the morning, gentle, misty. Tender.

It always was you, Tal, and it always will be!

Joy and dismay burst inside him with a hard, hot shock, robbing him of breath, as if he'd used crash cart paddles on himself. She loved him. Oh, man, she loved him—and they were both free. It was all he'd ever dreamed of—and he'd discovered it at the worst possible moment.

He should never have made love to Mary-Anne in the first place. They were both too emotionally involved to keep a clear perspective. If she were in danger now, he'd eat a bullet to save her—and if she got in any deeper with him she'd blow the mission for his sake, he knew it.

Too much was at stake, and too many lives on the line for him to let that happen. He had to do what he could to change that—even if it meant losing her again.

It was time for damage control.

Mary-Anne smiled and replied, *"No hay de qué,"* in halting Spanish under Flipper's tutelage to the boy's ecstatic parents for the return of their son.

The boy they now knew as Juan came to for a short period before lapsing back into sleep—enough for Flipper to ask him a few questions in Spanish. His intelligent if mumbled answers that yes, he was supposed to be fishing but wanted to check out the big boats, and please don't tell his parents, reassured Tal that the boy had no permanent brain damage.

"We've been invited to stay for supper, to thank us," Flipper informed them all. "We can't insult their hospitality."

"Then we'll stay," Anson said quietly, "and thank them for the invitation, please."

As Flipper did so, Mary-Anne sighed and scrubbed at her eyes. Their last evening alone together was gone.

Tal glanced at her. "This has been pretty intense. Let's walk. The boy's asleep, and will be for a while. Can you tell them we're on our honeymoon and we'll be back soon?"

Flipper relayed the message to the villagers, who nodded

and smiled, making "aaa-ahh," sounds of complete understanding. They pointed out a path leading to a cliff that was, Flipper told them with a grin, very secluded and private; a Lover's Leap.

Anson said quietly, "It would look odd if we didn't stay here. Take a radio and stay in contact. Are you armed?"

Tal nodded, and took Flipper's two-way from him. "Back soon."

He led her up the path to the ragged cliff at one end of the cove, overlooking mile upon mile of ocean back to the Spanish mainland. "Nice place, this island, isn't it?"

Mary-Anne smiled. His clumsy attempt to tame down her upset was so sweet. He was only eloquent in anger…or in bed. "Gorgeous," she agreed, surveying the half-tamed, part-ragged beauty of the island and ocean. "It's a lovely place."

"But it's not home," he said quietly. "I love Cowinda."

She sighed. "It's our last day before we go in. I just wanted one more night, without people crowding us."

"Yeah." He turned to her, resting his chin on her hair.

"It feels like ten years ago." She couldn't touch him; for the second time in her life she knew how it felt to die inside. "If you brought me here to tell me we're not going to make it, I know," she said softly. "No need to soften the blow."

He swore and lifted her chin, his eyes bleak and raw. "I wish to God I could see a way for us." He swore again, its stark hopelessness fitting the searing hollowness inside her. "We're too close to tomorrow. I'm calling the target tonight to announce our arrival. We have to be complete professionals from now on. If we make it past tomorrow, we'll talk."

Once more, there was only one thing to say, because he was right—but they both already knew it was over. "All right."

Like a question without answers, a shot rang out in the lost quiet.

"The cliff," Tal uttered tersely and bolted for the crumbling edge, pulling out a gun.

"Watch your leg," she cried.

He turned for a moment, put a finger to his lips then crept

to the cliff face. He curled his finger to her, but she was already beside him, looking to the ledge two hundred feet below.

A body lay sprawled on the rocks, arms and legs at an awkward angle. It seemed impossible he should be alive, and if by some strange quirk of fate he still breathed, the incoming tide would soon take care of it.

A speedboat was disappearing at a death-dealing rate of knots. As they watched, the dark cap flew off the driver's head, and long, bright blond hair streamed in the wind.

Tal grabbed his two-way and said urgently, "Situation on the western cliff face, two miles from the village. A man's been shot down on the rocks. Tide's coming in fast. Assailant appears to be a woman, Caucasian, blond, tall. We need rope and medical supplies for the victim, ASAP. Get a chopper here fast."

"Got it," was Ghost's terse reply. "I'll call in the chopper. ETA five minutes."

Mary-Anne grabbed his arm. "A chopper will give us away if anyone's watching us, Tal!"

"Someone *is* watching. Don't you get it? Unless this is an unlikely crime of passion, there's no other reason to shoot this guy here, right where we'd hear it and find him." He pulled a hypodermic and syringe from a waterproof case in his pocket. "I need to inject my leg before I can head down the cliff."

"But you could fall asleep with the muscle relaxant," she babbled, hearing the panic in her voice. "You'll kill yourself!"

He didn't even look up. "This is a local anesthetic, it's all I can afford to use right now. I won't go to sleep."

"But losing feeling is too dangerous when you're relying on your legs!"

"I'll be fully anchored. This is what the Nighthawk Search And Rescue units do, Mary-Anne." He pulled his jeans down and injected his thigh. "I've kept up my fitness levels as much as possible. I can do it this once."

Mary-Anne squatted on the cliff edge, feeling stupid and helpless and panicked. "This is crazy. Let Braveheart do it!"

The deep, rumbling bear's voice came beside her. "He knows I can't. Irish is our resident rock-climbing expert, and I carry two stone heavier. I might snap the line or send showers of rocks onto the victim." Braveheart tied the coil of smooth rope to his body. After a quick glance over the cliff, Ghost took one end of the line and tied it to the only available anchor, a tree trunk. "I'm always ballast for him, and Ghost is backup."

Ghost came back from tying the rope and spoke to Tal. "I'm almost certain that's one of our suspects, Jack, down there. Be careful. It might be a setup."

Tal nodded. He completed hooking himself to the rope via the safety jacket, shouldered the medical kit, and handed the pulley attached to the line to Anson. He stood at the cliff face, gave her a swift, serious glance and disappeared over it.

She choked down a burning ball of pain in her throat and steeled herself against leaning over the edge to watch. If the face crumbled at all, Tal could lose his life.

But the seconds crept by, punctuated by sounds: the sad, wailing sound of an unknown bird, the sea far below, the swishing sound of the line as it moved rhythmically in and out from the cliff. The scrabbling sounds of Tal's feet finding foothold. The occasional shower of falling pebbles.

She couldn't stand it. As if coming out of a dark dream, she stood at the cliff face already. Shaking, she peered over.

He was almost two-thirds of the way down, pushing away from the cliff, coming in too far down for his own safety. His gaze was on the ground below, to the man injured on the rocks.

Irish is awesome in action. He doesn't even remember himself, or his life: he just focuses on the job at hand, saving people.

Flipper's words came back to her with new emphasis, and she saw reborn in him what she'd known since childhood. Tal was born to be a doctor—and not in some cushy Sydney practice. He lived for this, being able to save people in a world out of control.

"Tide's racing in," Ghost muttered, echoing her dread. There was nowhere for Tal to run to safety, and he'd never leave a patient to die. *Please, please work fast and get out of there…*

Tal reached the base of the cliff, still forty feet below, by simply swinging out hard and dropping. Braveheart fed him more line and he landed on the rocks with a bone-shattering jolt that she knew he'd pay for later in agonizing pain. He dropped to his knees, searching the patient for injury.

Seconds later Ghost's phone bleeped. "Go on." He pressed a button so the others could hear.

"Bullet behind left occipital. Death instantaneous."

"How long since death?"

Tal's voice was grim. "Over half an hour, rigor mortis has begun in the extremities. Too long for the shot we heard to be the cause."

"Any ID on him?"

"An Australian passport taped to his chest. He's Peter James Russell from Melbourne. Face matches the photo exactly."

"Jack," Ghost muttered, and sighed. "It's Jack. Was the shooter definitely a woman?"

Mary-Anne answered, "The hat came off at a convenient time to ID them as a woman, but he or she was a big build. Very tall."

Flipper nodded. "Angel's blonde. Very blonde. And she's very tall and strong-built. With jeans and a bulky jacket she could pass for a man from a distance, but for her hair."

"A guy could use a wig and pin the job on her," Braveheart suggested quietly, looking at Wildman, who gave a short, jerky nod, but said nothing. "We can't name Angel yet."

Ghost gave a quick, jerky nod, almost seeming relieved at Braveheart's assessment. "Can you get the body up before the tide comes in? His family deserves to bury him. There's no closure without a body.'' The restrained anguish in his voice showed he knew how that felt from experience.

''I can't climb back up,'' Tal replied tersely. ''Water's coming in too fast. I'll anchor him to me with the spare cams. Anchor your end to the chopper. It's risky in this choppy wind and sea, but it's the only possible way to get us both out.''

Mary-Anne looked around at the four men, Ghost, Flipper, Braveheart and Wildman, and knew they'd all do as Tal was now, risking his life to honor a fallen comrade.

The Nighthawks were like that.

Ten minutes later the chopper lifted the wildly swaying bodies, Tal cradling Jack's head against his shoulder like a child, to keep further damage from his dead body.

They laid Jack on the ground, limbs by his side, as though asleep. They saluted him in silence before covering him, to send him home to his family. Mary-Anne burned with fierce pride and sorrow and wistfulness. Goodbye to a comrade she'd never known, an ode to an unknown soldier in this, their private war.

She and Tal turned away to prepare themselves for the next fight. Tomorrow night they'd go into the Embassy with a minimum of protection, knowing full well someone had watched them today.

Their cover was completely blown.

Chapter 16

It was time.

Mary-Anne took a deep breath, surveying herself in the full-length mirror. The green dress was the exact shade of her eyes, simple and elegant, falling to her feet in tight, molded glory. The uniform black high heels, slender, sexy, expensive. Her hair pulled up and tumbling over—she'd suffer the usual headache for the folly later—enough makeup for effect, a little perfume, and no jewelry except her wedding rings: Tal's ring on her left hand, Gil's adorning her right. Hot and sexual enough to distract men, cold and distant enough to entice: the famous persona of Verity West taking over. Songbird on active duty.

"Mary-Anne," Tal said quietly.

She closed her eyes at the deliberate reminder: there was one man who knew her. "Thank you." She turned to him.

He was superb. The tailored tux couldn't hide his physical strength. With his streaky blond hair tamed, the makeup turning his face back into what it had been, he looked like the Tal she'd loved so wildly as a girl, with the added allure of his natural maturity shining from the ironic look in his dark eyes.

Her perfect man.

His mouth twisted into his wry grin. "Here comes Outback Ken and Barbie ready for action, all dolled up and wearing their respective masks, off to play spy games with the spoiled brat black market set of the Mediterranean."

She giggled before she could control it.

He winked at her. "Come on, Barbie-girl. Let's walk into their Barbie world and laugh at it."

They walked off the yacht to the waiting limousine, and for the first time she faced the ordeal of a public appearance as a spy, knowing she truly wouldn't be alone.

Within a second of walking through the electronic detector devices either side of the carved double doors of the Embassy, they triggered alarms.

Security men swarmed on her. She stepped back, her face and eyes pure ice. "Don't touch me."

"Keep your hands off my wife, or I'll break every bone that touches her," Tal said, cold and deadly, behind her.

The men's hands dropped. "We have to search you both," one hulking man said, his voice sulky and threatening as he kept his eyes on her body in the thin sheath of a dress.

"I wouldn't recommend it." Tal stepped in front of her, big, rough and dangerous. Braveheart and Flipper, in the roles of bodyguards, stood at either side of them, ready to fight.

"Is there a problem?"

The smooth voice was gentle yet full of authority.

Mary-Anne looked at the man, taking his measure. Robert Falcone. Tall and elegant, he was handsome in a dark, deliberate smooth-to-perfection way. Two men with pieces in their ears and suspicious bulges under their dinner jackets hulked behind him, giving him an aura of vast wealth, incredible power and hidden insecurity. Typical of a man who'd made his money by living dirty—denying his mortality while keep-

ing on constant guard against it. Killing for the sake of fur-
thering profit and power.

The goons at the entry snapped to attention. "Mr. Falcone,
they set the alarm off. We have to search them."

"No, you won't," Tal growled, wrapping an arm around
her waist. "We'll leave first."

"Dr. O'Rierdan," Falcone purred, "you are most welcome
in my home, and will remain unmolested, certainly. But would
you mind telling me why you brought bodyguards with you,
and why you're wearing devices that set off my alarm system?"

Tal held his gaze. "With all due respect, we don't know
you. Why should we trust you?"

Mary-Anne added, "If we deactivate the devices, or anyone
interferes with the signals or our men, six more bodyguards
and the police will swarm the house within two minutes."
Please, someone, do it, she couldn't help thinking. Starting the
assault with only her, Tal, Braveheart and Flipper against a
hundred defied any odds. "If you don't want the inconvenience, we're happy to leave."

She held Falcone's gaze, waiting for the next move, knowing the enormous risk in her half-truth. The devices wired back
to Australia's top security firm—and relayed straight to Ghost,
waiting with a team of choppers half a minute away.

Falcone's cool gray eyes gleamed with irony. He knew who
they were and why they'd come, but he was all gracious ca-
pitulation. "I understand, Miss West. Naturally a star of your
caliber must protect yourself from unwanted intrusion at all
times. I hope this will be a most memorable evening of your
honeymoon." He nodded at his guards, who backed off.
"Please, come in."

The alarms went off again as soon as they moved through.
Falcone waved, and soon the only sounds they could hear were
the low hum of conversation and soft music.

"I'm Robert Falcone, Miss West, Dr. O'Rierdan." He held
out a hand to her first.

She took it with reluctance. This man was a snake who'd

brought her here to seduce her...or to take her against her will. Another bored, rich, middle-aged man chasing Verity West the star, who wanted to be the man to melt the Iceberg.

Yet it would be dangerous to underestimate him. He knew who they were. A sense of waiting, watching, touched her deepest instincts, a restrained fury she could barely associate with Falcone's creamy smile and cold-eyed gaze. Someone other than Falcone? Was it Burstall—or the rogue Nighthawk? The undercurrents felt like a riptide, pulling her into an unknown sea.

She released Falcone's hand, slipping hers into Tal's as he shook hands in turn. As their host led the way up the stairs, she whispered, "Something stinks here."

"I know," he whispered back. "Great work. I couldn't have got him to let us in." Playing the loving husband, he kissed the hand he held and smiled at her. Though she knew it was an act, her insides went mushy with emotion and need flared in her with the intimate touch. Wanting to touch his body beneath the gorgeous, tailored tux, have him slowly unzip her dress and—

"Don't look at me like that, Mary-Anne, even if it is just to put Falcone in his place." Tal lifted her hands to his lips, one after the other. "I like it just a bit too much, and I'm only human. Got to keep my mind on the job."

He'd done that to make her smile, to make her remember she wasn't alone. They were friends, they were lovers—they were together for this case, at least. He wouldn't let her down, wouldn't overestimate her skills or underestimate her strength.

For the first time since she'd joined the Nighthawks, she knew she could count on someone completely. Tal *knew* her. He knew what she could take, would cover for her when she faltered.

Braveheart and Flipper, ignored by Falcone and watched by his men, stationed themselves at the two exits of the grand ballroom, their eyes constantly on Tal and Mary-Anne.

Falcone began almost as soon as they reached the ballroom. "Dr. O'Rierdan, I'd like you to meet Dr. Susan Hing. Perhaps you've heard of her? She's a pioneer in the latest forms of reconstructive plastic surgery. I'm certain you two will have much to discuss, both with a surgical background. Leave it to me to introduce your lovely wife around." With a sleek smile he put a hand on Mary-Anne's back, ready to take her away.

The sense of watching and waiting grew...her skin rippled, the unseen scent of danger closing in. Falcone left Tal with an expert in plastics. *He knew.*

Tal slipped an arm around her waist, smiling as smoothly as Falcone. "My wife and I are hardly likely to separate on our honeymoon, Mr. Falcone."

Oh, he was *good*...words designed to break the man's control. Falcone's eyes shifted, with a hint of gritted teeth, and though he smiled and moved away, the shiver ran right down her spine.

Tal turned to the slender Eurasian doctor, beautiful in the exotic, timeless way of Asian women, who was watching him in open female admiration. "I beg your pardon, Dr. Hing. I don't have half your experience or expertise, and I'd love to hear about your research, if we include my wife in the conversation?"

Mary-Anne smiled, slipped her arm around Tal's waist and asked the doctor if her new surgery involved the use of lasers.

"Separate after dinner and begin your objectives." Ghost's whisper came in their ears through those state-of-the-art earpieces. *"Braveheart, Flipper, use your thermographic devices to count the bodies outside the ballroom. Your objective is to stop anyone following Irish. Cause a melee if necessary. Songbird, your objective is to distract Falcone, and keep everyone's eyes on you. Sing, flirt, play their game—anything to give Irish time to conduct his search and report."*

Mary-Anne shuddered. The reality of this mission hit her hard. She'd never truly faced danger before, not like this. She couldn't treat this as the game she always had before. This was Russian roulette—and Tal, far more than she, was looking down the barrel of that one bullet.

Dinner was the most unnerving meal she'd ever sat through—

Falcone's eyes burning-cold and assessing on her, and the sense of watching, waiting—the rage…and the presence of so many guards, all with their gaze trained on her and Tal. Closing in.

During port in the large antechamber, as she chatted with a mixture of fans and local black marketeers, Falcone tried again. "Miss West, I'd like you to meet Jonathan Trimble of Maximum Impact Music. You know the label, surely?"

Mary-Anne nodded and smiled, shaking hands with Trimble. Waiting for the spiel.

"Mr. Trimble came tonight in the hopes of meeting you," Falcone purred, his hand just touching her back.

"I am a huge fan, Miss West," the portly man said earnestly. "I don't know if your manager has contacted you with my offers…"

Her smile remained firmly in place. "He has, Mr. Trimble, but as he told you, I'm under a five-year contract. There are legal procedures involved with changing labels, as you know."

"Surely a star such as yourself can waive procedure?" Falcone purred in her ear.

Her fingers tightened on the stem of her wineglass, longing to throw its contents in his face. "Stars belong in the higher galaxy, and are beyond protocol, Mr. Falcone. I'm just a woman who sings for a living."

"I'm sure I could rebuff that humble notion if you'd give me a few minutes of your time alone. I could show you what a star you are in my prejudiced view," he murmured in that smooth voice, close to her ear. "But you know that, don't you, lovely Verity? Such a pretty name, far more suited to your burning-bright beauty than Mary-Anne. Does the doctor know of my deep admiration for you—and how far I'd go to prove it to you?"

A whisper came in her ear. *"Remember the mission, Songbird."*

Ghost's voice of reason jerked her back from her fury. "My *husband* knows everything about me," she replied, the essence of languid politeness in her tone. She smiled with cool sultriness, the don't-even-think-about-it that was Songbird's trademark. "We're terribly close, in *every* possible way. But then, I'm sure you know that, as well, Mr. Falcone."

"Good. Keep him guessing," Ghost's voice encouraged her. *"He likes the chase. Play the Iceberg for him—it's what he brought you there for—and he'll do anything to get you in bed."*

She'd never wanted to sock Ghost in his perfect nose more than now—and damn him, he probably knew it. And Tal, wearing a similar device in his ear, must know it, too.

"Excuse me, Mr. Falcone. Although I do love my work, I love a night or two off, as well." She turned to Tal, slipping her hand into his—after she unclenched the fist he'd made.

"Control your temper, Irish. In two minutes, it's time for recon. Surveillance is tight, so use the scrambler and take no more than three minutes."

Like hell, Tal mouthed. He'll make a move on her, and you know it!

"Irish, you will do as I say or you're pulled. I have four operatives in there waiting to take over. Falcone won't give a damn if you suddenly disappear—but it will leave Songbird alone in his eyes from then on. Now do as I say or get out."

He gathered her close and spoke into her ear, smiling for the sake of any spies, whispering presumably for privacy. "You want me to leave her alone with that creep, Boss?" he asked savagely. "Can't you see it's a setup?"

"Of course I know. Watch your own back, too. Flipper says Burstall's on the move. Take three minutes," was the inflexible reply. *"She can hardly be kidnapped in that space of time, in the middle of a crowd. And she's not alone. There's a boy's life at stake. You will not leave him to die! For the last time, go."*

She hadn't expected a reprieve. Ghost never cut any operative slack on a mission. She smiled and touched Tal's face, grateful he'd gone to bat for her. "I'm used to doing this."

"Doing this? Yeah. Handling it? I'm not so sure." Tal's

eyes searched hers, his blazing with fury and worry and warning. "If things get too hot, scream for me, and stuff the mission. You got that?" He bent to her, kissed her hard and fast and, with a murmured excuse about the bathroom, turned on his heel, heading for the exit leading to the long hallway. And as they both expected, nobody made a single move to stop him. *Oh, God, please keep him safe. Don't let Falcone have someone there to kill him!*

Thirty seconds later it started. "So the extremely attentive doctor has finally left you alone, my lovely Verity," came the hated purring voice in her ear. "I've been eager to speak with you alone, just the two of us, without his unwanted presence."

She wheeled around to face Falcone, head high, eyes flashing—her heart pounding so hard it hurt. Could he see it? *Distract him before he gives any orders regarding Tal. Play the game.* "I am not *your* anything, Mr. Falcone, except your guest, and I would appreciate the basic courtesy and respect a gentleman normally extends to a married woman on her honeymoon."

A low blow—Falcone, by all reports, prided himself on his manners—but a necessary one.

The thin, elegant man froze at her words. "I beg your pardon if I've offended you, Miss West."

She nodded with regal carelessness. "Apology accepted."

He smiled again, using all the charm he was famous for. "It's really your fault. Your beauty can turn a man's head… your perfume entices, and your talent completes an irresistible and radiant package. I am utterly under your spell." His hand slithered down her arm.

She stepped back. "I didn't cast a spell upon you by choice. My perfume is my husband's favorite, and my looks are no more my fault than your actions are attributable to me." *Give him the full treatment. If it's the Iceberg he wants…* "I'd appreciate it if you didn't stand so close, if you wouldn't speak to me or touch me in this familiar fashion—and please stop speaking of my husband as a minor inconvenience." She spoke with icy precision. "I don't know what kind of women you associate with, Mr. Falcone, but I find this kind of charm rather nauseating.''

The indrawn breath was almost a hiss. ''That is truly telling it as it is, is it not, Miss West?''

''Songbird, I said distract Falcone, not alienate him—and try not to remind him of Irish while he's on recon!''

Damn it, damn it, damn it...a swift glance revealed Braveheart and Flipper had left their stations by the doors—and they'd only been ordered to do so if Tal was in possible danger. *Three minutes...give Tal three minutes!* Thinking furiously, she smiled, cool and gracious. ''I beg your pardon— that was an atrocious lapse of manners. I am a guest in your home. You wished me to sing tonight, Mr. Falcone. Why don't we forget the past two minutes and start over?'' She held out her hand to him.

After a moment in which she held her breath, Falcone smiled back. ''Of course,'' he said with an ironic little bow. ''Starting over—a most apt term. People can start over. Circumstances and objectives can change. But it is time to entertain us with your superlative talent, lovely songbird.''

And that term, which seemed almost deliberate, chilled her to the core.

''Bingo,'' Tal whispered, using the heat detector/body imager along the ground floor of the Embassy. ''There's someone in a basement cavity behind what looks like a wine cellar, and he's not moving.'' He gave the exact location in the house. ''Look again at the architectural plans. Isn't there an external entry near that cellar, a weak spot in their defenses?''

''Only barred windows. Good work, Irish. You know the plan—the equipment's waiting in the car for you.''

''Right. Scrambler off, and returning to Songbird.''

''Recon another minute or two. No shadows following as yet, and Burstall's on the move. Falcone's study is down the hall. Check for information relating to—''

''Send the guys. I've been out three minutes fifteen seconds. I'm not leaving her alone longer.''

"She's about to sing. The men are fawning all over her. It's only a matter of time before someone says something indiscreet to impress her. We've got some serious Interpol file names here, Irish. Give her another couple of minutes to—"

"Not in my job description. I found your hostage. I'm going back to protect my wife from the sleazebags fawning over her, as you so aptly put it."

"Give me a break, Irish. She's not in any danger. She's used to this part of the assignment."

"You don't know her at all, do you?" Tal muttered, feeling sick. "Do you have any idea how much she hates strange men touching her? Do you know she spends the night crying and scrubbing herself off after that kind of thing happens to her?"

The silence echoed, buzzing in his ears like a disconnection.

"You could have asked me." He headed for the stairs. "For the past three years you could have asked me how she'd cope with this kind of stuff on missions. But you didn't care. You traded on her need to help people to get what you want, but you never cared about her as a person. I'm going upstairs."

This time there was no argument.

He stalked back up the stairs where he met Braveheart and Flipper who, against orders, stood on watch for anyone following him. Together they walked into the large, airy ballroom.

Tal walked up to where Mary-Anne stood waiting for him with a smile of sweet relief on her face. "You all right?"

He grinned. "What do you think?"

"The boy?" she whispered, pretending to kiss his ear.

A hot shiver ran through him. "Alive. Let's get out of here and go back in with the others—"

Muted applause came at that moment. "Miss West has graciously consented to sing for us tonight…"

She rolled her eyes discreetly. "Not yet. It's time to sing for my supper."

He grinned at her silly crack—she always made the most pathetic jokes when she was nervous—and cupped her face in his palm. "I'm here. I won't let them touch you."

Her gaze drank him in for a moment. "Thank you," she whispered. "I needed to hear that tonight."

She took in a breath, plastered a smile on her face and moved to the stage with a natural grace that all the wannabe pretenders to style and class here would never know. She froze out Falcone's guiding hand with the tiniest shrug, cool and proud, a touch disdainful.

What a woman…

The orchestra immediately struck up her biggest hit, "Making Memories." The room hushed as her glorious voice filled the room. Every eye fixed on her as the woman carved from ice came to warmth, love and life before their eyes.

> "Even with all I ever knew of me and you,
> Knowing my joy will soon be through,
> Still I'll stay another day, filled with love, lost in pain,
> Making memories with you."

The poignant song of love doomed by death from her album *After the Dove* came to its superb climax. Through enthusiastic, spellbound applause, she saw only him. Although she'd written the song for Gil, the words applied so well to their lives.

He tipped his glass to her, making silent applause against the exquisite crystal, smiling in pride. "Encore."

She bit her lip over the sweetest smile he'd ever seen, her eyes shining; then she turned to the orchestra, murmuring. "This was always my favorite," she said, turning back to the audience. She smiled at him alone as the music began. "This is our song."

With the first raw, unhealed refrains of "Farewell Innocence," something shattered inside him.

On this night, which could be the last night of their lives, she wasn't hiding from him anymore. She sang to him alone with a whimsical smile, her expression hovering on tender, bordering on faith. Double bluff to perfection—for while the radiant, happy-bride look on her lovely face suited their hon-eymoon status, and kept Falcone in a state of unbalanced rage and hunger, it was also the truth…a truth she told to him alone.

I love you, her every word said—yet another refrain, hidden beneath the joy, haunted his soul. *Goodbye, Tal.*

Loving her and losing her, once and again. It was over, and yet it would never end until death parted them. Could he ever forget her, even after death? Could she forget him?

The applauding crowd parted as she walked down the single step toward him. He took her hand in his. "It's time to go."

For once she didn't have the words to make it right. She just nodded and turned to Falcone, hovering behind them. "Thank you for a most interesting evening, Mr. Falcone."

Falcone took her hand and held on to it. "Oh, please don't leave yet, my lovely songbird," he purred. "If your Irish com-panion wants to leave, he is most welcome to go, but I do wish you would stay here a little longer."

Tal froze. With two words, Falcone had declared war. Would he attack them with so many people around?

"I don't think so," he growled. He clicked his fingers and Flipper and Braveheart were beside them—Nighthawks united, ready to swing into action. Tal wrapped his fingers around the wrist of the hand holding Mary-Anne's. "Let go of my wife."

"Why not let her decide?" Falcone's voice had lost a touch of its creaminess: edges rubbed against the smooth finish. "What do you say, lovely songbird? Will we allow the good doctor to leave alone, quietly?" *Still alive,* his tone clearly said. He clicked his fingers, as Tal had done, and six men surrounded them.

Mary-Anne looked sick with terror. "Go, Tal. I'll be fine."

"Like hell. Twenty-four," he yelled, hoping those Night-hawk plants were in the room this moment.

As one, the four in the center of the storm kicked out and up, taking down a man each, Braveheart and Flipper, nearest the other two goons, took them out with quick, hard uppercuts. An orchestra member knocked out two goons racing through the doors from the balcony, one with his fist, one with his double bass.

Tal threw a tiny dart-needle at Falcone's neck as he tried to edge outside with Mary-Anne. With a look of comical surprise on his face, Falcone fell to the ground.

"It's just a tranquilizer dart that'll only hold him for a few minutes. Let's go!" Tal yelled, grabbing Mary-Anne's hand and running like hell for the doors to the stairs.

From the other doors Darren Burstall suddenly appeared, with three men behind him. "Kill the others, but keep Miss West alive—and O'Rierdan's mine!"

"Ghost, enter the perimeter!" Tal snapped into his mouthpiece. "We'll never get a better opportunity than now."

"Halfway there," came the reassuring reply. *"ETA one minute."*

Tal could almost hear the distinctive *thwack* of the choppers arriving. "Let's hold them off." He pulled out a gun.

"Set up a forty-eight, boys, and run!" Mary-Anne shouted into her mouthpiece. She stumbled out of her heels, still running. Fully armed, Flipper and Braveheart covered their backs.

Tal bolted down the last of the stairs with the speed of adrenaline, ignoring the shooting darts of pain in his leg, and forced his feet to take him through the door.

On the first floor, two young waiters with trays of food and glasses appeared out of a door, knocking it right into two of the security men and stepping right into Burstall's running range. Startled by Burstall's vicious snarl to move, one dropped the food all over the floor. The other tripped, smashing glasses all over the stairwell. Burstall stumbled, slid on the sauce and fell down three stairs, landing right on the glass. He screamed as blood spurted from his leg. His gun went off. Someone above screamed as a glassed-in set of first editions shattered.

Burstall scrambled to his feet, his face and hands cut and torn, his expression dark and ugly. "Stop Dr. O'Rierdan and Miss West from leaving," he said into a microphone on his wrist.

"Mr. Burstall, the gates are smashed, our men are knocked out," a dazed voice answered. "I think they've gone."

Burstall snarled and turned to the young waiters, scrambling around to clean up the mess. "Hello, little Nighthawks. Looks like your famous operatives left you behind to take the rap."

"*Que?*"

Burstall frowned as the two pure-speaking natives, barely out of their teens, gave fumbling apologies in soft, shy Amalzan dialect. Meanwhile the head waiter, a highly recommended friend of someone in the catering firm, and the double bass player, had already disappeared from the Embassy.

Chapter 17

They watched from the thick belt of shrubbery as their car moved smoothly around a curve in the road, leaving them behind. After a final quick review of the Embassy's architectural plans Anson had left in the car, Tal nodded to her. "Go."

He injected his leg with local anesthetic and picked up the bag of tricks left in the car for him. She slithered out of the slinky dress, kicking it away, and put her hand out. With his back turned, Flipper handed her one of the new suits they were trialing for the Nighthawks's lab. The suits were light and fast to pull on, yet acted like lead lining, cutting out heat and light, slowing if not totally repelling bullets. She pulled on night-vision goggles and gloves that covered her last inches of exposed skin. "We'll recon at the basement, Irish. Go," Flipper murmured to Braveheart, and they disappeared into the night.

"He knows who we are," Tal mouthed into the lip piece.

She nodded. It was obvious he must have known all along. Men were searching for them on the grounds as well as Burstall's team outside, chasing the car.

"You okay to finish the job?"

She nodded again. *Keep a professional distance now.* "I'm trained for this, even if I haven't done it." Even she heard the uncertainty beneath the confident words.

He turned to her, his eyes strange beneath the snorkel-like equipment. "This is my show, Songbird. I've done this a hundred times. Trust me. Stay with me and do as I tell you."

"Yes, sir," she acknowledged, giving her life into his hands.

He slung the bag with the weapons and electronic pieces they'd need. "Fit your silencer on. And be prepared to use it."

She fitted the silencer, praying she wouldn't be forced to use it.

He led the way to the next patch of cover in a night that, lit by floodlights all around the Embassy, seemed almost as bright as daylight. Crouching, they flitted from shrub to tree. She felt like an "alien" actor from a B-grade 50's schlock movie, but—if Falcone caught her—

"We could do ads for this," came the whisper via the speaker in her ear. "See Outback Ken and Barbie turn into creatures from the black lagoon in seconds—only $19.95."

She choked on quiet laughter. The most illogical sense of calm filled her at his joke, coming from the lip mike into her mind, as though he were part of her. She needed him, and he was here. Just as he always was there for her when they were kids.

"Let's go," she whispered.

"We can't use any toys until we reach the house. Braveheart says the scrambler's unpredictable after five minutes, and using the laser will give us away fast."

She nodded, knowing what he didn't say. Using any toys at all also warned Falcone that they'd returned to the house. Once they were inside, they had three minutes at most to rescue the hostage and get out, or— She shuddered again.

"Are the choppers in the perimeter, Ghost?" she whispered into the lip mike. "We'll need backup within a minute of setting the scramblers and using the laser gun."

"Roger that. We're ready to land. Where are you?"

"Halfway to target," Tal whispered. "Going for frontal assault. They won't expect it. Catching them napping is our best chance of getting out of here intact. Go?"

"Permission granted," Anson said. *"Go."*

Never had four minutes seemed so long, flitting from bush to tree, crouched over double in gray froglike suits in the over-lit shades of night. Tal helped her all the way with a guiding hand, a pointing finger and whispered encouragement. "Flashlight at ten o'clock, Songbird. Duck. Still now. Four o'clock." Every time she did exactly what he said, melting into trees and bushes to hide from Falcone's goons.

"Take aim, six o'clock!"

She whirled to find two men running at them, gun in one hand, lifting walkie-talkies to their lips with the other. She took aim with a shaking hand—

He could have a wife and kids. Dear God, I can't do it!

Tal's shot was quick and silent. The man fell, unconscious, and she knew he'd used a tranquilizer dart instead of killing the man. A shot from his real gun took out the man's radio.

"Songbird! Tranquilizer dart! Four o'clock!"

As the second man took aim, she shot her tranquilizer gun at him, the dart hitting his neck, rendering him unconscious. Tal shot out the second portable.

"Refill your dart," Tal whispered. "If you can't kill 'em, don't waste time agonizing about it. Put 'em to sleep."

She shoved a refill dart into her gun and put the gun away, grateful he was still the same healer he'd always been.

"Target ahead, Ghost. Two men down, sleeping only, their communications taken out. The target's men will soon know they're not answering. Go?"

"Permission granted! Go! Choppers are visual."

Tal swore, glancing up at the approaching birds, clearly audible, visible even with their lights off. "Area seems clear. Get the choppers outside the cellar window—keep the goons off left flank. Run, Songbird—and don't stop if the targets find us. Cover my back when I have to set the scrambler."

She took off running, Tal right at her back. A man appeared at the door as they reached it, his gun right at her face.

She didn't hesitate this time. Diving for protection, she shot him with the tranquilizer. "Help me get him out of sight."

"No time." Tal took out the array of lights with the laser, and blew out the security camera. "Go left before the stairwell and into the servants' entry."

They bolted through the swinging doors and right down the cramped hallway. The sneezing sounds of Tal's gun as it took out the cameras startled the confused servants. A woman screamed. Another threw a ceramic bowl at them.

"Thirty seconds," Tal muttered, deflecting the clumsy shot. He pushed Mary-Anne to the cellar door, shooting out lights and cameras as he went. "Take out the lock. Laser the window bars as soon as we're in. When the hostage is safe, get out."

"You'll need me to—"

"No. You've done your job. It's you Falcone wants. You put us all in danger. If you're out we have an even chance."

She nodded and pushed the door open. She had to obey him without question, to be one hundred percent a Nighthawk.

"Songbird! Window!" Tal tossed the laser gun as he ran toward the boy slumped in a chair, bound with rope, bruises mottling his face and blood on his temple.

She caught the lethal weapon and ran for the windows. She melted the metal in moments—one bar gone. Eleven to go—ten—

"Hurry!"

The choppers landed outside the windows, their high-beam lights turning half-night to day, blinding her. She groped for the next bar and melted it, smashing glass with its heat.

"Choppers landed!"

A crashing oath, Tal, with the foreign minister's son slumped now fireman-lift style over one shoulder, took over. "He's alive, just contusions and concussion. Get the lock!"

The window was open and five bars gone by the time the first of Falcone's men hit the locked door and started crashing against it with obvious body weight.

"Drag the kid out the window. He's okay physically, but drugged. He can't help us." Tal burst through the seventh bar, burning his glove as he pulled it in and snapped it off. "You're small enough to get through the bars. I'll have to burn another two bars before I can make it. Go, or this kid will die!"

She grabbed the sill and vaulted through the window, a pair of big, capable hands pulled her safely through. She ripped off the hood of her suit and looked up at the dark, handsome face of Wildman. "Take the hostage from Irish!" was all she said.

Seconds later the boy was out and Wildman and Braveheart lifted him onto the chopper.

"Are you all right?" Wildman asked her quickly.

"Fine." She bolted back to the window. "Get out, Tal!" she cried, forgetting the Nighthawk rule about names. "Hurry—"

"I'm afraid he can't hurry, my lovely Verity. You see, he's trying a new and exciting role—a human shield." Falcone's smooth, smiling voice came from behind Tal's strained face, now devoid of his hood. "I do love the Catwoman look on you, my dear—elegant and sexual with a hint of danger. It showcases your glorious body to perfection. Just the kind of suit I admire…in private, of course."

Total silence descended over the noise of whirling choppers. They all knew the score. This was it. Exchange time.

"No!" Anson whispered as she moved to the window. *"Don't do it!"*

Wildman laid a hand on her shoulder. "He wouldn't want this."

Bile burned her throat, her heart's wild pounding made her shivering and sick. She looked in Wildman's troubled dark eyes. "If it were the person you love, would you hesitate? Would she?"

He winced; it was answer enough. "We can find another way—"

"Let me go," she ordered. Slowly, Wildman's hand fell.

Tal, struggling against the two men holding him, knew it would happen, knew her words even before she climbed into the window. "I'm here. Let him go."

"No, honey! I'm not worth it," Tal yelled, struggling harder against Falcone and his other goon, not even caring that the gun he held could go off at any second.

She looked deep in his eyes. *You are to me.* And she fell through the window.

Oh, dear, sweet Lord. He'd known, damn it…hadn't he known all along she'd sacrifice herself for him? He should have switched her for Wildman at the gates—

Falcone shoved him toward the window. "Go, Dr. O'Rierdan. You have thirty seconds before I shoot you."

"Go, Tal," she said coolly, moving into the restraining circle of Falcone's arm. "I don't need you now."

He looked back. Her eyes spoke to him, loud and clear, the same message he'd been giving her all week. *Trust me.*

She turned to Falcone with a cold, glittering smile. "So you finally stopped talking and made a move. It's about time. I really expected better than this from a man of your reputation."

Falcone's start was slight but noticeable.

She looked at Tal. "Sorry," she said awkwardly. "I never meant to hurt you. You're one of the good guys. I shouldn't have used you, or your people. But we were never going to last more than a few weeks. I've discovered I've got this weird kind of attraction to bad boys."

My God, what an act! If he hadn't seen the love in her eyes bare seconds ago, even Tal would believe it. It was the perfect response, given that her work in the Nighthawks included attending black market parties.

"That's why you insisted on coming to this party tonight?" he croaked, knowing he couldn't say too much.

She nodded and spoke to Falcone, who was staring at her in half-disbelieving fascination. "Marrying Tal seemed a good way to show the world that I was ready to kick the Iceberg rep out. But the world loves it. I had to be careful, and do it right. Tal and his cute little Mission Impossible group was the easiest route to change. It was fun, playing a spy for a month or two, getting the fitness and defense training. My body looks much sleeker now, don't you think?''

She pirouetted in front of him, running slow, proud hands over her waist and breasts. "For years I couldn't get a date without bad press wrecking my career. It got so frustrating, like a ghost on my back. Tal was a front-door solution. People would believe our marriage was real after the tabloid stuff about our affair." She smiled, with a pretty shrug. "So I went to him, played the siren, and he married me within a week. Poor Tal believed every word I told him."

Oh, clever girl! Unobtrusively putting his hand in his sleeve, Tal used the flat pager to message Anson. *Get in through the front door.* He made no move to climb through the window. Falcone had forgotten all about him. "You're a fabulous actress, aren't you, my dear?" he drawled, but even Tal could hear the note of doubt.

She nodded, with simple pride. "Yes, I'm a good actress— too good for poor Tal. He never had a chance. I'm even too good for you. I had you convinced I was a real spy!" Her eyes flicked to Tal. *Run!* "I'd love to break into movies, like *Moulin Rouge.*"

Falcone blinked. His men hovered, unsure what to do with Tal without a clear word from their boss. "But you do want children, don't you, my dear?"

She stared at him as though he'd grown another head. "Get real. Do you *know* how long it took to lose those sixty extra pounds I was carrying? My mother put on seventy-five pounds having kids. If I lose my body, I lose work. I'm not getting fat again."

Falcone's head looked as if it was literally spinning. "You don't want children?"

"Didn't I just say that? You got cotton in your ears? I thought you were supposed to be smart." She pulled a thoughtful face. "Maybe I'll adopt, like the other stars do. Not yet, though. I barely have time for my dog at the moment."

She sighed and rolled her eyes with a tiny sneer. "Don't tell me—you want me to have kids for you. Sorry, babe, not this little black duck. By the way, my hair's dyed, in case that was another of your little turn-ons about me. It went auburn years ago. I brighten it as part of my fire-and-ice routine. Some guys hate redheads, but a lot of guys go nuts over my hair. Well, if you're one of them, too bad," she snapped. "My body and my voice is all mine. I don't lip-sync—ever!"

Falcone opened his mouth and closed it. "Of course not."

"At least we have that established!" She tossed her hair back. "And one more thing. I'm no man's *Playboy* bunny, or the little woman in the kitchen. I don't cook, I don't clean, and I don't take orders. I go where I want, do what I want. No man tells me what to do. Got it?"

Tal felt it was time to help again, before Falcone remembered where he was, or that he still held a gun. Anson must be inside the house by now, ready to take Falcone down. "I don't mind if that's what you want, honey."

She closed her eyes and shuddered. "Tal, it's over. I'm sorry, you're a nice guy, you really are—but nice is boring. I got over it years ago." She sighed. "I'll give you fifty thousand if you'll go away! A hundred thousand. I'll put it in your bank tomorrow. Just leave me alone!"

Should he push the envelope? He decided to try once more. "But you could be pregnant! We didn't use anything—"

She flashed him a you're-so-stupid look. "I took care of that problem ages ago. I'm not going to risk my career for any man's warped little-woman fantasies of me."

He sneered at her, hoping his watery eyes from not blinking the past minute came over right. "My God, I thought the Iceberg was just an act—but you haven't got a heart anymore!"

"I'm just being honest," she said coldly. "I tried to tell you nicely. You used me all those years ago—now I've used you. *Cest la vie*. Get over it. We move in different worlds. Got the picture yet, or are you so dumb you need a color-by-numbers?"

"Damn you," he said, his voice shaking.

Sudden clapping made everyone start. "Nice one, Miss West—Dr. O'Rierdan, too," came an ironic voice from the burst-in doorway. "I haven't seen a better act since Julia Roberts in *Erin Brockovich*. But time's up, lady Nighthawk— you've been a spy the past three years. Don't try any neat little self-defense maneuvers on us, or I'll shoot your husband. And I won't just scar him this time—I'll bloody kill him."

Everyone turned to see Darren Burstall in the ruined doorway, cut and bruised, his clothes torn, standing with his feet apart and braced, an assault rifle in his hands and an ugly glint in his eyes. "Hello, Rambo." With a handkerchief, he rubbed the makeup from Tal's face. "I knew it was you. The voice gives you away." He grinned. "Glad to know I did such a good job of messing up your face. Unless you want your famous wife to die right now, you'd better get me what I want."

The game was played out and they'd lost. Time for the truth. "I can't get her for you," Tal said quietly.

With a scream, Burstall let loose, shooting upward, taking out half the ceiling. "Do it. I'll kill your wife, I swear it."

"We're in, Irish. All Falcone's goons rounded up bar those in the room with you. One final sweep and we're there," the reassuring whisper came in his earpiece.

That could be too late. He'd diagnosed Burstall without equipment. Brilliant and unbalanced and in obvious need of medication and treatment long before his twin sister's death, Burstall was lonely, heart-hungry—and desperate for the woman he wanted, even if it meant killing everyone in the room.

Dare he take the risk? He had no choice. "She can't come, Burstall. She's in hospital giving birth."

Burstall snarled, "So she betrayed me. I'll kill McCluskey. I'll kill all you Nighthawk do-gooders, starting with you!"

"I'll leave you to Mr. Burstall's tender mercies." Falcone pulled Mary-Anne backward. "Goodbye, Dr. O'Rierdan."

Go! Tal flew at Burstall's feet in a quick dive, stabbed him with a tranquilizer dart and, grabbing the rifle, rolled up and aimed the muzzle at Falcone in one movement. "Now try it,

you gutless bastard,'' he taunted Falcone as Burstall crumpled.
''You can't do anything on your own without a bunch of
brainless goons or poor, crazy Burstall to protect you, can
you? Move and I'll drop you like the bloody rabid dog you
are.''

Falcone froze, the smile plastered to his face; then, as quick
and casual as if he'd switched on a light, he shot the unconscious Burstall in the upper chest. ''A life-and-death decision,
Doctor,'' he mocked gently. ''Who do you save—the poor,
crazy man dying on the floor or the lovely lady?''

No more time. ''Nighthawks!'' he yelled. ''Twenty-four!''

Flipper, Braveheart and Wildman dived through the window
one after the other, covering Falcone's goons with assault ri-
fles more deadly than any they'd ever seen.

''Save Burstall, Tal!'' Mary-Anne cried. ''I can handle this
jerk on my own.''

''Please do handle me, lovely Verity,'' Falcone purred,
holding her from behind as protection. ''I do enjoy these little
power struggles with women. Having a woman on top is so
exciting—and then I show her who's in control.''

''Oh, yeah?'' With a swift, high kick she sent the gun spinning out of Falcone's hand, her elbow landed hard and fast in
his solar plexus. As he staggered and released her, she
stomped on his foot, twisted and thrust the heel of her palm
upward on his nose, then kicked into his chest, pushing him
to the ground, holding him down with her foot. She grinned
down at him. ''I'm on top. Are you enjoying yourself yet?''

''Mary-Anne, I need you!'' Tal yelled from the floor where
he was frantically working to save Burstall. Pushing down her
relief-filled adrenaline rush, she tapped Falcone's jaw hard to
knock him out, picked up his gun, tossed it at Wildman and
fell to her knees to help Tal.

At that moment Ghost, Braveheart and ten Amalzan police
flooded the room. ''Drop your weapons,'' Anson repeated, his
voice grim and cold.

Without argument Falcone's goons laid down their weapons. The Amalzan police hauled an unsteady Falcone to his feet, cuffed him and led him out, reading him his rights.

"Ghost! Get the full Medivac equipment from the chopper now if you want to keep him alive! And my bag from the car." Tal's hands pushed down on the wound site, desperately trying to stanch the bleeding with Burstall's torn shirt while Mary-Anne monitored the pulse and respirations. "Prep the chopper, Wildman. We need to evacuate him to a hospital stat!"

Anson looked down at the bloody scene. "Go!" he yelled, and Braveheart and Wildman launched through the window, one after the other, and bolted to the chopper.

Chapter 18

"Pulse thready and fast," Mary-Anne reported urgently, checking both venal and arterial pulses. "Respirations shallow and weak. We've got a hemorrhage here, guys."

"I need his blood pressure. Get the equipment," Tal yelled, beads of sweat running down his face. "We're going to have to operate on him here or lose him!" He glanced at her. "Are you up to scrub?"

Her nerves didn't flutter, they kicked her in the belly. Five years since she'd scrubbed for an OR... "I'd better be."

Flipper said quietly, "I'm 18-D trained, Irish. I can do the IV work and scout nursing. Songbird can do the hard stuff."

"Good." She turned to Nick and rapped, "Clear the room. Get some morphine from a local doctor—the tranquilizer dart won't see him through, at least three ampoules of five or ten milligrams each, plus an IV kit and some ampoules of penicillin. Check his medical records for known allergies. I need a blood-pressure kit ASAP. We need to check where the nearest hospital is, and ask them to prepare an OR and surgical team for our arrival. And get that equipment in here now!"

Without checking to see how Nick reacted to her orders, she returned to the patient's arterial pulse. "What else do we need?"

Tal muttered, "Bring Hartmann's or Ringer's lactate in the IV kit until we can get a cross-match done. Hemocel would be good in a pinch, but I doubt they'll have any here."

"I wrote it all down," Nick said. "I'm on my way." But words floated back to her in Nick's drawling baritone. "You can take the girl out of nursing, but obviously not the nurse out of the girl." Then he barked, his normal irascible self, "Braveheart, where the hell is that damn equipment?"

Three operatives ran in moments later with as much equipment as they could carry. Flipper, having taken the sphygmomanometer, reported, "Blood pressure eighty-five on forty."

"Pulse, one-oh-six," Mary-Anne added. "Tal, I think—"

"I know—internal hemorrhage. We need to stretcher him to the chopper now! We can notify the hospital en route. One, two, three!" Together they lifted Burstall on the stretcher, and carried him as quickly as care would allow to the chopper.

It was almost 0500 by the time Tal finally limped out of the OR of the Spanish hospital.

With no surgeon available within a ten-minute radius after midnight, the hospital gave him emergency VMO rights to operate on Burstall—but the following four hours taxed him to the limit. Once the adrenaline hit from the standoff and working to save a life had faded, exhaustion, leg weakness and pain hounded him; clawed at him like frisking puppies, demanding attention—but he couldn't give in to any of it yet. Right now he needed to find Mary-Anne, and just hold her for a little while. A few minutes...a few hours. A decade.

He found her curled up asleep in the staff room, probably to avoid newshounds—but she was on a wing chair instead of the bed. Tenderness filled him. So typical of her to leave it free for a tired doctor who might need it. Whatever he'd thought about her a week ago, he knew one thing—Verity

West was the best act she'd ever put on. She'd never left Mary-Anne behind. His girl had simply been in hiding, waiting like Sleeping Beauty for him to awaken her once more. "Come here, baby." He lifted her up in his arms and carried her to the bed, lying down with her.

"Mmm." She snuggled into him. "Did it go okay?"

He kissed her forehead, inhaling the soft rose-lavender scent rising from her hair. The sense of well-being and restfulness he'd always associate with being near her filled him. He could sleep now, with her in his arms. "He made it through the op. If he gets through the next three hours, he should be all right."

"I was so scared last night," she whispered into his shoulder. "I thought he or Falcone would kill you. I wouldn't want to live in a world without you, Tal…"

Oh, yeah, he related to that fear too well. He'd never been so terrified in his life as last night, thinking she could die or Falcone would take her as his sexual hostage. The price would come soon, the reaction would set in from too much stress. But for now, he just needed her and the peace having her close brought to him. "I'm here. We're both fine. Sleep, honey."

She snuggled in tighter, wrapping her arm around his waist. "I love you," she mumbled.

Weary, stressed to the point of overload and still on medical standby, sudden emotion grabbed him by the throat. He hadn't realized how damn much he'd needed to hear that right now— he'd only known he needed her, had to be with her.

Almost all his life if he'd needed anything, she'd provided it, and from shy girl to famous woman, she still did.

I love you, too, his heart whispered, cursing his stupid, stubborn tongue that refused to form the words aloud. He held her even tighter. The end was coming, but he'd hold it off as long as he could.

"So I finally found you both. I thought you might want to know that Falcone escaped from custody last night."

The words, in that rich, sexy Southern drawl, made them both jerk up off the bed to a sitting position at once.

"W-what?" Mary-Anne rubbed her eyes, smudging the makeup she hadn't yet had time to remove. "Ow." She peered through stinging eyes at him, closing one.

Nick's brows lifted. "Falcone fled the European mainland last night in the company of four of the Amalzan police. We think he's gone somewhere in South America. Oh, and he left a note for you, Mary-Anne. 'You were unworthy, lovely song-bird.' I guess that means you don't have to worry about him anymore."

"Or that he wants us to think so," Tal said quietly from behind her. "He wouldn't let her go that easy. We need to get him back in custody before he can try again."

Anson said harshly. "That's a given, Irish."

"Well, what's the plan?" Mary-Anne asked.

"Unfortunately for you, there is no plan—apart from going home, or continuing on tour. From the time you leave here you're officially released from what remains of your contract." His voice and face were rueful. "I'm sorry, but you knew the risks. Your cover blew sky-high last night—and now that Falcone's loose we have no way of knowing who he'll give the information to. You're too famous to fade into the woodwork and show up elsewhere, Mary-Anne. We can't use you anymore. The risks are too high."

So there it was. It was over. The warning given a week ago, seeming so insignificant compared to the task ahead, was now a reality she had to face.

Goodbye, Nighthawks. Farewell, Songbird. You've done your part for world peace, now move on.

She didn't know what to say now. What to do.

She felt Tal shrug beside her. "You have to finish your tour, anyway. You've got lots you can do, Mary-Anne. And I have my final operations. After that—"

"I never said *you* were released from contract, Irish. You have three years yet and by God, you're going to fulfill them."

Tal literally leaped over her out of bed. "What the *hell—?*" he gasped. "You know I can't be a field operative now."

Nick faced Tal down, his arms folded. "That's total crap. Your real, vital role on this mission and the people whose lives you've saved this week have proven otherwise. But that's no longer what we require from you. Your ability to see a pitfall in the most thorough plan is unparalleled, as well as your usefulness as a medical officer. I want you in both headquarters and on field from now on. You'll take my desk when I'm on assignment, and you're team commander for special SAR rescue ops, a surgeon for the injured on the field. Your experience in Tumah-ra showed headquarters we need a permanent medical officer on assignment who doesn't put his own life at risk."

Tal swore. Hard. "I don't want to sit twiddling my thumbs on bloody boats and choppers while others do the hard work!"

"You'd be a vital part of every mission, Irish. We want you to handpick a team of paramedics to go on the field when called by operatives that there are critically injured operatives or civilians. Like medics during wars, they bring them to your team, and you operate. You'd be the one coordinating the rescue efforts, directing the operatives on field, and saving the lives of innocent people. And if your pain comes back, there are fully trained medics to help you, and you can still direct them on how to treat the injured.

"And during the last year of your contract, if you decide not to re-sign with us, we'd want you to train your replacement, a qualified doctor of your own choice. Virginia wants you to train doctors for each base, so you'd be traveling to London, Nairobi and Seoul, as well. We need this scheme set up worldwide, and you're first choice for worldwide team commander." Nick grinned at Tal as he opened his mouth then closed it. "Sound like hard enough work for you? What do you say?"

Mary-Anne almost gaped with wonder. It was a dream come true for Tal—the chance to continue in the work he loved so much, taking into account his limitations and working around them, yet being an absolutely vital part of the team: commander, no less.

It was perfect for him…

So it won't be me leaving him behind, after all. It won't be him feeling useless or unnecessary. With a bittersweet smile of pride, love and loss, she gathered her things and slipped out of the room.

Tal felt dazed—overwhelmed. The door he'd thought closed and locked was not only open, but wide open with possibilities he'd never dreamed could happen for him since his accident. "Since I have no choice I guess I say, thanks, Boss." He grinned and held out his hand.

Anson gripped it. "Welcome back, Irish. I'm glad I finally got you to listen to me. I've had this in mind for a year now."

Now he was really speechless, floundering inside his inarticulate nature like a goldfish on dry land.

"For the next year, we'll work around your surgical and training schedules. Nightshift or Flipper can take point or the desk while you're in hospital if I'm called on a mission."

"What's the stats, Boss? How many for the team? What number of doctors and paramedics? What kind of equipment are we talking? Are we setting up ORs on a ship, portables in rescue choppers, or a jet?"

For the next few minutes they hammered out a few of the basics that Anson had in mind.

"This is an incredible offer," he finally said, still feeling awed by the magnitude of the task at hand—and thrilled.

"It wouldn't be on the table if you weren't the man you are," Anson replied quietly. "I can trust you one hundred percent—and that's a rare event for me. I know you can do it, Irish."

The sudden harsh bleeps of an emergency filled the room. Tal reacted without thought, wheeling around. "Mary-Anne!"

She was gone…and dread filled him. "Burstall. It's Burstall." He bolted down the hall as fast as his bad leg would allow.

Thundering echoes of feet behind him told him Anson followed, but they stopped at the door, where Mary-Anne straddled the bed, frantically performing single CPR on Burstall's inert form. "What happened?" Tal rapped. "Mary-Anne, what happened?"

"Suffocated, I think," she replied between compressions. "Five to one!"

Tal shone a torch in Burstall's eyes. "Pupils fixed and dilated, Mary-Anne. He's gone."

The sound of the shrieking *aaack, aaack* of the emergency button seemed obscene in the shocked silence. Anson walked around Tal and hit the button, stilling the noise. "Why do you diagnose suffocation, Mary-Anne?" he asked.

Tal saw the swift hurt that crossed her face. Anson's use of her real name told them both that he no longer considered her a Nighthawk, in any way. "There were cotton fibers in his mouth when I performed respiration on him."

Tal checked it out. "I'll order an autopsy, but you're right." He frowned. "Where are the cops guarding the door?"

Another strange expression crossed her face. "I'd say on their way to be with Falcone, wouldn't you?"

He sighed harshly. "Yeah, I would. Damn it, I shouldn't have left him with them!"

"If anyone's to blame here, it's me—I knew of Falcone's escape. I knew the danger for Burstall. I should have left operatives here guarding the doors instead of sending them all to chase Falcone. Burstall knew too much." Anson sighed. "So Falcone gets away—and our rogue is still safe in the ranks."

"Hell, this is a mess," Tal growled. "We've got to weed this guy out. He's bloody dangerous. So what's next, Boss? Where do we go from here?"

"I'd say our best chance lies with following up on the lead Falcone's obviously going to pursue—he's after his runaway wife. She was presumed dead five years ago after a body wearing her wedding ring was found in a burned out car in a ravine on the coast of Amalza, and their infant son was presumed dead and lost at sea. But Falcone never believed the story and never stopped hunting for them, and neither have we. We believe that she set up the accident somehow and disappeared with their son, along with ten million dollars and suspected evidence implicating Falcone in the murder of a U.S. senator, which were not found in or around the car.''

Tal nodded. "Sounds good to me. What about if—"

"I don't think you should be speaking about your plans in front of a civilian, gentlemen."

Startled, Tal swiveled around to her. She stood at the door, wearing ordinary jeans and a T-shirt, her face clean, her jacket slung over her shoulder and her bag in her hand. She wore the loveliest, saddest smile he'd ever seen. Her eyes shimmered with unshed tears. "I'll leave you to your discussion. I need to make arrangements to get back to Sydney for the rest of my shows there. And then move on, as always."

Shocked out of coherent thought, Tal groped for words to say. "No. Mary-Anne, you're still one of us...don't go—"

"Unfortunately, I'm not." She shook her head with that sad, crumpled smile. *Goodbye, Tal.* "You have work to do, and I have a tour to get on with. Can't let the fans down, you know."

"I can arrange transportation home for you," Anson said, his eyes dark and shadowed. "It's the least I can do."

"No thanks. I'll get a commercial flight home from Barcelona. There are always first-class seats available." She moved quietly to the men, holding out a hand to Anson. "It's been a joy and a privilege working with you, sir. I don't regret a minute of it."

"The privilege has been mine. You are one classy lady, Miss West." Anson kissed her cheek. "I'm going to miss working with you. Hell, I'll just miss you."

She grinned at him. "That's good to know, because I think I'll miss your grumpy face from time to time, too."

"I'll have a car waiting outside for you in five minutes," Anson said gruffly, fighting emotion of his own.

"Thank you." Then she turned to Tal, all her heartbreak hiding inside her brave, smiling eyes. She held out a hand to him. They walked outside the hospital to the warm, sunny day in the Spanish coastal countryside. She put down her bag and jacket, then she kissed his mouth. "'Bye, Tal. See you in Cowinda from time to time? We have to see the family together. Let me know when you want to go, and I'll coordinate the time."

So this was a panic attack? Heart racing, head spinning slow and heavy, wanting to puke, can't catch your breath enough to string a sentence together? All he knew was that she was going, and he couldn't—couldn't let her go, not now. Not ever. "Mary-Anne—no, honey, don't go! Can't you—"

A finger to his lips halted him. "Don't make me cry, Tal," she whispered. "Not now, okay?" But the first tear spilled over. "You have your life, your dream has come true, and I'm glad—so glad for you. It looks like we both got our dreams." Her smile wobbled. "You're Doctor O'Rierdan again, and you're Irish. And I'm Verity West. And never the twain shall m-meet…"

He pulled her into his arms, shaking. "Don't go, Mary-Anne. I love you, honey, I love you so much."

She dragged in air through her parted lips as tears spilled from her closed eyes. "Thank you," she whispered. "I've waited all my life to hear you say that."

Cupping her face in his hands, he kissed her, over and over. "I need you, baby. I don't think I can make it on my own."

"You did for years." A loose curl danced across her face, she looked lost and helpless and beautiful, lovelier than he'd ever seen her. "You'll be fine, Tal. I know it. You don't need me. You have so much to do now." Her voice was nearly gone, yet its lingering sweetness pierced his soul. "M-maybe we can catch up in London or Virginia while you're training the other doctors, if I'm there at the time? Or we can meet in Sydney sometimes. We'll need to coordinate calls to our parents from time to time if we want to convince them we're still together…" She made a fluttering movement to be free. "I—I have to go now, okay?"

"No," he rasped, his heart and soul shredding. Dear God, he'd never thought he'd ever need to beg her—but right now, he'd get down on his knees for another single moment with her.

"I have to go, Tal! Don't you get it?" she cried. "I can't be Verity West and your wife—that can't work for you. And I can't stay home and wait for you any more than you could for me. I was a Nighthawk, too! *Was*, but it's over for me, not for you…and even if I could stay with you without risking your life and cover, I'd watch you leave on missions and I'd ache and burn with wanting to be there. One day I'd resent you for always leaving me behind. And you're a dedicated doctor—this offer is everything you've ever wanted. You'd resent me if I asked you to stay for me." She gave a hopeless shrug. "I've loved you all my life—but it's always been me waiting for you, me coming to you, me compromising for you. I can't do it anymore. We love each other now. I couldn't stand to watch it die."

He wheeled away. There was nothing to say to that. She knew him too well. "If you ever change your mind…"

"I know my way to headquarters—but I'd need a pass to get in now." The words were light, self-mocking, but with a quiver of emotion. "Tal, if…if you meet someone else—"

He wanted to puke at the thought of it. "It's more likely to be you than me, Miss West."

She turned his face to hers. "I've loved you for twenty-four years. You climbed that tree for me, even though you knew the eggs wouldn't hatch. I knew then I'd found the love of my life. There will never be anyone else for me but you."

"You think it's any different for me?" He heard his voice, so rough and gravelly with pain. No, not a bit different—he'd loved her from that first day. He'd climbed the stupid tree to stop her tears—anything to stop the kid crying—and seeing her little freckled face so radiant with joy, her eyes so filled with shy admiration for him and the silly task he'd performed for her, something weird happened. It was as if he'd fallen inside her, body and soul, and he'd never found his way back out.

"If you do meet someone else…" she went on softly, her

voice shaking. "If you ever want…want a divorce, send me the papers and I'll sign them. Just…just don't tell me you love her." With a sudden, tiny cry, she collapsed into his chest. "Please, Tal, promise me that much. Just don't tell me you love her!"

He had to say it; the wait was killing her. "Okay," he said slowly, knowing he'd never have to fulfill the promise.

"Thank you. I—I can't—" She grabbed her stuff, turned and bolted down the path to the waiting car.

He watched her leave, watched the car pull away from the curb and roll smoothly down the street, as if by fixing his gaze on it he could make a miracle happen and she'd come back to him, tell him she'd found a way for them to be together, forever.

When the car finally dwindled into the horizon on the long, unwinding road leading to Barcelona, he turned back to the hospital, his limp getting stronger as he allowed the physical agony to take him over, his exhaustion to win—and he made himself think of the upcoming autopsy on Burstall. He'd probably have to perform it himself.

A gross thought, but he'd rather think of that than go back a minute in time. Anything was preferable right now than the memory just burned into his brain, of watching her leaving his life.

"'Tis better to have loved and lost, than never to have loved at all…"

"What a load of crap," he muttered, and slammed the swinging doors open and stalked back into the staff room to inject his leg pain into temporary oblivion.

But he didn't have any relief, temporary or permanent, for the life-draining anguish inside his heart.

Chapter 19

Canberra, five months later

"Use the fins harder. Your patient's going under! This is not a dress rehearsal, men. *Swim for his life!*" Flipper shouted from beside the pool. Artificial crashing waves and sounds of thunder filled the aquatic training facility. Flipper knew how to push the armed-service-recruited paramedics learning combat swimming/rescue techniques to the limits of endurance.

Tal, leaning on his cane beside Flipper, nodded. "This lot will make it. They're almost ready to send out."

"You're rescuing the man, Jones, not breaking his neck! How many weeks do they have to go with the advanced medic's course?" Flipper went from yelling at a recruit to asking Tal the question without skipping a beat.

"They're finished. They passed the exams and practical stints with high credit to distinction." He scrutinized the trainees carefully, looking for any signs of fear, of hesitation or loss of concentration that could cause a patient to lose their life. "If they pass the physical, they're ready for their first assignments. Group two begins their course in three weeks."

Flipper spoke the thought that came to his own mind at that moment. "You think West will make it through, Irish? I have my doubts. He's strong and fit enough, but the stress is showing."

Tal's heart did the usual stop-start whenever West's name came up. Nice guy, but he'd be glad when he was on assignment, he'd get a code name and his name wouldn't be in his face and filling his ears every day. "I don't know. The cracks are getting stronger. He's got a big heart, though. He *wants* to do this so bad. I think he might get through."

"If he doesn't freak out when he faces the real thing out there," Flipper returned with strong doubt in his voice.

Tal shrugged. "Didn't you freak out the first time?"

Flipper turned to him, chuckling. "If I had, they'd have turfed me out on my ass. SEALs don't tolerate wimps. No personal problems on the job. No fear. No excuses. Not ever."

And without that attitude the past two months, without Flipper beside him on the survival skills course for the trainee Nighthawk Evacuation Rescue team, Tal would have fallen apart.

They'd come to know each other well. As field commanders of equal status, they had to thoroughly acquaint each other with their backgrounds and skills, to assess which team they needed on what field at any given time. A kid from the meaner streets of L.A., a former gang member turned pilot turned SEAL, Flipper was a complete man of action. He seemed almost as inhuman as Anson at times. Flipper didn't just live for the job; he *was* the job. It defined him.

He wished he had that tunnel vision, that absolute one-hundred-percent-at-all-times dedication to the job. Then he'd sleep better at night, not waking up drenched in erotic or terrified sweat from one dream after another of her. Sometimes he thought he'd give anything for one night's sleep—just sleep. No 0100, 0200, 0300 and 0400 heart, gut and body-punching wake-up calls that she was gone, and she wasn't coming back. Loving her or losing her, every night was the same…he just couldn't forget, not even for an hour. Not even in sleep.

"Irish. Flipper. Report to head office stat."

The disembodied voice filtered through their earpieces and jerked Tal out of memories. "Right. Out, men," he shouted. "Thirty-minute lunch break, then back into the jungle facility for simulation enemy territory training."

Without a word, the men swam through the choppy waters to the side, vaulted out and headed for the change room. Meal and sleep times were their only breaks, and they didn't waste time talking about it or complaining: they knew they'd be shown the door if they couldn't handle any single part of the training course.

Tal and Flipper left the facility, hopped in the Jeep and headed north toward central Canberra and Anson's office in silence. Neither man was the kind to waste words in speculation. They'd know why Anson wanted them soon enough.

"You're on assignment," Anson told them as soon as the doors to his office closed. "Both of you. Effective immediately."

Tal blinked. "Boss, the course is almost done—"

Anson nodded impatiently. "No time for that."

Intrigued, he asked, "Where are we going?"

Anson turned to Flipper. "New Zealand for you. We've found a strong probable for both Delia de Souza Falcone and her son hiding out in the Bay of Islands in the north island."

"New Zealand? She's in New Zealand?"

Tal, hearing the strange note in Flipper's voice, glanced at his friend. He was pale, yet his eyes burned. His fists were so tight-clenched he looked as though he'd break something any second.

So Flipper had an Achilles' heel after all…

Anson nodded, seeming uninterested in Flipper's reaction. "A town called Renegade River. She calls herself Elizabeth Silver. Fly in yourself—the N.Z. military's given you clearance—and play the tourist. Try to get close—you met her on

your first assignment, right? Check her reaction. Work fast—
if we've found her, I doubt Falcone's men will be far behind.
He wants his son and everything she stole from him when she
ran. Gain her trust and get that evidence. We want an affidavit,
plus Mrs. Falcone and her son in protective custody, ASAP.''
Anson held out a sheaf of papers. ''Here's what we know
about her and the area. Get what you need and don't hesitate.
If this woman is Delia de Souza, she's invaluable to us.''

''Yes, sir.'' Flipper took the assignment sheets.

''This is stat, Flipper. I've already made arrangements for
Tapper and Shadow to take over with the trainees for now.''

''Yes, sir. Consider me gone.'' Flipper turned and stalked
out of the room as though chased by his own private demons.

Tal could relate to that.

''I gather I'm not going to New Zealand, sir?''

''No. London,'' Anson said briefly.

His heart jacked up into his mouth. That's where Mary-
Anne was now on the final week of her tour. He hadn't seen
her in over two months, since their last fifteen-minute reunion
in New York to call their parents together. ''What's the deal,
boss?'' he asked bluntly.

Anson looked up then, with a small smile. ''She used to
say that to me all the time. 'What's the deal?' were always
her first words whenever I called her in on assignment.''

Tal gave a deep, harsh sigh. Another little trip down memory lane was more than he could stand right now. ''Is this
about Mary-Anne? If so, sir, we'd both appreciate it if you
wouldn't interfere with our personal lives.''

His face blank of emotion, Anson handed him a photo.
''Now tell me I'm interfering.''

Tal took the picture, and stared at it. The world started tilt-
ing around him in slow, crazy arcs. ''When was this?''

''Last night, just after the show,'' Anson replied, his tone
grim. ''Get over there, Tal. She needs you.''

Anson's use of his real name registered in a kind of vague,
brief shock—but his other words hit him with the relentless
force of a jackhammer. ''I want the jet.''

"It's fueled up and waiting for you at the airstrip." Anson hesitated. "The disguise is waiting, too, if you decide you need it. I thought, with the press speculation—her career might suffer. She's already lost enough."

Tal nodded. "Thanks, boss." He'd wear the goop—he'd do that and more—to make it to her. He knew what he had to do, whether she wanted it right now or not.

London

"Miss West. Miss West! Encore!"

Mary-Anne started as the urgent hiss penetrated her brain. She looked around the stage from the wings, almost bewildered, and slowly walked on to thunderous applause.

Was the show over? Had she actually gone through another entire show on autopilot?

Had it come to this, that her brilliant career could mean so little to her?

The cheers of the audience told her it made no difference to them. They didn't know, couldn't see the ice had reached right down to her heart—and if it did, it hadn't changed her voice and looks, and that was all they cared about. They preferred her this way, fulfilling the legend they expected to find when they bought their tickets. Verity West was even colder than before, totally inhuman, the Iceberg sculpted into a perfect maiden of frost...but she could still sing, so who cared?

Distance was the only armor she had left, and she clung to it with the grim desperation of a drowning woman.

Verity West's Secret Marriage Fails After One Week. Iceberg Freezes Her Husband Out, the headlines mocked.

She'd always thought she was a pro at the game—now she realized what a novice she'd been, protected by society's innate respect for the widow's mantle. As a woman separated from her husband after a week she'd become fair game: from socialites to journalists to photographers and interviewers. Men crowded her, touched her, propositioned her with greater impertinence than before. The challenge was back on: who would melt the Iceberg after she'd driven away her second husband?

The media constantly asked her about Tal's disappearance. How could she lose her husband after only a week?

She couldn't tell them. She was too busy breathing from one day to the next. Busy pacing her room at night, night after night after waking up reaching out to emptiness, her body aching for the release and love that it, and she, couldn't have.

Visions of him smiling at her, with his crooked pirate's grin. Taking her in his arms, kissing her mouth, and her body. Needing her touch when the pain hit him. *You have healing hands, honey.* Throwing her on the bed—

Wild, sweet loving, her body on fire, her heart filled with joy and love.

Tal, oh, Tal…

So she was alone again in her pretend world. Verity West, the glorious princess, immersed in her ivory tower like Snow White or Sleeping Beauty. Just breathing. Back in emotional slumber, waiting for the prince who would never ride in on his white horse to save her…

Deep silence recalled her to now. Slowly she looked around, feeling as though she was crawling through a thick murk. The quiet was so heavy it buzzed in her ears. The audience, the cast, even the stagehands blinked at her, slow and confused. Waiting for her to do something, say something.

And without warning the world did the kaleidoscope thing again, she couldn't focus her eyes. What…what—

Her legs gave way. She felt herself crumple to the floor as darkness fell down on her.

Tal sat in the special box reserved for family in mounting horror. He'd only arrived in London in time to make the start of her performance. He'd asked the theater manager to keep his presence a secret—he wanted to surprise his wife after the show, and didn't want to distract her.

Now, he wished he had. He'd seen her in live performances

more often than she'd ever know…and watching this one felt as if he was getting a well-deserved kick in the guts.

She was reed-thin, her eyes hollow with fatigue and stress. She all but stumbled in her heels as she danced and strutted around the stage; her hands looked as though they needed something solid to hang on to. The tremors weren't strong enough to hit headlines—maybe only he could see them because he knew her so well. But he suspected only her dauntless spirit kept her on her feet and her glorious voice from faltering.

Dear God, had losing him done this to her?

He saw the moment when she started losing it—at the encore call. Her eyes blinked a few times and she looked around as if she had no idea where she was. She swayed on her feet.

And he started running.

"Move! Get out of my bloody way!" He elbowed his way through the crowd milling in front of her dressing room. "Move! I'm Verity West's husband, and if I don't get in there someone's going to be hurt!"

His tone, even to himself, was rough-edged and filled with danger. The crowd took one look at him, parted, and he stalked through them into the dressing room.

"You can't come in here, sir." A hulking security guy blocked his way in, his voice authoritative. "Miss West is unwell."

He flipped out his ID. "Miss West is my wife. Now move or I'll move you."

The guy gave a glance back, then moved aside. "Of course, sir. I'm sorry, I didn't recognize you."

Tal didn't waste words. He pushed past the guy and walked in.

She was on the bed in the corner, her bright hair a fiery slash against a face so pale, and still it scared him. As well as two men and a woman hovering around her, a man was checking her over. "Move," was all he said.

The thin, middle-aged man checking her swiveled around,

his face startled. "Who the hell do you think you are, ordering me to move? I'm her doctor—"

"So am I. And I'm her husband." His voice was as taut as his emotions as he pushed past the guy to kneel beside her.

One of the men hovering around her came to him with his hand out. "Dr. O'Rierdan, it's wonderful to meet you. I'm Michael Mathieson, Verity's agent—"

"*Verity* doesn't exist. Her name is Mary-Anne." He checked her pulse, the condition of her skin. Too hot, clammy. "I'd leave now if I were you—all of you—before I belt the hell out of you for letting her get into this state. You're supposed to bloody look after her, not work her into illness!"

Mathieson backed off—and no wonder, if he looked half as violent as he felt right now—but the doctor, though he had the grace to look guilty, stood his ground. "It's Miss West's right to decide who stays or goes." He turned back to Mary-Anne's inert form. "Miss West. Miss West!"

They all began chanting the words like mindless parrots, standing at a distance, as if they were scared of touching her. *Miss West. Miss West.*

Didn't anyone in this crowd know who she was?

Gently he took her hand in his, felt the trembling and fever even in her palm. "Mary-Anne?" He lifted the palm to his lips, kissing her over and over. "Mary-Anne? Honey, it's me."

She stirred, with a tiny groan. "Tal?" she murmured, her soft voice touched with disbelief, with wonder.

"Yeah, it's me." Tenderly, using a nearby damp cloth, he wiped off the makeup on her face—a face so thin the angles showed in stark contrast to the soft fullness of her mouth. He checked her over. Stress and exhaustion had taken its toll, and she hadn't been eating enough. She'd been sick for weeks by the looks of it, denying it and trying to work through it—but thank God, it was fixable—in time. "What have you been doing to yourself while my back was turned, kid?"

She sighed. "No...not Tal. Dreaming again." Tears trickled from beneath her closed lids. "Want it too much..."

His throat constricted with love and longing. Oh, how he understood that, and he knew what she needed now—because he needed it, needed it more than his next breath. Letting go of her hand, and drinking in her tiny cry of loss, he lifted her in his arms, cradling her like a newborn and just as infinitely precious to him. "Touch me, kid," he murmured huskily. "I'm really here. I'm not going anywhere again without you."

Her eyes fluttered open and she saw him smiling at her. A slow, shaking hand touched his face, cupping it in her palm as though he was a priceless treasure. "Tal?" she cried softly, her gaze filled with a joy so intense, his whole body seized up with love. "Is it really you?"

"Yeah, it's really me." He kissed her mouth with all the tenderness he could give her.

Her head fell to his shoulder. "You came to me, Tal," she sighed. "You finally came for me..."

"Yeah," he muttered gruffly. "I came for you, honey." *Even if it was a few months too late.* He felt like slamming his own head against a convenient brick wall. He took full blame for the state she was in, but she didn't need his self-recrimination. She needed him to be strong for her, and by God, he'd hold it together. "You'll be better soon. I'll take care of you."

Flashing lights recalled him to where they were.

He turned his head to see the gaping Verity West entourage, whoever the hell they all were—and the press taking shot after ecstatic shot of them. And he lost it. "That does it." Keeping her in his arms, he snatched up her bag and coat and headed for the exit. "Move," he growled at the hovering people in a tone that brooked no denial. "Get out of the bloody way, I said!"

"Where are you taking Miss West? She has a show tomorrow night! It's her closing night!" a yapping guy in a monkey suit kept saying over and over.

He looked at the silly jerk over his shoulder. "So sue me for your losses. I'll foot the bill—but she isn't singing again until she's well."

"But I have my reputation to consider! Miss West wouldn't want this—she never lets anyone down. She's just tired, I'm sure. Tell her I need her here tomorrow night—it's her closing night, and there's so many important people—"

Tal just kept walking, ignoring the cameras, the questions. He said one word, and that only when someone shoved a mike or camera in his face, or stepped in front of him.

"Move!"

Finally they reached the waiting Nighthawk limo. He slid in with slow care, still cradling her against his heart...and he wasn't planning on putting her down for a long, long time.

Her cell phone started ringing. He fumbled in her bag, found it. Her manager's name flashed on the screen. He disconnected it, but it rang again within seconds. Now the name of the theater manager came up. Moments later, it was someone else—her personal assistant, he thought.

He opened the window and threw the damn phone out of the car with an awkward backhanded toss, so as not to disturb her. He watched it bounce on the road and smash with no remorse at all.

"You'll be fine now, kid," he whispered into her hair. "I've got you. I won't let them get to you."

She stirred in his arms, looked up and frowned, fighting sleep. "Why have you got that goop on your face again? You hate it. Makes you itch."

He fought laughter and tears at once. So typical of her to notice, even when she was exhausted, and want to fix it for him. "For you, kid. I had to face the cameras to get you."

Her frown deepened; she looked bewildered. "So?" Her hand fluttered up, ineffectually rubbing at it. "Take it off."

His heart almost burst then. He pulled out a handkerchief and wiped off as much as he could. "Is that better?"

She touched hot, trembling lips to the almost-faded scars. "Yes. It's you. Just as you are. My Tal." She sighed and snuggled back into him. "Take me home, Tal...please..."

He choked down the emotion threatening to overwhelm

him. "You're on your way, Mary-Anne. You're coming home."

"With you, Tal?" she whispered, falling back into sleep. "Can I stay with you for a little while? Please?"

Hold it in. Hold it in…

A single tear fell onto her forehead. He wiped it off with a tender finger. He was a jerk, a tongue-tied fool totally unworthy of her—but for a reason he'd never be able to fathom, she loved him. She loved him and she needed him, and he'd damn well be there for her—for the rest of her life. And he'd tell her he loved her every day—and he'd thank God every day for the rest of his life for that single miracle, the priceless gift of her love. "Yes, baby," he muttered gruffly, holding it all in. "You're coming home with me."

Chapter 20

She was in her beloved Eden...

As soon as he thought she was fit to travel, he'd bundled her into the Nighthawks' jet and brought her home. Her feet never touched the ground. He'd carried her like a child, stalking past rabid photographers and screaming journalists without a word.

And now she was home at last. Home with Tal.

The dream of a lifetime had finally come true. For the past five days she'd woken up in Eden, Tal lying beside her in the bed, softly snoring. Her billabong was clearly visible from their bedroom window, shimmering in tranquil beauty beside its single old, twisted tree and the wildflowers that were really weeds, but so natural and lovely to her.

She was home, home with her Tal in her beautiful Cowinda.

The families finally knew about Tal's accident. Uncle Dal and Aunt Sheila had done their crying—tears of shame for not being there for their son, for making him feel responsible for their happiness because of Kathy's death.

Now they were determined to be there for Tal—and for her,

too. Along with her parents and half the town, they spent every day patrolling Cowinda for strangers, and directing them away from where Mary-Anne and Tal were. They were getting the honeymoon snatched from them in Amalza.

Aunt Sheila and Mum cosseted them, fed them, made sure they rested, walked and had privacy when they needed it. Aunt Sheila and Uncle Dal were even bunking with Mum and Dad for the week, until Tal had to go back to work—to his ship, as they thought.

She'd never felt so contented, so blessed or so loved in her life.

"Come on, honey—it's your favorite. Chocolate mousse," Tal coaxed her now with a crooked half smile on his face, as they sat at the old, cracked dining table in the eat-in kitchen. "You didn't eat much lunch. Aren't you just a little bit hungry?"

Instead of looking at the dessert, she watched him smiling at her, and she caught her breath. For five days he'd controlled himself to the max, only holding her at night, determined to feed her, make her rest and nurse her back to health...and while she could feel her body gaining strength every day, she could also feel the yearning for completion, to have him inside her once again, building up to a crescendo. "Yes, I'm hungry," she said softly, her gaze on his eyes, his mouth. "But chocolate mousse isn't really my favorite anymore."

The disappointment on his face gave her a little pang. "What do you want? If it's not too fancy, I can get it..."

"You can easily get it." She let her gaze travel along his body. "You gave it to me all the time in Amalza, and I've been dying to taste some more of it."

He groaned and closed his eyes. "I'm trying so hard not to think about that, honey. I want to make you well here."

"Then make me well." She leaned forward, parting her lips. "I'm sure I'll be a lot hungrier if you make me happy. Touch me, Tal. Kiss me. Heal me."

"I want you to eat!" But his voice, rasping with need, told her he was sinking, and he knew it, too.

"I want to play." She nuzzled his lips; then a slow smile curved her mouth. "I know. We'll compromise." She dipped her index finger in the mousse. "I eat, you kiss me. Deal?"

"Huh?" He was too busy watching her slowly licking the mousse from her finger. "What?"

A thrill of hot excitement rippled through her whole body. Feeling wicked and wanton, she dipped her finger in the rich chocolate again, and with teasing deliberation, smeared it across his mouth. "Yum," she whispered, and gently licked and sucked the dessert away. "I ate," she announced, smiling, her body thudding with delicious need. "You have to kiss me now."

"That's cheating, woman," he growled, but he pulled her onto his lap and kissed her, deep, hot and edged in male need.

She bit down on her smile. Oh, yeah, her Irish lover was hard, primed and ready for action. "I never promised to play fair," she murmured, aching. "I just promised to play." She dipped her finger in the dessert again…and this time she smeared it across his throat. "Oh, yum," she whispered again. "Yeah, I'm definitely getting hungry now." She nibbled it away, smothering his throat in slow, hot kisses. Then she looked up into his eyes, knowing hers were fiery with the desire she didn't want to deny. "Take your shirt off."

His eyes mirroring hers for raw sexuality, he stripped off his shirt, revealing his strong, golden-brown chest with rippling muscles. The sight made the fire flickering inside her crank up to a furnace. She felt him watching her as she first smeared, then licked and nibbled the mousse from his chest, with special attention to his flat nipples. "Hmm…" She twisted so that she straddled him, wriggling against his arousal, filled with an anguished pleasure-pain, aching to have him inside her. "Chocolate mousse is definitely my favorite on *this* plate."

"I'll keep our fridge stocked," he groaned, his hands in her hair to keep her there. "Yes, honey, that's so good…"

Sudden emotion swamped her as she kissed him over his thundering heart. "I love you, Tal."

He lifted her face, his eyes dark, warm, soft. "I love you, too." Without warning he moved her leg over and scooped her up in his arms. "Get that mousse, kid. Ve haf vays of making you eat," he uttered in an atrocious German accent, "and I remember getting distinct permission to play connect-the-dots."

She laughed and snatched up the bowl as he carried her to the bedroom.

"That's it. Go. Go!"

Mary-Anne watched from the single row of bleachers as the new recruits raced for the "patient" rimmed by a ring of fire in the simulated battlefield. Holding pure wool blankets in front of them as fire shields, they wrapped the blankets around their bodies to go inside the fire to save the patient.

A massive *buzz, buzz* filled the air as Tal called the exercise to a halt. "Recall!"

The recruits fell in line, facing Tal. "Someone tell me why I did that!" he snapped.

Everyone looked at one man, who reddened, his face half-defiant, half-embarrassed. "Jackaroo didn't go in with a partner, sir!" one of the men yelled—Farmboy or Rodeo, she wasn't sure. All the men here were full Nighthawks, they had their code names now, ready for their first field assignments. "Never enter a life-threatening rescue op without backup, sir!"

"If you're injured you can't save the patient! Patient is always our first priority, sir!"

Tal nodded. "Jackaroo. Out on the bleachers until you decide to stop playing cowboy and work as a team member!"

His face sulky, Jackaroo sat out beside Mary-Anne. "Control freak," he muttered, kicking at the dirt with his steel-capped foot. "Perfectionist. I just wanted to try—"

"Irish is a perfectionist for your sake," she said gently. She had no idea why Tal had brought her here, or why Nick had given permission to show her all aspects of the new training program, but she reveled in being back. It was as though she'd come home again. "You don't know what it's like out there. You don't want to live with regrets if your innovations don't work."

Startled, he turned to look at her. "Pardon me, Mrs. Irish, ma'am. I didn't mean to pick on your husband, ma'am."

She grinned. "Mrs. Irish" was the only name the recruits knew her by, and they knew she was a former operative, but if they knew she was Verity West with her now shorter hair up in a pigtail, wearing jeans, T-shirt, her glasses and no makeup, they didn't show it. "He's hard on you because it's vital on the field to be an unquestioning member of the team. One mistake can end in death. I mostly did undercover work, but I was on assignment with him earlier this year."

"You—oh, sh— I mean, you're *Songbird*, aren't you, ma'am?" He kept gulping between words. "We've all heard about you. You're a legend around the lockers. People still talk about the things you did on assignment, and—you're Verity West!"

She lifted a finger to her lips. "Don't tell everyone. Irish and Ghost wouldn't appreciate it. I only told you so you understand that I *do* know what I'm talking about. Irish is right about cowboys. Until you can prove you're a member of the team, they won't let you on assignment…and you'll never be a commander. And if you get out there and think you can do things differently, you might survive—but someone else might pay for your decision with their life. Is that what you want?"

Slowly he shook his head. "You're right, ma'am." He sounded humble, awkward, embarrassed. "I won't do it again, ma'am."

That night at Tal's farm on the southwestern slopes of Canberra, lying twined together in the afterglow of loving, she sighed. "You're doing an amazing job with the recruits, Tal. The simultaneous training can't be easy on them, or on you, especially when everyone else is out on assignment, like now."

He chuckled. "I love it, to be honest. Jackaroo's right. I am a control freak. I like running the office and the training program without interference from the others.'' He hesitated. ''You could help me, though.''

She frowned. ''How? I'm not an operative anymore.'' A pang ripped through her once more—the sense of identity lost.

''You could be again, Mary-Anne.''

''What?'' She stared up at him. ''But...my cover is gone...''

''It would be different work this time.'' Obviously nervous, he paused again. ''It'd be nothing like your old work.''

''Well?'' she asked, impatient to hear it. Being a Nighthawk again—just the thought of coming back made her burn inside with anticipation, with joy. ''Tal, tell me!''

He sighed. ''I don't know how you'll take this, so bear with me, okay?'' He gently disengaged himself from her arms and sat up, not looking at her. ''I can train the doctors, the medics. I can do the on-field discipline. But we need nurses: nurses with guts and the dedication to work in extremely tough situations without complaint.'' He turned to her. ''We need someone to train them, not in nursing techniques, but in how to cope with the worst conditions. We need a qualified Nighthawk nurse to show them how to make do with whatever we face at the time and to improvise with equipment. How to assist while the doctor or medic is operating on a cliff wall or deep in enemy territory—or how to operate themselves, and how to go down that cliff, too, to rescue people if they have to.''

Her excitement grew with every word he said. Oh, this was something she could do, something she'd *love* to do. No more undercover work, no theft, no playing the siren. This wasn't Verity West's work—this was Mary-Anne's. She bounced up in the bed. ''I'd need to take refresher courses, both in surgical nursing and in fieldwork. You'd have to teach me a lot I don't know.'' She twisted around and grabbed his hands. ''Can you teach me how to rappel, and how to cope behind enemy lines? I'd need a lot of help before I could train anyone...''

''That's what I'm here for.'' His grin seemed fair to split his face. ''I gather you want the assignment?''

"Of course I do! You don't know how much I've missed this, Tal. I'm aching to be a part of things again. And this is something I can do!"

"You'll be perfect for the job." He squeezed her hands. "But think carefully, kid—because this would mean giving up Verity West. You couldn't do both anymore. For the safety of other operatives, you'd have to fade into obscurity."

She didn't even hesitate. "I haven't liked being Verity West for a long time," she said quietly. "Not since Gil died. I tried so hard to cope with it all, but the only way was by being the Iceberg. Until Nick asked me to join the Nighthawks, I didn't know what else to do with my life. Nursing didn't seem an option when everyone knew who I was. I didn't particularly like what Nick asked me to do, but I felt it had a higher purpose, so I did it." She smiled up at him. "Then I was on assignment with you and I felt, for the first time in a long time, that I was where I was meant to be. I wasn't only a thief or a distraction or a sexual attraction. I worked on the field. I helped you save lives. And I loved every minute of it. Then my cover blew and it was over, and I didn't know what else to do but to go back to the old life." She sat beside him, legs dangling over the bed. "None of it made sense to me, Tal. I didn't know why I was there anymore. I just kept going, kept working, and crying every night until you came to me." Suddenly she bounced on the bed. "I can't believe I'm coming back! I'm so happy!"

"What about your commitments with that life?"

She shrugged. "I'd just finished making *Blue Straits* when I started our assignment. My contract stated I must make three albums in five years, and I have. I've done the tours. I'm free." She turned her face to him, awed. "I'm free," she whispered. "I don't have to sign the new contract. I can walk away."

"And you're sure you want to? You won't regret it?"

She laughed at his serious face. "You dork!" She dived on him, wrestling him backward on the bed, tickling him. "What do you think? I get a job I love, I get peace and quiet, and I get to be a Nighthawk again. What's not to like?''

He grinned, already aroused. "You get one more thing in the deal—me. And when we've had enough, we can retire from fieldwork and have a few kids. How does that sound?''

Her heart melted at the anxiety he was trying not to show. "Doofus." She smiled with total love. "What do you think? I've only wanted you all my life, and to be the mother of your babies." She wriggled against his arousal. "Mmm. Yes, please…''

With a deft flip he was on top of her and, after a deep, hot kiss, was inside her. "Welcome home, Songbird," he whispered.

Afterward, twined together once more, he spoke in the warm darkness. "I love you, Mary-Anne. Will you marry me?''

She laughed at him. "I love you, too, but…um, Tal, unless I missed something, we *are* married.''

"Yeah, but you got cheated of your dreams. I want you to have them." He tilted up her face and kissed her. "I want to marry you again—properly this time, at the billabong, with our family and friends all there.''

She gasped, choked on the tide of emotion surging up from her heart, and stammered, "Tal—oh, Tal…''

And when she wept in quiet joy against his chest, neither of them had to speak.

Everyone kept their secret, right up until their wedding day two weeks later. The only reporter to cover the event was from the cash-strapped local bush rag. The scoop of the year, sold to newspapers, magazines and TV stations around the world: the sunset wedding by the billabong of the handsome, scarred local hero and the woman who'd turned her back on fame to share her life with the man she loved.

"You may kiss your bride," the local minister proclaimed, smiling at them both.

Tal drew her into his arms and touched the simple lace of

her dress. "I love you," he murmured, and she whispered it back. Then he kissed her, to the cheering joy of their families and the laconic, understated approval of the Cowinda community.

And the silent, smiling man standing in the shadow of a tree well away from the other guests, who couldn't afford to be seen in public or in any photo, gave them a nod of approval, and left his gift on the wedding table. He stifled the yank of unwanted pain inside his empty heart and climbed into his unmarked sedan, to return to his dangerous and isolated world, where he could keep pretending that saving the world was enough.

In the quiet of an Outback evening, the man who no longer existed drove alone in a government car toward a plane that would take him to a city that wasn't home, to a house that wasn't his, in a world barely anyone knew about and none in the know dared acknowledge. And when the coldness of night came to him, surrounding him like the loved ones around Mary-Anne and Tal, he knew this was all the comfort he'd ever know—the satisfaction of a job well done, and seeing others find their happiness.

Annie was gone. Forever.

With his adoring wife still in the circle of his arms, his mouth still filled with the taste of her kisses, Tal quietly watched Anson slip away into the violet shadows of dusk, like the ghost he'd become so long ago. An instinct as deep and abiding as the one he'd had at eight years old, that told him he'd belong to Mary-Anne forever, filled him, touching the edges of his joy. He could see it, see the shadows of dark memory seeming to follow Ghost, gathering all around him, quiet and malevolent, biding their time.

The storm was coming...

And when it came, he and Mary-Anne would be standing beside him, facing it shoulder to shoulder. The Nighthawks were like that.

"Tal?"

The soft, pure voice recalled him to now. He smiled down at the beautiful, radiant woman in his arms. "I'm here, honey. Now and always." He took her hand. Together they led the way to the big old barn in Eden, decked out for an old-fashioned hoedown, to celebrate the marriage, not of the year, but of a lifetime.

* * * * *

Don't miss Melissa James's next thrilling read,
DANGEROUS ILLUSION
The exciting story of
Nighthawk Brendan McCall.
Coming in April 2004
From Silhouette Intimate Moments

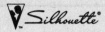

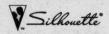

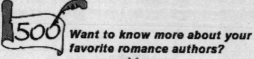

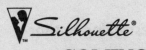

COMING NEXT MONTH